TUNDRA KILL

Also by the author

White Sky, Black Ice
Shaman Pass
Frozen Sun
Village of the Ghost Bears

with Sharon Bushell
The Spill: Personal Stories from the Exxon Valdez
Disaster

TUNDRA KILL

A novel

Stan Jones

Published by
Bowhead Press LLC
Box 240212
Anchorage AK 99524

Tundra Kill: a Nathan Active Mystery / Stan Jones

ISBN 978-0-9799803-8-1 (hardcover)
1. Police—Alaska—Fiction. 2. Inupiat—Fiction.
3. Alaska—Fiction I. Title

Library of Congress Control Number 2015907826

10 9 8 7 6 5 4 3 2 1

THIS BOOK IS dedicated to the late anthropologist Ernest Burch, whose work on the Inupiat of Northwest Alaska not only makes fascinating reading, but also has long been one of my chief aids in understanding the origins and traditions of the culture I write about.

ACKNOWLEDGMENTS

THE AUTHOR WISHES to express his heartfelt gratitude to the following people, whose support and assistance made this book possible:

John Creed and Susan Andrews of Kotzebue, for sharing their expertise about life in the Alaska Bush and for their many other kindnesses in helping bring this book to life.

The officers of the Kotzebue Police Department, for providing much useful information on how policing works in the Alaska Bush, and for letting me ride along on patrol on spring evenings in the Arctic.

Chief Leon Boyea of of the North Slope Borough Police Department for information how things work when a rural borough takes on police powers.

Keenan Powell of Anchorage, attorney par excellence and wise counselor on many a legal issue, especially the various sizes and flavors of murder and homicide in Alaska, and the workings of spousal privilege.

Bill Cummings, my oldest friend and another attorney par excellence, for his helpful expertise on Child in Need of Aid cases in Alaska.

Jimmy Evak of Kotzebue, for his help with the Inupiaq language.

Michael Faubion, for allowing me to adapt and use the lyrics from his song, "Ice Road." The adapted version appears in Chapter Nine.

And, friends and fellow writers too numerous to name, including my wife, son, and daughter, who reviewed the manuscript along the way and recommended countless improvements.

THE ICING STORY in Chapter Six is adapted from "Superheroes Only Live in Comic Books," a story in *CloudDancer's Alaskan Chronicles Vol. III, The Tragedies*. It is used with the author's permission.

A NOTE ON LANGUAGE

"ESKIMO" IS THE BEST-KNOWN TERM for the Native Americans depicted in this book, but it did not originate with them. In their language, they call themselves "Inupiat," meaning "the people." "Eskimo," a term brought into Alaska by white men, is what certain Indian tribes in eastern Canada called their neighbors to the north. It probably meant "eaters of raw flesh."

Nonetheless, "Eskimo" and "Inupiat" are used more or less interchangeably in northwest Alaska today, at least when English is spoken, and that is the usage followed in this book.

The Inupiat call their language Inupiaq. A few words in it—those commonly mixed with English in northwest Alaska—appear in the book, along with some local colloquialisms in English. They are defined below. As spelling varies among Inupiaq-English dictionaries, I have used when possible the most phonetic spellings for the benefit of non-Inupiaq readers.

A NORTHWEST ALASKA GLOSSARY

aaka (AH-): mother

aana (AH-nuh): old lady, grandmother

aanaga (UH-nah-gah): auntie

aaqaa! (ah-CAH): you stink!

agnauraq (ug-NOR-uq): little woman, slang for gay man

angatquq (AHNG-ut-cook): shaman

aqpattuq (UQ-put-tuq): runs

arigaa! (AH-de-gah): it's good!

arii! (ah-DEE): ouch! it hurts!

atiqluk (ah-TEEK-luk): woman's flowered parka

bunnik (BUN-nuk): affectionate term for daughter. The actual Inupiaq word is **paniq**.

inuksuk (IN-uk-suk): a stone trail marker erected by Eskimo peoples all around the circumpolar world. By tradition, an *inuksuk* meant, "You are on the right path."

Inupiaq (in-OO-pyock): one Eskimo; the Eskimo language

Inupiat (IN-you-pyat): more than one Inupiaq; the Inupiat people

ivu (EE-voo): ice override, ice pushed onshore by storm winds

kunnichuk (KUH-nee-chuck): Arctic entry, or vestibule

muktuk (MUCK-tuck): whale hide with a layer of fat attached

naluaqmiiyaaq (nuh-LOCK-me-ock): someone who acts almost white

naluaqmiu, naluaqmiut (nuh-LOCK-me): white person, white race

nuliagatigiik (NU-lee-AG-ah-teek): co-husbands; two men who have sex with the same woman

pibloktoq (pib-LOCK-tock): Arctic hysteria

pukuk (PUH-kuk): get into things

qaaq (cock): marijuana

qiviktuq (KIV-ick-tuck): suicide

quaq (kwok): frozen fish

quiyuk (KWEE-yuck): sex

quyaana (kwee-YAH-nuh): thank you

sheefish: a delicious freshwater whitefish that can reach 60 pounds in size

snerts: a rambunctious multi-player variant of solitaire

Suka (SOO-ka): derived from *sukattuk*, Inupiaq for fast

tuuq (tuke): long-handled ice chisel for making sheefishing holes

ulu (oo-loo): traditional Eskimo woman's knife, shaped like a slice of pizza with the cutting edge at the rim

yoi! (yoy): so lucky

He came in unto me to lie with me, and I cried with a loud voice.

— Genesis 39:14

CHAPTER ONE

Tuesday, April 15

"YOU SEE, CHIEF?" Alan Long pointed at the corpse on the snow. "What I said on the radio? He was lying right there when he got hit. He must have been passed out, all right."

Nathan Active continued his study of the dead man without comment. The wind blasted snow past them and a Cessna 207 labored past on climb-out from the Chukchi airport a half-mile west.

The victim sprawled face-down on the snow a couple of yards off the trail that ran east from Chukchi to the villages up the Isignaq River. He was bundled in well used but serviceable winter gear, right down to the stained legs of his black snowgo suit—probably from kneeling in blood and guts to cut up game—and a patch of duct tape on the right shoulder of his parka. From a rip in the collar, a tuft of goose down was working its way out. He was tall for an Inupiaq—taller than Long, about the same height as Active. What little of his hair could be seen was jet black, no trace of gray.

Active crouched beside the victim's head, which had rolled to one side. Judging from his injuries, a snowmobile had hit him from behind and to the left. The cleated drive track had evidently run up his legs and back, then torn through the neoprene face mask he had worn against the wind. The cleats had peeled the skin off the left side of his head from crown to jaw, leaving exposed flesh like raw hamburger. Bone glinted white in spots. A patch of scalp was gone above the left ear. Through the gap bulged a fold of reddish-gray pulp that Active took to be brain matter. The rest of his head was still covered by the mask.

Active stood and looked down the trail toward the village in the morning light. "I don't think so."

"Think what?"

"I don't think he was passed out when he got hit."

"Ah?" Long came closer.

"Smell any booze on him? See any bottles around?" Active pointed at the snow nearby. "Or snowgo tracks leading up to him? I think he was on the trail when he was hit and the impact knocked him over here. That means he was on his feet."

Long sniffed the air, put his head closer to the victim and sniffed again, then squinted the Inupiaq no. "What difference is it? He's walking along the trail sober and a snowgo knocks him over here. Maybe the guy on the snowgo was drunk, then."

Active nodded. "Probably. What do you make of those?" He pointed at a set of snowgo tracks that passed within a few feet of the victim.

Long took a look. "Maybe there was two of them?"

"Yeah, or only one and he came back to check."

"And didn't even help him. *Arii*, some people." Long squinted again, this time in dismay.

Active studied the tundra around them. This close to town, snowgo tracks laced and crisscrossed the main trail in a tangle of loops and whorls and side trails. "Just get pictures of the body and those tracks and everything around here, OK?"

Long lifted his eyebrows in the Eskimo 'yes,' pulled a Nikon from the folds of his parka and went to work.

"You recognize him?" Active asked.

Long squinted the no. "His face is too chewed up, the part you can see, anyway."

The near-total absence of blood said the victim hadn't lived long after he was hit, but Active had checked for a pulse anyway. As Long had reported by radio, there was no sign of life.

From the airport came a muted roar as a Boeing 737 taxied out from the Alaska Airlines terminal. Active wondered if the crew or passengers would spot the two cops and the corpse on the tundra.

"He's cooled off some and there's a little snow blown over him," Active said. "But not much snow and he's not frozen yet, so—"

"So he probably wasn't here all night?"

"Probably not," Active said. "You check for ID?"

"You said not to touch him if he was already dead."

Active grunted approval. He thought of going through the corpse's pockets but decided against it. Best to disturb nothing until Long finished shooting. He stepped back a few paces to think.

The dead man had been discovered by a family from the village of Ebrulik on their way to Chukchi on snowgos, dog sleds hitched behind for passengers and cargo. Trimble Sundown, the patriarch of the clan, had pulled off the trail to relieve himself on the tundra, only to stumble upon the corpse.

Trimble had checked for signs of life, found none, and then, having neither cell phone nor radio in his gear, had cranked up his Arctic Cat, resumed the journey with his family, and reported the find via a call from his mother's house in Chukchi.

Exactly what had happened next was a puzzle to be sorted out later. The report that had reached Active was of a drunk passed out on the Isignaq trail east of the airport. He had dispatched Long by snowgo with an EMT kit and a couple of sleeping bags in a tub-like ahkio cargo sled to retrieve the sleeper. Active conjectured that the dispatcher at public safety—white, like most of the force—had misunderstood Trimble's village English. In any event, Long had reached the scene, radioed back to say they in fact had what looked like a fatal hit-and-run, and Active had mounted his own department Yamaha and headed out.

Long finished shooting, came to Active's side, and handed him the Nikon. Active surfed through the pictures on the display, nodded, and passed the camera back. The roar from the airport built as the Alaska 737 started its takeoff roll at the west end of Chukchi's main runway.

"What was he doing out here?" Active said. "No snowgo, nobody with him. Who walks this far by himself that early in the morning? Especially sober."

"Good question, Chief."

"You don't have to call me 'Chief.' It's understood."

"Sure, Chief."

Active grimaced.

"Sorry, uh...boss?"

"'Nathan' would be better."

Long squinted another 'no.' "*Arii*, I dunno."

"All right, call me 'boss.' Unless we're arresting somebody or questioning them. Then you can call me 'Chief.' How's that?"

Long raised his eyebrows.

"You talk to Trimble yet?"

Long nodded. "I called him at his mom's house."

"And he didn't see any snowgos around when he made his relief stop? Didn't meet any back up the trail?"

Long squinted no.

The Alaska jet was close now, almost overhead. At first they couldn't see it, because of the blowing snow picked up from the surface. But the layer was shallow and the sky above was a blue bowl with a white rim

Thunder rumbled in Active's chest. Long looked up as the 737 became visible above them. The rumble started to fade as the jet passed over the crosses of the village's ridge-top cemetery and vanished into the haze.

"That's her plane, ah?"

Active looked up, too. "Yes, and thank God for it. Imagine having that woman in our hair while we try to sort this out."

CHAPTER TWO

Friday, April 11

Four Days Earlier

"ME GUARD THAT woman?" Active looked across his desk at Patrick Carnaby, commander of the Alaska State Trooper post in Chukchi. "Let me explain it this way: No. That's a Trooper job. It's not a job for borough public safety."

"Nathan, Nathan." Carnaby's face took on an expression of charitable piety. He tapped the green folder he had just dropped on the desk. "This is a marvelous opportunity, guaranteed to put you and your fledgling department on the map right out of the gate."

Carnaby waved his coffee cup at the move-in clutter around them in what, a few weeks earlier, had been the office of the chief of police for the city of Chukchi.

Now it was the office of Nathan Active, newly appointed chief of public safety for the newly created Chukchi Regional Borough. The borough had absorbed the police functions of the city of Chukchi and acquired jurisdiction over the surrounding eleven villages in the patch of Arctic coastline, tundra, mountains, rivers, and lakes known as the Chukchi region. The borough was bigger than fifteen of the United States, and now one-time Alaska State Trooper Nathan Active was responsible for the public's safety on every square foot of it.

"Not to mention on the evening news," Carnaby went on. "And cable news, talk radio, the New York Times,

Flitter, and—what do they call those Internet things, globs?"

"The word is blogs. And it's Facebook or Twitter, not Flitter."

"That's it," Carnaby said with a twinkle in his eye. "Twitface. Anyway, you spend a couple of days bouncing around the countryside with our gorgeous governor in Cowboy's Cessna and you'll be an international celebrity. Your face will be on the cover of People Magazine right beside hers."

"Not so much," Active said. "The media don't follow her around like they used to. She only makes national news when she does something ridiculous and the papers here find out and it blows up. Remember when her limo hit the cat and the Juneau paper reported it and PETA got all over her?"

Carnaby chuckled. "Admittedly, her last try at national office was unfortunate. How many countries did she want to invade?"

Active shrugged. "I lost count."

"So did she, I suspect," Carnaby said. "The point is, she's determined to fight her way back into the headlines. Helen Mercer does not know the meaning of the word 'quit.'"

"Or 'mercy,' either, from what I hear," Active said.

Carnaby nodded. "When she played high-school ball here—well, that's when they started calling her Helen Wheels. Which takes us back to you, young man. You really want to stand in her way?"

"I just wanna dodge this bullet."

"Coming home to Chukchi to watch her husband win the Isignaq 400 is part of her master comeback strategy." Carnaby patted the green folder again. "You help the governor show herself heroically braving the Arctic skies in a tiny Bush plane while playing the loyal spouse and you get yourself not only her undying gratitude but, what, at least ninety seconds on Fox News? "

"Coming home? Ha. How long since she really lived here?"

Carnaby waved a hand in dismissal. "Granted, it's been some years since she graduated from mayor to the state legislature and then to the governor's mansion. But there's no place like home and now she's back and she wants you to watch her body."

"All right, let me explain it a different way," Active said. "No chance, no hope, and no thanks. It's a suicide mission and we both know it. My plan is to avoid her presence, cross my fingers, and hope she gets out of town safely. I've got all I can do right here in Chukchi trying to keep the lid on till the race is over, anyway. Plus, I need to go up to Katonak on the honeybucket murder—"

"Honeybucket murder? Do I know about this one?"

"No reason you should, I guess. Only happened last night and the guy turned himself in already. Apparently he and a buddy got into a fight over the ownership of an Igloo cooler full of homebrew, the honeybucket got kicked over in the fight and then there was another fight over that. And when the first guy woke up and saw his buddy dead, he staggered over to my village safety officer's house and turned himself in. Actually, he said he was sorry and begged my guy to shoot him, but all he got was arrested. And now I have to bring him down here."

Carnaby waved it off. "Let Alan go. Or have the safety officer bring him down. Sounds open-and-shut."

Active shook his head. "Thanks, but, I still gotta pass on this one. I want to check in with my safety officer up there and ask a few questions before I button it up."

"You may not exactly have a choice. She—" The door banged open and Carnaby jumped out of his chair. "Why, here she is now! Welcome home, Governor, this is Chief Active. Nathan, have you met our governor?"

Active masked his astonishment as she swept into the room, complete with the scarlet Helly-Hansen parka, the rectangle glasses, the weapons-grade cheekbones, and a cloud of the famous perfume, though he couldn't remember what it was called. And the calf-length high-heel boots—what was the brand? Something weird and a little suggestive, if he remembered.

She crossed the office, hand out. He rose without conscious effort and his hand met hers of its own accord.

"Chief Active." She shook his hand and held it a moment longer than necessary. "What a pleasure!"

Active stifled simultaneous impulses to ask why, and to punch Carnaby in the face. "The pleasure's all mine, Governor," he managed.

"Good to see you again, Governor." Carnaby put out his hand. Mercer turned her head away. The Trooper captain gave a slight eye roll. "Governor, I was just—"

Mercer shot him a frown and he shut up. Carnaby retreated to the only other chair in the office, which was against the back wall. She took his seat in front of Active's desk.

"Sit, Nathan, sit, we need to talk. We haven't met yet, right?"

Active dropped into his own chair behind the desk. "No, ma'am, you were already governor when I got here and—"

"I know, I know, I'm not home nearly as much as I'd like to be. It's so hard to do that, now, much as I love my Chukchi and I guess...well, our paths just haven't crossed."

"No, ma'am."

"Has Captain Carnaby told you how much I need you?"

"He was just starting to exp—"

"Yes, I want you for my bodyguard while I fly the Isignaq 400 and cheer my husband on for the next couple days."

Active gave Carnaby a fast look. The trooper threw up his hands in the international symbol for bureaucratic surrender.

"But, Governor, I think you'll be perfectly safe in Chukchi and the villages. And, anyway, don't the troopers usually—"

He froze at Mercer's look. Too late, he noticed Carnaby's grimace and warning head shake from behind the governor.

"I will not have a trooper anywhere near me." Mercer swung on Carnaby. His expression dissolved into bland impassivity. She turned back to Active. "The last one was guarding my body, all right. Especially my butt when I climbed the stairs to my office. I sent him back to Juneau this morning."

Behind her, Carnaby circled his ear with a fingertip.

"Of course my department will be happy to help in any way possible, Governor." Active snapped his fingers. "In fact, one of our officers, Alan Long, was born in a fish camp up the Isignaq and I'm sure he'd be only too happy—"

"No."

"I'm sorry?"

"I don't want Alan Long. I want you."

"Me?"

"Posilutely." She nodded and gave him the smile made famous on her campaign posters and book covers. "So we're all set!"

He shot another quick glance at Carnaby, who winked.

"May I ask how you chose me for this honor? I had no idea you were even aware—"

"Oh, I'm very aware of you, Nathan. I still have my sources here. You can take the girl out of the village, but you can't take the village out of the girl, am I right?"

"So they say."

"To be exact, I was very impressed by your interview with Roger Kennelly on Kay-Chuck the other night."

"You pick up Chukchi public radio in Juneau? I didn't know—"

"They stream it on the Internet, duh! Modern times, Nathan."

"Of course, what was I thinking?" He slapped his forehead, as she seemed to expect.

She shot him another grin. "I liked what I heard about your ideas for the new department you're creating here. I liked it very much. So much so that I've suggested to our commissioner of public safety that you might make a good director of state troopers in Anchorage the next time the job opens up. Which I anticipate will be soon."

Active rubbed his eyes. "Director of the Alaska State Troopers." He gave Carnaby a vengeful look. "Meaning I'd be Captain Carnaby's supervisor?"

Carnaby shuddered behind Mercer's back.

"Come to think of it, you would!" She shot Carnaby another blood-freezing glare, then turned back to Active with an expectant air.

"It's a great honor, Governor, but—"

"Suka."

"I'm sorry?"

"Please. Call me Suka. That was my nickname when I played basketball here. It comes from the Eskimo word for 'fast' and it's what my friends use." She leaned across the desk and touched his forearm. "I hope you'll be my friend now?"

"Of course, Gov—er, Suka. But there's so much I need to do here." He waved at the litter of file boxes and office equipment on his floor. "I just took over. We're still getting moved in."

Mercer glanced at the clutter and sighed. "The director's job can wait, I suppose. But when you're ready, you just let me know."

"Of course, Governor. Of course."

"And, meantime, you'll be my bodyguard for the race?" She widened her eyes and waited. "You have a reputation as a guy who won't back off, no matter what. That's exactly what I want if things go sideways out there, right?" She waited some more. "Look, Nathan, I, that is, the state, of course, we do fund over half your department's budget, right? And this seems like such a small thing to ask. You know, as one friend to another."

Active faked a delighted grin. "Of course, Suka. Absolutely. Your wish is my command."

She nodded with a gratified look. "Now, where was I? Oh, yes, your interview on Kay-Chuck. That network of women's centers you and Grace Palmer want to set up around the region? I am totally in support of women's rights, other than contraception for girls, of course, and abortion. But if you need an additional appropriation, just let me—well, here." She scribbled something on a business card and handed it to him. "That's my personal cell number. You call me absolutely any time you need absolutely anything." She touched his arm again. "Anything at all, any time at all. You've got a friend in Juneau, Nathan. A true friend? Okay?"

Active nodded.

Mercer rose and swung on Carnaby, who let his game face slip a little under the pressure. "You have the information my staff emailed up?"

Carnaby pointed at the green folder on the desk. "I printed it all out."

"And you'll brief Chief Active on my schedule and make sure he has all the state resources he needs?"

Carnaby nodded again and started out of his chair.

"No! Don't get up!"

Carnaby sank back down.

Mercer turned back to Active. "Nathan, great to finally meetcha, I can't wait to fly the race with you and watch Brad win his third Isignaq 400! My staff arrives on the noon jet tomorrow. We'll meet them and get organized, and then we'll be off up the river with the legendary Cowboy Decker. Brad should hit Isignaq tomorrow afternoon to give his dogs their last mandatory rest stop, and cross the finish line here in Chukchi the day after, so we should be out for just the one night and two days. All good, Chief Active?" She snapped him a mock salute.

To his shock, he found himself picturing her in a tight sailor suit, the blouse open except for a knot at her bellybutton. Christ, what was this mojo she had? "All good, Suka," he said.

She wheeled and swept out of the office in another cloud of perfume. Active and Carnaby listened as her footsteps clacked down the hall. After a few seconds, Carnaby rose and peered after her.

"She gone?"

"Gone." Carnaby dropped into the chair before Active's desk and let out an exhausted breath.

Active waved the business card at him. "And I have her personal cell number."

"Not my circus, not my monkeys," Carnaby said. "Not any more."

CHAPTER THREE

Friday, April 11

ACTIVE TUCKED THE card into his shirt pocket. "But what the hell was it about?"

"You heard what I heard. She wants you to guard her body."

"Because one of your Troopers looked at her butt? Seriously, her butt?"

"She thinks every man looks at her butt," Carnaby said. "Which most of them do, probably. Also, don't forget, she told that TV reporter she doesn't like people judging her by her chest size. So, don't get in front of her or behind her, and you'll be fine."

"But—"

"And I definitely wouldn't use that word around her."

"Jesus," Active said. "She's even crazier than people say."

Carnaby's eyes twinkled. "I hear she can see the White House from her house. You'd think we would have learned our lesson from the last woman governor we elected. But, no, we had to do it again."

"I mean, I heard the Juneau guys talk about her when I worked for you, but—"

"That's our governor," Carnaby said. "A woman of iron whim. Not for nothing is she known as Helen Wheels even to this day."

"I'm doomed. I ride around for two days with her in Cowboy's Cessna, she's gonna think I'm looking at her butt or her boo—er, ah, chest, for sure."

"Actually," Carnaby said, "you want my theory? It

may not be the butt-checking at all. Maybe what it is, she does get any news coverage while she's out here in the Bush, she wants to make sure there's a Native face in the picture, so as to broaden her appeal in this multicultural society of ours. Mad she may be, but there's usually some method in it."

"Her husband's half Inupiaq," Active said. "Why does she need me?"

"The lady demographic maybe? You do wear a uniform and a Glock, and I don't have to tell you what that does to some women." Carnaby grinned. "But seriously. I didn't know this guy she just fired very well, but I'm told he was in all fairness somewhat lacking in emotional intelligence—an area where you excel, I might point out."

Active studied the trooper captain in the spring sun flooding through the third-floor windows. The Super Trooper, as he had been known when Active was at the public safety academy in Sitka, was six-two, square-jawed, and still looked fit at age sixty or so. But there was a hint of jowl under the jaw these days, a little gravel in the voice, a little more salt than pepper in the hair and mustache. The bifocals that had appeared a year earlier were pushed up on his forehead.

When Carnaby had first arrived in Chukchi, as Active understood it, he had a family in Anchorage and plans to return to it in a couple of years. But here he still was, with a live-in girlfriend, a boat, and a plane, and no word lately of the Anchorage family. And now he was retiring, what with the Chukchi Borough taking on the police powers once wielded by the Troopers. So far, he showed every sign of staying on in Chukchi. Maybe he had missed too many planes, as the saying went, to go home again.

Carnaby cocked an ear. "We got company?"

There was a rustle outside, then a tap.

Active grimaced. "Come in, Lucy."

The door swung open to admit Lucy Brophy, one-time dispatcher and office manager for the Chukchi police department, now office manager for the new borough public safety department. A blue folder rested on her prominent belly. "I wasn't listening when the governor was here," she said.

"Of course not," Active said. "The thought never crossed our minds."

"Not for one moment," Carnaby said.

"*Arii*, I wasn't. She's sure pretty, ah?" Lucy said it with what struck Active as studied casualness. He didn't respond. "I read she's a size six. I wish I was a size six." She laid the folder on Active's blotter. "Maybe I'll go on Amazon and order some Naughty Monkeys, too. You have to sign the paychecks."

"I do?"

"Sure, it comes with your new job. Finance sent them over." She snuffled a little as she said it, and felt around in the pockets of her sweater.

"You got a cold?" Active said

"No, it's just my allergies."

He handed her his handkerchief. She looked at it, then at him.

"Don't worry, it's clean."

"*Arii*, I know." She took it and dabbed her eyes, then blew her nose.

Active opened the folder and looked at the top of the stack. "I sign my own paycheck? Isn't that a conflict of interest or something?"

"Not if it's under fifteen thousand. Then the mayor has to sign it."

Active signed checks. Lucy looked at Carnaby. "Is Nathan going to Anchorage?"

"I thought you weren't listening," Carnaby said.

"I heard on accident," Lucy said.

"He's not going anywhere any time soon," Carnaby said. "You heard wrong."

"I don't think so," Lucy said. "I have really sharp ears."

Active handed her the folder. She offered him the handkerchief, which he declined.

She left and closed the door behind her. Carnaby looked at Active, then at the door, and raised his eyebrows.

"Thank you, Lucy," Active said in his command voice. "That'll be all."

They heard a bustle outside, then footsteps receded down the hall.

Carnaby chuckled. "Interesting life you lead, Chief Active. Your ex-girlfriend is your office manager?"

"She came with the package," Active said. "It's fine. She's a blissfully happy married woman now."

"And pregnant again," Carnaby said. "How far along? And how many is this?"

Active scratched his temple. "Six or seven months, and number two."

"And suffering from allergies, it seems. But in April? With everything still frozen solid? When did that start?"

"How would I know?"

"Maybe it started right outside the door when she heard you might go to Anchorage to run the Troopers."

"And maybe it's none of your business. Like I said, married, blissfully happy, number two on the way."

"And what are these Naughty Monkeys she wants?"

"That's it!" Active snapped his fingers. "The boots the governor was wearing."

"Mm-hmm. Well, you and Lucy have fun with your shiny new cop shop. Where were we, now? Oh, yes, your flight-seeing expedition with the governor."

"Oh, God."

"Assuming you can resist the temptation to induct her into the Mile-High Club in the back of Cowboy's Cessna, there may be a way out of this."

"What way?"

"If history is any guide, a few days in your company will be enough for our governor to get quite enough of you. She'll move on to something else. Or someone."

"How is it a way out if she ends up hating me? The state money for my department could go up in a puff of smoke. Like that bodyguard."

Carnaby tented his fingers and beamed over them at Active, who groaned. "It's all a matter of calibration, Nathan. Turn that emotional intelligence of yours up to 'stun' and make sure you're just cooperative enough while you're with her, but not more so. Gracious but reserved, if you will."

"What the hell does that mean?"

"You'll figure it out." Carnaby leaned forward, grinned, and touched his forearm just like the governor had done. "If not, you do have her cell number."

Active slapped away Carnaby's hand. "Maybe I could be sick tomorrow and send Alan Long."

Carnaby's eyebrows shot up. "That nitwit? After what she said about him?"

"He's not a nitwit," Active said. "You just—"

"You just have to watch him," Carnaby said. "I know. We've all had guys like that. In fact, I once supervised a young trooper who jumped out of Cowboy Decker's Super Cub in mid-air. Without a parachute."

"It was not mid-air and I did not jump," Active said. "Cowboy was hovering in a high wind and I stepped out onto a snow bank."

"And dislocated your shoulder."

"A gust caught us, is all."

Carnaby waved a hand in dismissal. "The point is, the governor likes you. Play it right and you'll be fine."

He flipped open the folder and ran his finger down the schedule for the week. "See, she got in yesterday to drop the starting flag for the race and she and her kids are staying at their place here in town tonight. Like she said, the race leaders will overnight in Isignaq tomorrow, Saturday, and finish here in Chukchi the next day. She'll park her daughters with her parents while you and Cowboy will fly her and the videographer, who happens to be her son, out to watch Brad mush into Isignaq. Then, while he looks to his dogs and sets up camp for the night, the governor stays with the family of the Episcopal minister there in Isignaq. The next day, Sunday, she barnstorms a couple of the upriver villages for *muktuk* eating and Eskimo dancing and such, then Cowboy does a 180 and whisks her back to Chukchi in time to cheer Brad on as he leads the pack down Beach Street, after which they spend the evening celebrating his victory in a manner not appropriate for minions like ourselves to speculate upon, however tempting the prospect might be. The evening of the next day, Monday, is the mushers' banquet, where she passes out the trophies, and the morning after that she jets off to Juneau, restoring peace and tranquility to our little hamlet on the tundra."

He passed over the folder. "Until next time."

CHAPTER FOUR

Friday, April 11

ACTIVE WALKED DOWN two flights of stairs to the ground floor of the public safety building and out into the brilliant April sun. He fumbled through his parka pockets for the mirror sunglasses essential to survival this time of year and slipped them on as he climbed into the new Chevy crew-cab that had come with the new job.

One thing he had to give Chukchi was April. The village might have winters that lasted most of the year with months of near-continuous darkness and a relentless west wind that blew for weeks on end, but then would come April.

There was no better day in life than a fine Arctic day in early April, for his money. The snowdrifts were still intact and they incandesced like titanium in the sun. Daytime temperatures soared up near plus twenty, so warm you could leave your parka unzipped in the sunlight. Even at night, the mercury didn't drop much below zero.

He started the Chevy, drove west on Church Avenue to Beach Street and turned north along the seawall being built to protect the village from the Chukchi Sea.

At the south end of Beach Street was Chukchi Region Inc.'s newly renovated Arctic Inn, modern as anything in Anchorage, right down to an espresso stand, free wi-fi, and rooms with pay-per-view porn and professional sports on cable.

After that came a stretch of log cabins crumbling

back to nature, some with caribou antlers lining the eaves as had been the custom until a few years ago. In front of the old cabins, cars, trucks, outboard motors, and snowgos rusted away—slowly in the dry, northern climate—in their effort to return to iron ore. A few were draped in abandoned mattresses, soggy and mildewed in summer, hard-frozen under the snow in winter.

The north end was marked by the towering cranes of the Chukchi docks, where everything that sustained the village arrived if it wasn't so urgent it had to come by air.

Beach Street was, in its way, a museum of Chukchi's past and present. Even its future, if you counted the near-complete seawall on along the shore.

The ice of the bay was still solid in front of the village. Kids and *aanas* jigged for tomcod fifty yards offshore, and farther out, a snowgo headed inland with a dogsled-load of family and gear. Most likely, Active figured, they were in pursuit of the fat white sheefish that schooled up under the ice around the mouth of the Katonak River this time of year.

Grace's house was far up the street, almost to the docks. It shared an alley with the high school where her father had been a teacher, then principal, until her mother had shot him to keep him from molesting Nita, the daughter he had sired by Grace.

Active blinked behind his mirrors to clear away the story, so dark and immense that to survive it was, he had come to understand, the central effort of Grace Palmer's life. Her job, she had explained, was to get up every day and go out and play a normal woman and not let her past suck her down like the cold restless current always at work under the sea ice.

As he pulled up at the Palmer house, he saw Grace at work with a power drill on the clapboard wall beside the front door. He rolled down his window and leaned out to watch. She hadn't noticed him yet, probably because the drill had drowned out the sound of his arrival. She bit her lower lip and squinted in concentration.

The sun that angled in from the southwest picked out auburn highlights in her hair—he'd never noticed those before—and, when she turned just the right way, brushed the corners of the foxlike eyes behind her sunglasses. He honked the Chevy's horn. She didn't react. He turned on the siren for a couple of hoots. She lowered the drill and turned and pulled out earplugs.

"Hey, baby!" they said at the same time.

He left the pickup, and climbed the steps to the deck. "What's all this?" he said before he noticed the sign that leaned against the wall.

She stepped back and they looked at the sign together: Chukchi Region Women's Crisis Center.

"Pretty nice, huh? The kids from the high school shop class brought it over a couple hours ago."

"Pretty nice, all right," he said. "And not a moment too soon. The ribbon-cutting still on for next week?"

She nodded. "Yep, Friday. I'm just about packed up and ready to move out of this place to live in sin with my favorite cop."

"Here's to sin," he said.

She gave him an elbow in the ribs and a kiss that was pretty long and hot for a public venue like the front steps of her home. But when he put some pelvis into it she stiffened and pulled back. "Maybe when I'm out of this house."

"That's what I'm thinking," he said. "And hoping."

"I know, baby. Fingers crossed." She opened the door and waved him in like an usher. "Come on, dinner is ready.

"Sonny!" she yelled when they were inside. "You

staying for dinner?"

"Sorry, Gracie, I gotta bounce," said Sonny Johnson, Active's half brother, as he came out of the back room where the center's computers lived. "But your new network's set up. All secure and everything like the government wants. You can tell them to test it now."

"Thanks, again, it would break us trying get somebody up from Anchorage to do this. Sure I can't pay you? The center does have some money for this kind of stuff."

"Nah, that wouldn't be right, charging family."

"Not even a sheefish dinner?"

"*Arii*, I got basketball practice, all right. But I think Mom's got some, too, for when I get home. Hey, Nathan, how you doing?" Sonny extended a fist for the bump that was replacing Chukchi's customary single-pump handshake among the younger generation.

Active bumped. "Not bad for a cop. You?"

Sonny shrugged and opened the door. "You know. It's Chukchi."

"Bounce? Where do they learn to talk like that?" Grace said as Active shut the door.

"TV, the Internet, the gym, Eskimo soul travel, who knows?

He followed her toward the kitchen, enjoying the view as her backside rolled in her jeans and hoping this latest move to escape her own story would pan out. She had donated the house she'd inherited upon her mother's death to the new borough to serve as the women's shelter, then gotten herself hired to run it and wangled a state grant to buy the house next door for an annex and set up a network of smaller crisis centers in the villages. Now she and Nita were moving into the house he'd rented on the lagoon behind town till they could buy or build one of their own.

She pulled a pair of sheefish salads from the

refrigerator and set out a stack of pancake-sized pilot bread saltines, plus a Diet Pepsi for him and a pot of green tea for herself. He dropped his briefcase onto a chair and himself into another.

"Nita still at school, is she? I don't see any mac and cheese on the table."

"Mm-hmm," Grace said around a mouthful of pilot bread. "Study group for a big social studies test."

"On a Friday afternoon? Her zeal is commendable."

"There's a cute boy in it."

Active raised his eyebrows in inquiry.

"A wise mom knows when not to ask."

"Ah."

Grace paused with a forkful of salad halfway to her lips and looked at the sea of packing boxes around them in the kitchen and in the hallway outside the door. "With any luck at all, that sign out front and what's happening to this house will make the son of a bitch spin in his grave."

Active nodded, then brooded. It had to be healthy for Grace to get out of her father's house, at least at night when they'd be together in the new place on the lagoon.

And if she spent her days inside the house, helping women who were victims of men like her father, that had to be healthy, too, right?

Then why did it feel so unhealthy? The unprocessed rage behind that last remark, maybe. *Make the son of a bitch spin in his grave.* A remark triggered, to all appearances, by his mention of Nita.

"What?"

He started, a little. "What what?"

"What's on your mind, duh."

"Oh, I had a mildly interesting conversation just now, is all."

"How interesting, exactly?"

"There's good news and bad news." He shrugged.

"Stop that! Stand and deliver, Chief Active."

He grinned. "It seems the governor wants me."

Her eyes widened. "And that's the good news or the bad?"

"Bad, I guess. It seems she heard my radio interview with Roger Kennelly and now she wants me to be the next director of the state troopers."

"Jesus! That woman!"

In Active's experience, no one in the state was neutral on its governor. Alaskans, particularly female Alaskans, either loved or hated Helen Mercer. Grace fell with great passion into the latter camp.

Active himself was the only exception he knew of. He neither hated nor loved the governor. Rather, he regarded Mercer, with her incomprehensible charisma and the passions it aroused, as one more dangerous natural phenomenon. Like rotting sea ice under a snowgo or deteriorating weather in mid-flight in a Bush plane, Helen Mercer was something to be accepted and coped with. Especially since the run for vice president on something called the Free America ticket that seemed to have stuck her manic personality in permanent overdrive.

"Yes, that woman," he said. "But the good news is, I may be able to get out of it."

"Hurray for that. I don't wanna move to Anchorage. Do you wanna move to Anchorage?"

"Some days I think about going back there," Active said. "It still feels more like home than this place, sometimes."

Grace's face registered such alarm that Active grinned and said, "But not on a sunny day in April. Who could want to leave the Arctic on a day like this?"

Grace rolled her eyes. "You said you might be able to

get out of it?"

"She wants me to be her bodyguard while she's here to cheer Brad on in the Isignaq 400." He fished Carnaby's green folder out of the briefcase and laid it on the table.

"Hah!"

"Hey, there's nothing funny about the 400. It's a grueling test of man and mutt."

"And a few women!"

"All right, a grueling test of man, mutt, and maiden. But it's still not funny."

"The 'hah' wasn't for the race. It was for the hype that she's coming here to cheer Brad on. She hasn't been back to Chukchi more than twice since she got elected governor. She's only here now so she can announce for president. Right in her home town, and right on the basketball court where she starred as a student and coached as a teacher."

"What? Where did you hear—wait a minute, you've been reading the blogs again!"

"Busted." She hung her head in mock shame. "They get things right, sometimes."

"Yeah, and if you put a million monkeys at keyboards, they'd eventually write all of Shakespeare. Not to mention 'Fifty Shades of Grey,' probably. But that doesn't mean Helen Mercer's going to run for president. Not after what happened the last time she tried national politics. She'd have to be..."

"Crazy? You were going to say 'crazy,' weren't you? But you stopped because you know she already is, don't you?" Grace beamed in triumph.

"No, I got some pilot bread stuck in my throat is all. I think I need a drink." He gulped at the Diet Pepsi. "Now, where were we?"

"You were going to explain why you have to guard

Helen Mercer's body, which I'm sure you don't mind one bit, right?"

"Why, whatever do you mean?" he said. He wanted to keep it light, but there was no light in Grace's face.

"You don't find her attractive?"

He tried to think over the din of alarm bells going off in his head. Finally, he thought he spotted a way through. "Actually, I find her terrifying."

Grace nodded. "I've heard she fires people on the slightest whim. And not just from bloggers."

He nodded. "That one does seem to be true."

"Anyway," Grace mused, "how big a deal can the bodyguard thing be? She spends some time in the state building here, makes a few public appearances, does a meet-and-greet at the mushers' banquet after the race, hands out the trophies, and she's outta here, right?"

She caught the look on his face. "No?"

"Not quite." He tapped the briefing folder.

She cocked her head and shot him the stink eye. "OK, what?"

"She's chartered Cowboy Decker so she can follow the last two days of the race from the air."

"And you'll be riding along with them?"

Active cleared his throat. "I will, yes."

"And do I recall correctly that this race includes overnights in the villages along the route?"

"It does, yes."

"And the governor will be overnighting, too?"

"She will, yes. But only once, at Isignaq village, which is the last mandatory rest stop in the race."

"And will she be sleeping with Brad?"

"I understand he prefers to sleep in a tent among his dogs."

"And the governor?"

"I don't believe the governor sleeps with the dogs, no."

"So you and the governor will be overnighting together?"

"Of course not," Active said. "I mean, we'll be together in the sense of being in the same village at the same time. But not in any other way, of course. She'll be staying with a minister and his family. Cowboy and I will be sleeping at the school. And, anyway, I'm a happily committed guy. And she's a happily married woman."

"Hah!" Grace said. "They're filing for divorce any day now. You should read the blogs. "

Active shook his head. "No doubt I should. Be that as it may, she asked me to be her bodyguard and I don't think I can refuse. Half my budget comes from the state."

"But why you? Isn't this a trooper job?"

Active took Grace through the butt-watching incident and the other intricacies of the governor's toxic relationship with the Alaska State Troopers. "You see now? All I have to do is flunk my tryout without making her so mad she cuts my budget, then things will get back to normal and I won't have to go to Anchorage."

"OK, fine." She picked up the three quarters of her salad not eaten, covered it in plastic wrap, and put it in the refrigerator. "You do as you think best. I'll be fine, just fine. Right here, all by myself, getting us moved into the new place."

What now? Should he try, "You're cute when you're jealous"? No, probably not. Then he remembered. "There is some good news, actually."

Grace eyed him with a skeptical expression. "Yes?"

"It seems she heard me mention our plan for the village crisis centers on the radio and is highly supportive."

Interest and suspicion wrestled for control of Grace's

expression. "Seriously?"

"So she said."

"So if I loan you to that woman for a few days, I get funding for my crisis centers?"

"I could even ask her about cutting the ribbon at your women's shelter next week."

"You know," Grace said after some reflection. "Life's a bitch. And then one gets elected governor. And you have to be nice to her."

Grace cleaned up the lunch things at the sink. Forks rattled, plates clanked, water ran, she said nothing. And her body language wasn't good.

"So," he said. "We all right? If not, are we gonna be?"

"Watch yourself around her," Grace said after a long thoughtful silence. "She may have summer in her eyes, but that heart is pure winter."

CHAPTER FIVE

Saturday, April 12

"GRACE, TOO? I thought it was just my wife." Cowboy Decker closed the access panel on the engine cowling of one of Lienhofer's Cessnas and muttered "Oil's good, anyway." The west wind flipped the panel back up. He swore, caught it, slapped it down again, and pushed on it with both gloved hands till it latched, then pulled the rear edge of the greasy orange engine cover back into place over the panel.

"Yep, Grace, too," Active said. "She actually used the f-word."

"Not 'fine'."

Active raised his eyebrows in the Eskimo yes. "Three times."

"The most terrifying word that ever came out of a woman's mouth," Cowboy said. "Linda used it right before I left. 'Fine, then. Fly all over the country with that woman if that's what you want.' "

The pilot checked the power cord for the electric heater he had put inside the engine compartment the night before. "Guess we better leave it in there for now. Pretty damned cold for April."

Cowboy was right about that. Ten below, with maybe twenty-five miles an hour of wind off the Chukchi Sea. A chill factor of minus forty, according to the morning report on Kay-Chuck.

It was so cold that even Cowboy had dressed for it. He wore the usual Ray-Ban sunglasses and ball cap, but his trademark leather bomber jacket was nowhere in sight. Instead, he was bundled up in Sorel boots, insulated rust-colored Carhartt overalls, and an oil-stained green parka patched in several spots with shiny gray duct tape. Heavy mittens dangled at his side on lanyards; he had flipped them off to use the woolen gloves he wore underneath when he checked the oil in the Cessna. Active was dressed to match, except that his overalls were green RefrigiWear, his parka was red, and he wore a fur hat with ear flaps instead of a baseball cap.

Cowboy turned and surveyed the sky east of the airport for sign of the Alaska Airlines jet that would deposit the governor's staff in Chukchi. There was no evidence of a Boeing 737, only the morning sun clearing the horizon.

"Late as usual," Cowboy grunted. He never missed a chance to show his contempt for the nitwits and incompetents who operated major airlines and big jets, particularly the pilots.

"Maybe if we handcuffed ourselves together and left the key with Grace or Linda," Active mused. "Then we could vouch for each other. The women would have to believe us."

"Yeah, right," Cowboy said with the familiar grin. "At times like this, a woman thinks with her hormones, not her brain."

Active gave a noncommittal grunt

Cowboy started his walk-around and Active stepped back to watch the ancient, lover-like ritual between plane and pilot. Cowboy ran a gloved hand along the front edge of the propeller to check for fresh damage from the gravel airstrips where Chukchi's Bush pilots did most of their business. Then he checked the fronts of the wings with the same tenderness, shook the wing struts, moved the ailerons at the back of the wings, waggled the tail flaps up and down, and swung the tail fin back and forth.

"Think it'll fly?"

"Posilutely." Cowboy punctuated it with a pretty good imitation of the governor's wink.

Active turned to look down the runway. "Hear that?"

Cowboy cupped a hand to his ear, peered east, and grimaced. Like most Bush pilots who'd been at it long, he'd lost some hearing. Active sometimes had to shout to be heard.

Together they watched the sky over the snow-covered folds of tundra past the runway's end. Then Cowboy pointed southeast. "Got 'im. Right there, see?"

Active picked it up, too—a landing light, glowing dull orange through the snow haze kicked up by the wind.

They watched as the pilot rolled his wings level on final approach, set the 737 down with a chirp from the tires, and taxied for the Alaska Airlines terminal.

Active looked at Cowboy. "Here we go."

"I guess," Cowboy said.

They walked from the tarmac through the Lienhofer office and out the customer door into the parking lot, where they climbed into Active's Chevy.

Two minutes later, they pulled up at the terminal and Active switched off the truck as the jet's turbines whined down. They went inside and watched as the 737's rear door swung open and a truck-mounted airstair rolled up.

For a while nothing happened, then Mercer pulled up outside in a bronze Ford Expedition with a teenage boy in the passenger seat and a decal from the late City of Chukchi on the door. Mercer stepped down, dressed in a snug black snowgo suit and scarlet down parka with a sunburst ruff of wolf fur, and hurried into the terminal. The teenager rushed after her with a video camera on his back and Mercer somehow talked herself and the boy through security and onto the apron. Mercer hurried up the airstair while the teenager positioned himself at the foot.

Cowboy looked at Active. "What's she doing?"

"Beats me," Active said. "She just told me to meet her here when the noon jet came in. What's with that old city Expedition, anyway?"

"I guess how our former mayor ended up with it when she left office to go to the legislature."

"Ah, that would explain it. And that's her son with her?"

"Right. 'Pudu,' they call him."

"Wait, she's not..."

Mercer stepped out the doorway of the jet with a curly-haired white man Active recognized as Phil Ackerman, her chief of staff. She paused at the top of the airstair, Ackerman at her elbow, to don sunglasses and wave at her son and his video camera as the wind pulled at the ruff of her parka.

"My God, she's faking her own arrival," Active said.

Cowboy chuckled. "I guess the press mob doesn't follow her around like they used to."

"Not so much, no."

"But she's gonna make the big announcement while she's here, right?"

"Maybe. Or maybe she just put out that rumor in hopes the reporters will show up when she hits the primaries Outside."

Behind the governor, other passengers were visible as they waited, more or less patiently, for her to get out of the way.

Mercer pulled out a phone, pressed it to her ear and started down the steps. She waved at the imaginary crowd a few more times, then gave Pudu a throat-slashing gesture to turn off his camera. Finally she entered the terminal.

There were a few cries of "Suka" as people recognized her. A teenager put up an iPhone and got some video as the governor caught Active's eye and walked over.

"Chief Active, Cowboy." She gave them the campaign grin. "All set for our big adventure?"

"Yes, ma'am," Cowboy said. "The plane's ready to go. In fact, it's the ladies—"

"No! Do not tell me it's my favorite Cessna! With the purple livery?"

Cowboy nodded. "Yes, ma'am, Five-Five-Two-Five-Sierra. The ladies' model."

"No way!"

"Yes, ma'am, I thought you'd want it. For old times' sake."

"Same old Cowboy Decker, I see." The videographer moved up and trained the camera on the governor. Mercer beamed and said, "Gosh, it's good to be back in Chukchi! Oh, and, Nathan, this is my son, Pudu."

The videographer bumped Active's fist and grunted a hello to Cowboy.

Ackerman stepped up and spoke into Mercer's ear. She nodded and the aide took a seat in the terminal's waiting area.

The governor turned to Active. "You guys wanna move my stuff and Pudu's from the Expedition to your rig and we'll get going?"

"Do we need to drop Mr. Ackerman somewhere?" Active asked.

"Oh, no," Mercer said. "He won't be staying. He just flew up to give me a status report on things in Juneau. He's flying right out again."

Active and Cowboy headed out to the Expedition. "Some status report," Cowboy muttered as they unloaded gear and transferred it to Active's Chevy.

"Ackerman's just here for show," Active said. "So it'll look like she's actually doing something while she's here."

"Ah," Cowboy said. "Good honest work, politics."

"Always and evermore. But what was that about the ladies' model? For old times' sake? Anything you need to tell me here?"

"Keep the customer happy," Cowboy said. "That's the Lienhofer motto. Always has been." He pulled the brim of the ball cap over his eyes and wouldn't meet Active's gaze.

In a couple of minutes, the Chevy was loaded and they were rolling, with Mercer in front beside Active and Cowboy and Pudu in back.

Active started to turn right for the half-block trip to Lienhofer's but Mercer touched his arm and pointed uptown. "Can we take a minute to look at the seawall project, Nathan? I want Pudu to get some video. My Reagan for Rushmore petition already got nearly a million Likes on Facebook, but I need a good solid local accomplishment in my ads too when I hit the primary states in a couple of weeks."

Active nodded and threaded the maze of little streets near the airport, worked his way to Beach Street, and started along the rampart of boulders and corrugated steel that in theory would save the street, perhaps the whole village, from the fall storms that howled in from the Chukchi and battered the shoreline with ice floes. The work was on winter hiatus, with a few remaining stacks of rock and steel guarded by orange traffic cones.

Active felt her hand on his arm again. "Let's stop here."

He parked the truck on the ocean side of the street.

"How's the project going?" she asked.

"Well enough, I think. They're supposed to wrap it up right after breakup. It's mostly cleanup left now."

"And that date's pretty solid?"

"As solid as anything gets around here." He shrugged.

Mercer's eyes frosted over. He sensed he had let a little too much Chukchi into his attitude.

"The borough's doing everything possible to make the deadline," he said. "The whole town's thrilled that you got us the money to protect Beach Street. In fact, the mayor's giving you an award at the mushers' banquet, but you're not supposed to officially know about it."

"Then I officially don't," Mercer said with a satisfied nod. Active relaxed a notch. The governor craned her neck to look into the back seat. "Pudu, let's get some video, OK?"

Pudu peered out at the snow whirling off the drifts and wrinkled his nose in reluctance. "*Arii*, this wind will get in the mike. The audio will be too noisy."

"That's OK. I can do a voice-over later."

"The camera might be too cold already from being in the back of the truck and the buildings are blocking the sun."

"Then you shouldn't have left it back there."

"*Arii*," Pudu said again, but he went to the rear and dropped the tailgate.

Mercer checked her makeup with the selfie camera in her phone, then put her hand on Active's sleeve again. "Nathan, do you mind? Walk with me along the shore here and explain the project while Pudu shoots."

"What? Me? Don't you want the mayor or somebody? Public safety's not really involved."

"Come on, I'll make ya famous!" She shot him a grin.

"Of course." Active flipped up his hood, climbed out of the truck, and went to the tailgate, where Pudu was putting a battery into the big Canon video camera. "Any way I can help?"

"She's the one you better help." Pudu cut his eyes toward Mercer in the passenger seat.

Active took a look. The governor's body language suggested a measure of impatience.

"You're supposed to open the door for her," Pudu said.

"Seriously?"

Pudu raised his eyebrows. "You're the bodyguard, ah?"

Active put on his game face, walked to the Chevy's passenger door, and pulled it open. "May I?" He put out his hand.

Mercer stepped down, put her arm through his, and drew him to the edge of the street. Pudu came around the truck with the camera and Mercer became all business. She unlinked arms and said, "Could you stand on my other side, please?"

When Active didn't get it, she pointed at Pudu and raised her eyebrows with an apologetic look.

Then Active understood. He was between Mercer and the camera. He stepped around her to the edge of the seawall and they waited. Then Pudu said, "OK, we're rolling, Mom."

"All right," Mercer told Active. "We'll just walk along here. You point at the sheet piling, up and down the waterfront, that kind of thing, and say whatever comes into your head."

Active pointed north, up the waterfront toward the cranes at the freight docks, as Pudu shot away, then swept his arm to point south. "As you know, Governor, we have a pretty serious combination of currents along the beach here, some of it from the Katonak River mouth a few miles north and some of it tidal currents from the Chukchi Sea, and all of it apparently exacerbated by global warming…"

He stopped as the governor squeezed his arm and pointed at the sheet piling below their vantage point on top of the seawall. He bent over to see what she was pointing at. "Officially speaking, Nathan, I don't believe in global warming," she said. "Luckily, we're not wearing mikes, but…"

"Ah," Active said. He fake-pointed where Mercer had fake-pointed and they resumed their stroll. "And down here we have the sheet piling, thanks to your own efforts, of course."

"And it's working, I see." She pointed at the slabs of ice jumbled against the seawall.

"It is indeed. We had a big storm from the southwest right after freezeup last fall, and the ice slammed in pretty hard."

Mercer nodded and gazed up Beach Street. "In the old days, we'd get what they call *ivu* and that stuff would ride up the shore and right out on the street like an uphill avalanche. Couple times, it even knocked into some of the houses."

"Our engineers assure us it will hold off the river and the ocean for at least thirty to fifty years."

"Especially since we don't have to worry about global warming?" Mercer asked with the grin.

"Exactly," Active said.

They were far enough down the beach that the videographer was behind them. "You don't have to point and wave now," Mercer said. "We can just chat."

"OK."

"First," she said, "thanks again for agreeing to be my bodyguard. It's overkill for Chukchi, I know, but it seems to come with the job."

"No problem. It'll be good to check in with my village safety officer in Isignaq."

She nodded. "And how are you feeling about the director's job today? We really could use some new blood in that office."

"I'm giving it serious thought, Governor. Thank you for considering me."

"Nathan."

He froze. Time stopped. It appeared the hammer was about to fall.

"Keep moving," she said. "Pudu's still rolling. And call me Suka, remember?"

"Look, er, Suka," he said. "I really am grateful. But I have things here—"

"Grace and her little girl?"

"Nita?" he asked. "She's actually Grace's cousin. Grace adopted Nita after her mother, Grace's aunt, died in a plane crash."

Mercer nodded. "I saw something about that in the records. Tragic, absolutely tragic. And Grace's father dying like he did. What a sad, unlucky family."

The records? Mercer had looked into the records of the Jason Palmer case? He was still groping for words when Mercer caught his expression and touched his arm.

"Just due diligence before I offered you the job. You can't be too careful these days." She turned and looked back up Beach Street. "Think that's enough footage, Pudu?"

"I'll try check." Pudu worked the buttons on the camera for a few seconds, then peered into the viewfinder. "It's good, all right. We could go now." He headed for the truck.

Mercer watched him go. "You know, he can talk white when he wants to. But he wants to talk Chukchi."

Active again could think of nothing to say.

"I can't get him to stay in Juneau, he just wants to be up here. One day he'll be like the rest of them—how's huntin', how's fishin', how's the weather? And basketball, of course."

"It is a religion here."

Mercer brightened. "Let's hit the trail, shall we?

CHAPTER SIX

Saturday, April 12

"LOOK LIKE A water sky, ah?" Pudu shaded his eyes and squinted west through the haze.

Active tried it with his sunglasses on, then off. The wind whipped the guard hairs of his wolfskin ruff into his eyes. He blinked away the tears. "What? I don't see it."

"That dark place out there?" Pudu pointed across the ice.

Active stared over the fuselage of Cowboy's Cessna 207 again. Maybe there was a black band along the horizon, maybe not. If so, it was far out to sea.

"Water sky?" Mercer said. "What's that?"

"It's when there's open water somewhere out in the ice, Mom," Pudu said. "The clouds over it are real dark. You remember, ah?"

"Thank you, Pudu, but I was asking our pilot. Cowboy?"

Cowboy shoved up his Ray Bans to survey the horizon, then shook his head. "Could be."

"Open water?" Active said. "In this cold? Does that—"

"Yeah, it probably means weather coming." Cowboy dropped the sunglasses over his eyes again. "Fog, a little snow maybe, warmer probably. We go, we might wish we hadn't."

"It's certainly not warm now," Mercer said with a shudder. "Can we go back inside while we make up our minds?"

Cowboy led them into the Lienhofer office with its

smells of cigarette smoke, ancient vinyl furniture, and the oil heater in a corner. At least it was warm, Active thought.

Cowboy spread the aviation chart for northwest Alaska on the counter and swept a hand along the coast from Nome to Cape Prince of Wales, where Alaska almost touched Siberia. "They're already getting it a little bit along here—Nome, Port Clarence, Tin City." He ran his hand north up the shore toward Chukchi. "The FAA says we'll probably have it in a couple-three days."

"But we'll be back tomorrow," Mercer said.

"Sometimes the weather gets ahead of the forecast."

Mercer rattled scarlet fingernails on the counter. "Or it never shows up. This is the Arctic. It could stay clear for the next week. Right, Cowboy?"

"It could," Cowboy said. "But I don't know how likely that is."

"Governor, ah, Suka, maybe you should just wait here in Chukchi for the race to finish," Active said. Could the water sky get him out of the bodyguard assignment?

Mercer looked at Pudu, who still had the video camera slung over his shoulder, then at Active. "We've got plenty of video of me walking around Chukchi. I didn't come all this way to be grounded by a little weather that may not even happen."

She turned summer eyes and the campaign smile on Cowboy. "You can get us through, right, Cowboy? You're the famous Bush pilot. Don't I remember the village girls calling you Clouddancer?"

Pudu snickered. Did Cowboy blush under the leathery skin he had acquired from years of Arctic sun and wind?

"Sure, yeah," the pilot said with a shrug. "Weather craps out on us, we can sneak into one of the villages upriver till it blows over."

Mercer looked at Pudu, then Cowboy. "All right, then. Let's do this!"

They trooped out to the plane, where a brief discussion arose about seating arrangements.

Mercer wanted to sit in front, beside Cowboy. Pudu pointed out that he would have to shoot from behind, which would permit no good angle to capture the governor's profile as she viewed the tundra, mountains, mushers, dog teams, and her husband.

"Good point, Pudu," Mercer said. Pudu climbed into the right front seat with his camera and Cowboy swung into the pilot's seat beside him. Mercer took the left rear seat, Active the right, and they donned headsets.

Mercer looked out the 207's side window, then forward at Pudu. "This angle gonna work for ya, Pudu?"

Pudu twisted in his seat, pointed the camera at Mercer, and peered into the viewfinder. "I think so, Mom. *Arii*, it's kinda dark inside this plane, though. I might have to use my light so you're not too backlit against the snow."

He pressed a button on the camera and a light came on above the lens. In the glare, Mercer looked like a suspect in a mug shot.

Pudu checked the viewfinder again. "Yeah, that should be good."

Active wondered, but Mercer gave a thumbs up and turned the smile on him. "Off we go, eh, Nathan?"

"Absolutely, Suka." Active cast a sidelong glance to see if the summer would leave her eyes. She took a tiny lapel mike from Pudu and clipped it to her parka hood.

As they taxied from the Lienhofer apron eastward down the runway, the west wind rattled the 207 from behind so hard that Active wondered if the flaps would come off. After all, from the Cessna's perspective, it was flying backward at thirty or thirty-five miles an hour.

Cowboy didn't seem to notice. He spoke into his headset and scrawled notes on a clipboard strapped to his right thigh. Active assumed he was filing a flight plan and going over the forecast again with the FAA.

Halfway down the runway, Cowboy hit the left brake. The plane spun on its main gear and stopped with the nose pointed down a belt of asphalt ending at the shore of the Chukchi Sea. The wings rocked in the river of frozen air rolling off the ice. Active was a little more convinced he could see the water sky.

Cowboy voice came over their headsets. "All set? Everybody strapped in?"

"Posilutely," Mercer said.

"Good here," Active said.

"Me, too," Pudu said from the front.

Cowboy pushed the throttle forward, the engine snarled, and the 207 leapt into the sky like a startled cat. Before Active could check on the water sky, Cowboy banked right and wheeled over the village to head across the Burton Peninsula and the inlet behind it, toward the mouth of the Isignaq River. In a few miles, they ran out of the coastal haze. Ahead now was only incandescent spring sun and the broad white embrace of the Isignaq Valley, the meanders, sloughs, and cutoffs of the big river still deep in hibernation in the brush-nubbled bottomlands.

A HALF-HOUR UPSTREAM, Isignaq village came into view, a pretty hamlet perched on the north bank of the Isignaq River where Siksrik Creek came in.

Active gazed over Mercer's shoulder as the village's hilltop airstrip crawled across the bottom of the 207's side window. He glanced forward and saw from Cowboy's profile that the pilot was also hooked on the sight. Active hoped Cowboy would let it pass in silence, but, no, he spoke.

"Takes you back, huh?" came his voice in the earphones.

Active looked at Mercer and at the back of Pudu's head. Neither showed any sign they had heard Cowboy.

"Is this just us?" Active asked.

"Roger that," Cowboy said. "I got the other two switched off."

"Yeah, it takes you back." Isignaq strip was where Cowboy had crashed and killed Grace's aunt, Aggie Iktillik. That event had delivered Nita into the hands of Grace's father, which had yanked Grace back to Chukchi from shell-shocked exile in the Aleutian fishing port of Dutch Harbor.

And then Grace's father, Jason Palmer, had ended up shot to death, supposedly by Grace's cancer-ridden and dying mother, who supposedly did it to keep him from raping Nita the same way he had raped Grace all those years ago and fathered Nita.

Active took the story on faith, because he would take anything on faith if Grace Palmer said it while she looked at him with those quicksilver eyes. Besides, Jason Palmer's killing was a city case, and Active had been a state trooper at the time, so it had been mostly not his problem.

But the cancer had finished off Grace's mother before the case came to trial. So it was still open as a technical matter, still buried somewhere in the archive boxes Active had inherited with the new job from the late Jim Silver, who had been Chukchi police chief at the time. Now it was Nathan Active's case, glowing like a radioactive ember in those archive boxes.

Active realized Cowboy hadn't said anything more. "You all right, buddy?"

"As much as I ever will be, I guess." Cowboy's voice was husky in the headphones. "If I just hadn't pushed so hard."

"If it hadn't happened, Grace would still be in Dutch Harbor and I'd still be...still be sleeping with perfectly nice village girls who deserved a lot more than I had to give them."

"Like Lucy."

"Exactly," Active said. "Like Lucy."

"Who can figure this shit out?" Cowboy said after a while.

"Not me," Active said.

"Me neither." There was a click, then static spritzed over the headsets. When Cowboy came back on, he was himself again. Or playing himself.

"So, folks, if you'll look out the left side of the aircraft, you'll see beautiful downtown Isignaq, tonight's rest stop for the mushers of the Isignaq 400. Speaking of which, we should pick up the race leaders in another half hour or so."

Cowboy followed the main channel of the Isignaq upstream, a thousand feet or so above the riverbed, wings about level with the tops of the bluffs and ridges lining the banks. Here and there, bands of caribou worked their way up the slopes, buglike with distance as they drifted north in the spring weather toward the calving grounds on the coastal plain of the Beaufort Sea.

Once they came upon an ancient Chevy Suburban speeding upstream along the well beaten trail on the river ice. "Hey, it's Roland Sweetsir," Cowboy said. "Must have some folks going up to watch the racers come by."

He dropped the Cessna's nose, dived down to treetop level and roared past the rusty old rig, wings rocking.

"Roland's still running Isignaq Ready-Ride?" Mercer asked. "Get out!"

Active looked back at the Suburban and saw an arm emerge from the driver's side, waving back at the Cessna.

"Oh, yeah," Cowboy said. "His river taxi business is still going strong. Roland's a lot cheaper than a 207 and he can go in worse weather than us. Of course he's a lot slower, too, plus you never know when he's gonna hit overflow and go through, but the village folk keep riding with him."

They spotted the first dog team twenty-five minutes past Isignaq village, a string of the compact little huskies that had proved best for long-distance races. The musher at the back of the sled kicked with one foot and stood with the other on a runner.

"That's not Brad," Mercer said from beside Active. "Why isn't he in the lead?"

Active studied the team as they roared over and Cowboy dropped the Cessna's nose to swing around for another look. "Not Brad?" Active said. "You could tell? I didn't even have time to count the dogs."

Mercer shot him a look and even Pudu pulled his eye from the viewfinder long enough to give Active a warning glance.

"Brad's all red," Mercer said. "Red parka, red snow pants, red sled bag, red harness on the dogs, red everything. His sponsor is Dodge, you know, and they like red. It's the power color, Nathan." She pointed out the window as Cowboy pulled past the team again. "This guy's got a blue bag and blue harnesses on the dogs and...my God, tell me he is not wearing Carhartts! What is he, homeless?"

"That's Bunky Ivanoff, ma'am," Cowboy said. "You remember him. He's got a camp way up the valley by a caribou crossing there, a few miles this side of Tuttuvak. Lives out most of the year, hunts and fishes all the time, gets a lot of respect. I brought him and his dogs down to Chukchi last week."

"Sounds like one of them old-time Eskimos, all right," Pudu said. "From early days ago."

Mercer was silent. "Oh, Bunky Ivanoff, yes, I think I do remember him. A fine Alaskan and a credit to...the entire Chukchi region!"

Active was pretty sure Mercer had been about to say "to his people" until she noticed the camera on her.

"Hell of a musher," Cowboy said. "Great guy, too. He runs—"

"I'm sure he is," Mercer said. "But where is Brad? We need some footage of me waving at Brad. I told him not to use Buster."

"Buster?" Active said. "Is that one of—"

"Buster's good enough as a team dog or a even swing dog, but he's no leader. I told Brad not to put him in the lead, but would he listen to me? Duh!"

"There's a problem with Buster?" Active said.

Mercer and Pudu shot him more looks.

"He's male," Cowboy said.

Mercer touched Active's arm. "Females make the best leaders, Nathan. Or, as dog breeders call them, the bitches. Everybody knows that."

She seemed to expect an answer, but Active couldn't think of one.

"Everybody but you and Brad, apparently," Mercer said at last. But she gave him a smile. "All right, Cowboy, let's see if we can find him. What on earth is his problem this time?"

Cowboy wheeled the Cessna into a wide, easy circle over the brush and snow banks of the riverbed and they continued upstream.

A mile farther along, they encountered another team, this one with green dog harnesses and sled bag. Another mile, and they spotted the team with the red rigging. There at the back, kicking from the runners in his red parka, was Brad Mercer, now known as the First Mate, thanks to an anonymous blogger called Tundrabunny who had stuck him with the nickname. The First Mate's leader was the biggest animal in the team and very masculine-looking. Active surmised this must be the inadequate Buster.

"Humph," Mercer said. "Third place. How's that gonna look? How far do they have to go, Cowboy?"

Cowboy studied his instrument panel and pulled at his chin. "Trail miles? Ah, maybe one-forty to the mandibles on Beach Street."

"So he could pass Bunky before they finish."

"Yeah, right," Pudu seemed to mutter. Mercer didn't hear.

"I'm sure he will, ma'am," Cowboy said.

"He better," Mercer said.

The First Mate spotted them and made a big show of waving as they approached.

The governor made a big show of smiling and waving back as they roared past. "Yep, that's Buster," she said with a grimace. "Dammit, the man will not listen. You get that, Pudu?"

"*Arii*, Mom. I was kinda shooting into the sun, all right. Cowboy, could you go around so we're coming the other way when I shoot him?"

"Roger that." Cowboy started a big turn to the left and soon the First Mate and his team came into view through Mercer's window again. This time, the plane's right wing, not the left, pointed at the sun.

Mercer repeated the wave and the smile for the camera. "How was that one?"

"Pretty good, all right," Pudu said. "But maybe one more, ah?"

"One more!" Cowboy groaned over the headsets. "We're—"

"One more will be fine," Mercer said. "Right, Cowboy?"

Cowboy didn't answer, but he circled for a third pass.

After this one, Pudu said he had enough video and Cowboy asked what his passengers wanted to do next.

"Walker village is another ten or twelve miles up the river," he said. "If anybody needs a, er, ah, rest break, we could set down there for a few minutes. Or, we could boom on back to Isignaq for the night."

"Oh, Isignaq by all means," Mercer said. "Pudu and I have several events this afternoon, then I have to greet Brad when he pulls in for the night. We certainly didn't drink any coffee this morning and I'm sure a couple of bush rats like you two wouldn't do it before getting in a Cessna, right?"

"Not me," Cowboy said.

"Not me," Active lied. But he figured his bladder could tough it out for another half hour or so.

"Roger that." Cowboy pushed the throttle forward, the note of the engine deepened, and soon they were topping the cliffs along the river again.

"What the hell is that?" Cowboy said over the headsets as they cleared the last treeless, snow-breasted ridge blocking their view downstream.

Then the intercom went silent. Active surmised Cowboy had switched over to the Cessna's radio to talk to the FAA about the thick batt of wool that blanketed the lower end of the Isignaq Valley.

Cowboy clicked back onto the headsets. "The FAA says the weather got a little ahead of itself. Chukchi's flat on its back and Isignaq village ain't a whole lot better." He rolled the Cessna into a turn. "Looks like it's Walker for us tonight." He came out of the turn and aimed the Cessna's nose upstream again at the Isignaq valley's radiant uplands. The pilot's shoulders relaxed. Active realized he hadn't noticed they were hunched.

"Cowboy," Mercer said. "Pudu and I need to get into Isignaq. You're the original scud-runner?"

Long seconds passed before Cowboy answered. "I did my share of that when I was young and wild. Now I'm old and careful."

More silence crackled over the headsets. Mercer twisted in her seat and peered back at sea of fog behind them. "Oh, Cowboy, you're overexaggerating. It doesn't look that bad."

Cowboy's voice clicked on. "Yo, Nathan. It's just us now. Any thoughts here?"

"Me? What do I know? You're the pilot. What's your gut telling you?"

"It's telling me I did what the governor wants a hundred times back in the day, and here I still am."

"And here you still are," Active said. "Your call."

"That stuff's only a couple-three thousand feet deep. If things go sideways on us, I guess we can punch up through it and get into the clear and head back up to Walker."

They glimpsed a scatter of buildings basking in the sunlight on the left bank of the river four or five miles ahead. "That Walker?" Active asked.

"That's Walker," Cowboy said. The right wing dropped, the Cessna started another turn, and Walker vanished behind them.

The headsets sprayed more static and Cowboy crackled on again. "I guess it can't hurt to take a look." The Cessna rolled out of the turn, its nose pointed at the gray-black wall downstream. Cowboy added power and the nose angled up. "We'll head for Isignaq village on top and see if we got enough visibility down through this stuff to land."

"And if we can't?" Mercer asked.

"Then we'll come back up here, drop down to treetop level and do some good old-fashioned scud-running."

"Excellent," Mercer said. "I'm sure we'll make it in. I get a little testimony whenever God has something in mind for me."

Active shot her a sidewise glance. A little testimony? If she was kidding, it didn't show.

Ten minutes later the upstream edge of the scud passed under their wings and the river, ridges, and tundra vanished beneath them. Active peered downward and saw only an impenetrable gray murk. It was like looking into three thousand feet of dirty dishwater.

"*Arii*," Pudu said. "I never see nothing down there. "

"Me, neither," Active said.

"Cowboy?" Mercer said.

The Cessna's left wing dropped and Cowboy stared down into the fog. "Scud-running it is," he said. The Cessna did another one-eighty and a few minutes later they crossed the upstream margin of the fog bank. Cowboy chopped power and put the Cessna into a wide spiral toward the sunlit, blue-shadowed riverbed. He ran a finger over the chart on his knee, scanned the ridges along the banks and nodded. "Got it," he said over the intercom. "We're about five miles upstream of Shelukshuk Canyon. Pretty easy run from here down to Isignaq village if ya got even a quarter mile of visibility."

He leveled off a couple of hundred feet over the brush and lowered the wing flaps for slow flight. They sailed toward the fog bank, so solid and forbidding that Active found himself bracing for impact as they hurtled into the wall of mist.

Now he could see the riverbed when he looked straight down, but the terrain to either side vanished within a couple hundred yards. A quarter mile of visibility? He wondered if Cowboy had half that.

He looked forward. Cowboy's shoulders were hunched again and he strained into the seat harness, his head on a swivel. Ten seconds straight ahead, a glance left, then right, then ahead for another ten seconds.

Then Active noticed that Cowboy didn't just look down at the river bed when he glanced sideways; he also looked at the wing struts and the undersides of the wings. And he spent more time looking sideways. Now it was the path ahead that got the glance, then it was back to the wing.

Active looked where Cowboy looked and in an instant understood the pilot's hunched shoulders. Ice sheathed the leading edges of the struts and the underside of the wing. Even as Active watched, the ice under the wing seemed to get a little thicker and creep back a little farther.

Active glanced ahead to check Cowboy's shoulders and saw why the pilot wasn't looking forward any more. Ice now glazed most of the windshield. Cowboy could see only sideways.

Active had been aboard before when a Bush plane encountered icing, usually just a thin white rime on the struts and wings, with no hunched shoulders involved.

But he had never seen ice like this, not so rough and building up so fast. Always before, Cowboy and every other Bush pilot Active had flown with had turned back at the first sign of serious ice, or shoved the throttle forward to climb through the clouds into the sunlight above. This kind of ice weighed down the plane and spoiled the airflow over the wings. This kind of ice could drag a plane out of—"

"Shit, Nathan," Cowboy said over the headset, his voice high and tight. "We got fucking freezing rain here. The weather service didn't say anything about freezing rain."

There was a flurry of clicks and Cowboy, sounding more himself now, spoke again as the engine roared to full throttle and the nose lifted. "Sorry, folks, this ain't gonna work. We've gotta get on top and go back up to Walker to wait this out."

"But, Cowboy—" Mercer began.

"Sorry, Governor. The weather's in charge today."

Mercer gazed out her window as the riverbed faded into the mist. "Couldn't we just turn around and follow the river upstream till we're out of it again?"

"Not safe to make a turn down in this canyon with visibility this low," Cowboy growled.

The riverbed sank into the dishwater and then it was the four of them and their thoughts and the snarl of the engine as the Cessna labored upward and the ice crept backward under the wings and thickened on the struts.

Pudu pulled his camera back onto his lap and stared into the void. "*Arii*, Mom. I don't like this."

"Be a man," Mercer gritted. "And keep that damned camera rolling."

"OK, Mom." He swiveled in his seat and aimed that camera at her.

Mercer looked straight into it and flashed a campaign

grin. "Yee-ha!"

Active leaned over and peered between Cowboy and Pudu's shoulders for any lightening above that would mean they were about to break out on top, about to burst into that luminous heaven of sunlight and blue sky above the clouds, free of the fog and freezing rain and ice that wanted to turn Cowboy's 207 into a falling coffin.

Nothing, no change in the gray mass overhead.

He shifted his gaze forward and peered past Cowboy's shoulder at the instrument that told the story of the Cessna's struggle to get above the icing. The instrument was called the vertical speed indicator, if Active remembered right. It had a black dial with white numbers and a white needle that pointed straight left if the plane was in level flight. If the needle angled upward, that meant the plane was climbing. If it angled downward, that meant the plane was diving.

Just now, the white needle was angled up, but not by much. Active was too far back to read the dial in the half-light of the cabin, but it looked like the needle was indicating maybe four hundred feet a minute of climb. At that rate, they should get through three thousand feet of cloud in seven or eight minutes.

The problem was, a Cessna 207 on a cold day should climb a lot faster, even with four people on board. Active was pretty sure he had seen this very Cessna climb seven or eight hundred feet a minute with a similar load. If the ice had already cut the climb rate in half, what were their chances of getting on top before the plane became unable to climb at all?

As Active watched, the white needle dropped a little towards the horizontal. Cowboy glanced at it, then at a part of the instrument panel Active couldn't see, then lowered the nose a little. The white needle dropped a little closer to horizontal. Now they were climbing two hundred feet a minute if they were lucky, Active figured. He watched, paralyzed, as the needle continued to drop until it finally pointed straight left. Zero climb, and the engine screaming at full power.

He leaned his head against the side window and craned his neck to look up again. Still no sign they were close to breaking out. He tried to read the altimeter, which was right above the vertical speed indicator. Did it really say they were only at two thousand feet?

Cowboy clicked onto the headsets as the vertical speed indicator dropped below horizontal. "Listen, folks. This airplane's given about all it's got and we're not gonna come out on top of this stuff. We have go back down through it till we spot the terrain and I can find a place to set us down. So everybody look out your window and keep your eyes peeled for anything that looks like a hill or a rock or a bush or a creek bank. And when you see it, yell out real loud and say which side."

The pilot dropped the nose a notch and backed off the throttle as the airspeed built. The engine note eased and the needle on the vertical speed indicator slid downward until it stabilized at what looked to Active like a descent rate of a couple hundred feet per minute. Then he remembered Cowboy's instructions and fixed his gaze on the gray chaos outside his window. Gray chaos with slabs of jagged granite in it.

Time crawled past. What if they hit a mountain and he never saw Grace Palmer again? How much thicker was the ice on the wing? Had they been droning down through these ice clouds for five minutes or thirty? Would Grace Palmer end up on back on the street if he didn't make it through this? What if he'd taken up with Lucy, spent his life in the glow of that sunny normalcy of hers, instead of with the irresistible and damaged

Grace Palmer? Would he be any happi—

"Cowboy!" Pudu shouted. "Isn't that Shelukshuk Mountain? On the right! On the right!"

Cowboy shot a fast glance out Pudu's window. "Yeah, and that's Shelukshuk Creek," he said. Then he backed off the power, nudged the ice-crippled Cessna into a gentle left turn, and they started down.

Now Active could see it, too, a brush-bearded furrow of white crossing a slope toward the Isignaq River, invisible and an unknown distance away in the fog.

"We can work our way down to the Isignaq, then follow the bank upstream to Walker," Cowboy said. He glanced at the ice on the underside of the wing. "Assuming we stay in the air long enough to get out of this crap."

Cowboy nursed the Cessna along the thread of the creek until the bank of the Isignaq swam dimly into view, then eased into another turn and started upstream, shoulders hunched harder than ever against the harness.

The pilot added power again and again in the effort to keep the Cessna in the air. The roar of the engine built up, the ice built up, and, Active sensed, the airspeed dropped. Cowboy lowered the wing flaps a notch farther and that seemed to stabilize the situation for a minute or two. Then the airspeed began to bleed away once more.

"It's just us, Nathan," Cowboy said over the headset. His voice was high and tight again. He didn't sound like Cowboy. "I'm about out of airspeed, altitude and ideas here. We gotta set down and I need you to do what you can for the governor back there. Try to help her with what I'm gonna say next."

Another click, and Cowboy was back on the intercom to all of them. Somehow, he had recovered his Bush pilot drawl. "Folks, this airplane's about done flying, so we're going to have to land. There's a slough about a mile ahead that usually blows clear of snow this time of year, and I'm gonna head for that. So slide your seat as far back as it will go, buckle in tight, and hold something soft in front of your face if you can find it."

Active put his arm over the seat back and fumbled through gear in the Cessna's cargo space. Finally he fished a down mummy bag through the safety webbing and passed it to Mercer, who cradled it in front of her. Active couldn't reach anything for himself, so he crossed his arms in front of his own chest.

Cowboy lifted his right hand from the throttle and raised his arm over his head. "Everybody look up here. You see my arm? There's a good chance we'll finish this upside down. If we do, wait till we come to a stop, then brace one arm hard against the ceiling over your head like I'm doing now to help break the fall, then unbuckle your seat belt. Everybody got that? Governor, Nathan, take anything sharp out of your pockets and put it in the seat back in front of you. Pudu, you give your camera to Nathan and let him put it in the cargo space behind the seats."

There was a scramble in the cockpit as everyone complied, then another click, then silence. Then a hurricane howled in as Cowboy swung the bottom of his window out a few inches and peered ahead through the resulting slot.

"*Arii*," Pudu said.

"What's going to happen?" Mercer asked over the intercom. "Cowboy?"

More silence.

"I think he switched off so he could concentrate," Active said. He pointed at Cowboy, his face in the hurricane as he nursed the plane through the fog with only—as far as Active could see—a fringe of willows and alders along the riverbank for navigation.

Slower and slower, lower and lower, the Cessna slogged through the murk. Then the plane jerked into a left turn and a squeal sounded that Active recognized as the stall warning.

"Cowboy?" Mercer said.

The 207 shuddered and sagged out of the air. Active braced for impact, but it never came, and he realized they were rumbling across a field of river ice, bare except for a spiderweb of snowdrifts a few inches high.

Cowboy raised the flaps, brought the plane to a halt, pushed open his door, and vomited into the blast from the propeller.

No one spoke as he pulled his head back in, closed the door, stopped the engine, and flipped switches to "OFF".

Active looked out at the wing and strut on his side of the plane. The ice had to be an inch thick in places. He could see one propeller blade on his side. It was sheathed with ice on the leading edge, too.

Cowboy still hadn't said anything. Neither had Pudu or the governor.

"Thanks, Cowboy," Active said into the thunderous silence. "Nobody else would have—"

"Would have gotten us into this mess?" The pilot sounded at once bitter and mournful, a man who had pushed himself past the limits of his competence, as when he had killed Aggie Iktillik.

"Would have gotten us down in one piece, I was going to say."

"I knew you could do it, Cowboy." Mercer's tone was bright. She sounded like a mom taping a child's drawing of a rainbow to the refrigerator.

"Just doing my job, ma'am," Cowboy said, back in

Bush pilot mode.

"Now what?" Mercer asked.

"Now we wait," Cowboy said. "The FAA in Chukchi knows where we are, at least generally. I told them what we were doing before we started down. I'll turn on our emergency beacon and a satellite will tell 'em exactly where we are in a few minutes." Cowboy reached out and flipped another switch on the instrument panel, this time to ON.

"And then what?" Mercer asked. "Will they send a helicopter?"

Cowboy shook his head. "Not even a helicopter can fly in this crud. They'll probably send snowgos from Isignaq. Or Walker, maybe."

"What? How long will that take?"

"Hard to say," Cowboy said. "Sometime tonight, maybe tomorrow."

"No, I have appointments and events."

Cowboy opened his door, swung his legs out, looked back at Mercer, and raised his eyebrows. "Right now, I gotta cover this engine and then hit the bushes. There's tissues in the seat backs if anybody else needs to."

He climbed out, zipped the oil-stained Bush-pilot parka with its duct-tape patch, pulled up the hood, dug the orange engine cover out of the baggage compartment in the plane's nose, and bungeed it into place.

Then he trudged off across the slough, Sorels crunching on the snow as he faded into the murk.

"Nathan!" Mercer's tone was outraged. "Can't you do anything?"

Not a damned thing, Active said to himself. To Mercer he said, "I think he needs a moment. I'll go talk to him in a bit."

Mercer said nothing, just pulled her phone out of a pocket.

He debated telling her the odds of getting cell bars on the upper Isignaq but decided against it and stepped out of the plane.

Mercer put the phone away with a "hmmph!" She looked ready to snap, but she climbed out and zipped up. She reached into the pouch behind the front passenger seat and came up with a packet of Kleenex, then climbed down and stalked off in the opposite direction from where Cowboy had gone.

Active climbed out, zipped up and covered up, then swung around to what must be south, as that was where the murk was lightest. The sun was still above the horizon, but the long slow slide into evening would come in a few hours and their slough would be black as only the Arctic wilderness could be on a foggy night. At least it wasn't too cold—five below at most, he estimated—with just a light breeze moving. Either the wind hadn't reached this far upriver yet, or it was petering out as it spread inland. Snow sifted down, snow with pinpricks of sleet in it when it hit his cheek. He started across the ice after Cowboy.

He found the pilot sitting on a downed spruce, a Marlboro between his lips and a lost look on his face.

"Hey, buddy."

Cowboy dragged on the Marlboro and didn't speak for a long time. "A man is what he does," he said. "And when he can't do it anymore, then he's not."

"You can still do it. You just had the governor of Alaska on your case."

"Yeah, but why did I listen?"

"She's got something."

"I know, but what?"

"Charisma," Active said. "Something. You want to do what she wants."

Cowboy nodded, took a drag, and exhaled. "And you

think she'll think you're not a man if you don't do it."

"Mm-hmm," Active said.

Cowboy smoked. "And a man is what he does."

Active stepped a few paces away from the lost cause and relieved himself. Cowboy would have to extricate himself from the conundrum.

"Be getting dark before long," Active said.

Nothing from Cowboy.

"We need to do any organizing here?" Active motioned at the Cessna, a ghost plane in the fog. "Put up a tent or something?"

"Whatever she wants." Cowboy shrugged. "I got an Arctic Oven in my emergency stuff. But we could wait it out in the plane. We've got enough gas to keep warm by running the engine every couple hours. I'll taxi over close to the brush here and we'll build a fire. Nothing like a fire to brighten things up. Plus, I got some pilot bread and freeze-dry in my emergency stuff, mac-and-cheese, chili, I don't know what-all."

"*Arigaa*, real bellywarmers," Active said.

Cowboy stood and stretched and they headed for the plane, Sorels crunching in the fog. "She puts some kind of whammy on you," he said.

"Mm-hmm."

Their heads jerked up as one.

"What the hell!" Cowboy said.

"Was that a rifle?"

The crack came again, then again and again. Active broke into a run.

CHAPTER SEVEN

Saturday, April 12

ACTIVE REACHED THE Cessna first.

Cowboy puffed to a stop beside him a few seconds later. The plane was deserted. "Where the hell are they?"

Active peered into the fog and shook his head. He made a megaphone of his hands and shouted into the murk. "Governor? Pudu? Hello-o-o-o-o?"

No answer, then the rifle cracked again.

"Come on," Cowboy said. "I think I got a direction on it." He sprinted off the same way Mercer had gone minutes earlier. Active followed, noticing now that a trail of boot tracks led the same way.

"Over here, guys," came the governor's voice. "I got us a caribou for dinner!"

The trail led to the edge of the slough, up the snowy bank, and into the willows, where they found Mercer and Pudu standing over the downed caribou, a big-bellied female with spiky little antlers. Judging from the blood on the gray-brown fur, she had been hit once in the stomach and once in the ear. And judging from the red snow, she had thrashed out her last moments in agony until someone had put the kill shot through her ear.

"Come on, Pudu, get some more video." Mercer put her foot and the butt of a rifle on the caribou's shoulder. "I spotted a little band in the toolie bushes here while I was using the facilities, so I went back to the plane and looked, and sure enough, you had this trusty old

.308 in your survival gear, Cowboy, so I got Pudu and his camera and we came back with the rifle and I shot the caribou and Pudu got it all on tape and now we've got ourselves a real Bush Alaska dinner! And it's gonna look great on YouTube." Mercer beamed at her son.

"*Arii*, Mom, I told you not to shoot a cow, they've got their babies in them now." Pudu poked the animal's swollen belly with a boot. A rivulet of half-digested reindeer moss oozed out. "And you gut-shot her."

"Oh, never mind that," Mercer said. "Leave it out of the frame. Just get me and the caribou's head and shoulders in the shot."

"And then I had to finish her off for you because you didn't want blood on your clothes!"

"Pudu. Get your camera."

Pudu thrust gloved hands into the pockets of his snowgo suit and glared at his mother. "This is dumb."

"I said, GET. YOUR. CAMERA."

Pudu dropped his gaze and turned to pull the Canon from its case on the snow a few feet away.

"Teenagers!" Mercer said with a bright smile.

"Governors," Active muttered to Cowboy.

Pudu flicked on the camera's light and taped for a minute or so as Mercer posed in the glare.

"You want me to get some video of you cutting it?"

"Please, Pudu. I'm pro-life, remember? You're seriously asking if I want to be on camera when that calf gets cut out if its mother's belly? Seriously? Is that what you want?"

"*Arii*, Mom," Pudu said. He put the camera away, pulled an Old Timer folding knife from a zipper pocket on the leg of his snowgo suit and opened the blade, muttering what Active thought might be, "Like you could cut caribou anyway."

Mercer didn't hear, or pretended not to. She turned

the bright smile on Decker. "So, Cowboy, whatcha got in that survival kit we could throw in the pot for some caribou stew?"

The pilot shot Active a resigned glance before he spoke. "A lot of Mountain House. I guess there's some chili mac in there, maybe some potatoes and broccoli?"

"Mmm," Mercer said. "Pudu, you bring up the backstrap and we'll be eatin' like real Alaskans tonight!"

Pudu grunted and slid the blade in at the cow's anus, then drew it up the midline of the belly, deftly parting the hide without puncturing the stomach lining underneath. He flipped off his gloves and began separating hide from muscle with bladelike motions of his hands.

"Um, Governor?" Nathan said as they started for the plane. "He will bring all the meat, right? Otherwise, Tundrabunny and the other bloggers will be all over you for wanton waste."

"Of course," Mercer said. "We'll take it with us to Isignaq and Pudu can get video of me giving it to the elders."

Active nodded, feeling a little dizzy. There was no end to the woman. "And, um, you do have a hunting license, right? Otherwise, Tundrabunny—"

"Of course, Nathan. I'm the governor of Alaska. And call me Suka, OK? Like I said?"

"OK," Active said. "Suka."

"Governors," Cowboy muttered.

"I GOTTA HAND it to you, Governor," Cowboy said an hour later as he lit a Marlboro. "You make a mean caribou stew."

They were sitting on bedrolls and spruce boughs around a pretty nice campfire Pudu had made by scavenging wood from deadfalls. Cowboy had thrown a cup of avgas from the Cessna's tanks on top of the pile and tossed on a match to start what he called a Bush pilot fire. Beside it, the remnants of the stew were freezing to the sides of the pot on Cowboy's camp stove.

As they cleaned their bowls and licked their spoons dry, Cowboy's face lit up. "Wait a minute, I think I've got dessert."

He dug into the survival kit again and came up with a Ziploc bag of Butterfingers. Active peeled his open and reflected that there probably were, in fact, worse places on earth to be than huddled around a campfire in the fog on a slough somewhere along the Isignaq River with a bowlful of caribou stew in his stomach and that first salty, chocolaty, sugary bite of Butterfinger sliding down his throat.

Pudu scooped the stewpot full of snow and fired up the stove again to melt water for what little dish washing would be done, then hiked off into the willows to answer the call of nature.

"We probably should think about sleeping arrangements," Mercer said. "How big's your tent, Cowboy?"

"Actually, we can all sleep in the plane, if you don't mind sitting up."

"I do," Mercer said. "So, the tent?"

"It'll take two easy, three maybe. Four could be a problem. But you and Pudu can have the Arctic Oven and we boys can sleep in Two-Five-Sierra, right, Nathan? I'll hafta run the engine now and again to keep her alive, which will warm up the interior, plus my sleeping bags are pretty good."

Active nodded.

"I don't know," Mercer said. "I think Pudu—"

Just then the boy crunched back up from his trip to the woods.

"They want you to sleep in the tent, Pudu," she said. "Don't you need to back up your memory cards and charge your batteries?"

"Oh, yeah," Pudu said. "Every night, all right. I gotta be in the plane."

Mercer raised her eyebrows. "Looks like it's the Arctic Oven for you and me, Nathan."

"Us? In the tent? All night? Won't Tundrabunny and the bloggers...you know?"

"Let'em. They're gonna sexualize everything I do, anyway. Better they say I spent a night in a tent with a cop than my own son." She brightened. "I know—I'll bring in Cowboy's rifle and put it between us!"

Active could think of nothing to say, so he said, "Cowboy's rifle."

"Posilutely," Mercer said.

"My rifle," Cowboy said.

Mercer nodded. "That way, if Nathan tries anything in the Arctic Oven, I'm all set." She flashed them the campaign grin. "And if the bloggers try to make something out of it, well, by golly, I'll show 'em my rifle and you can show'em your great big Glock. Right, Nathan?"

"Right, Suka." Active hoped he sounded less doomed than he felt as he pictured himself explaining this to Grace. "I'll get the tent."

Active set up the Arctic Oven over a mat of spruce boughs as snow sifted down, and the murk deepened. Mercer waited by the fire and Cowboy and Pudu pulled the seats out of the 207 and set up their own beds on the cabin floor.

"Been kind of a taxing day," Active said when the tent was ready. "I guess I should unroll the sleeping bags. You got a light, Cowboy?"

The pilot handed over an LED flashlight, then rummaged in the back of the plane and came up with two sleeping pads and a puffy, down-filled sleeping bag.

"Just one?" Active muttered. "I'm not sharing a bag with that wo—" he glanced at Pudu and Mercer, who might or might not be within earshot "—with the governor."

"It's a Woods double-single," Cowboy muttered back. "It's all in how you zip it. Strictly your choice, Nathan." He looked at Mercer, eyes aglow in the firelight. "Or hers."

Active headed back to the tent. As he passed the fire, Mercer spotted the Woods.

"Just one?" she asked. "That'll be cozy."

"Don't worry, Suka. It zips apart into two singles."

"Oh, the double will be fine," she said as he pushed into the Arctic Oven.

Active pulled his head out of the tent. "Seriously? The double?"

"Of course. After all, I've got Cowboy's trusty .308." She patted the rifle propped on the log beside her.

Active stooped into the Arctic Oven, tucked the flashlight under his chin, laid out the pads, and unfurled the bag in the center of the floor so they could get in and out without crawling over each other. He shucked off his parka and rolled it up for a pillow, kicked off his Sorels, then slid into the bag in his RefrigiWear and stocking feet. "All set in here," he called out.

Mercer came into the tent on all fours, then turned and closed the flaps in the beam of his flashlight.

He debated turning off the light so she could undress if she wanted to. Then he decided he didn't want her to, and left it on. He watched in unease as she studied the layout, taking in the parka rolled up under his head and the straps of the snowgo suit looped over his shoulders.

She took off her own parka, wadded it up, and dropped it at the head of her side of the bag. She hesitated, tapping her lips with a forefinger.

He waited, then caved. "Would you like the light off?"

"No, this'll be fine." She kicked off her own Sorels and slid into the bag in her snowgo suit. "Good night, Nathan. And thanks for everything."

"My pleasure." He switched off the flashlight and tucked it into a pocket of his RefrigiWear to keep the batteries warm.

An alarm bell went off in his head. He pulled out the flashlight and switched it on again. "Did you forget the rifle?"

Mercer raised her head and peered around the tent. "Did I? Gosh, I guess so." She gazed at him. "But surely I'm safe with a sworn officer of the law." She rolled away and pulled the bag over her head.

"You should leave a breathing hole," Active said after another debate with himself. "Otherwise the bag will ice up."

"I'm from around here. Remember?"

"Of course, sorry." He switched off the light, rolled away from Mercer, covered his own head, and made his own breathing hole.

"It's OK, Nathan. I'm not a complete twit, no matter what they say in the lamestream media."

Boots crunched up to the tent in the dark. "Hey, guys, don't panic, but I'm gonna warm up Two-Five-Sierra before Pudu and I bed down," Cowboy said.

"No problem, Cowboy," Mercer said.

"You two sleep tight in there," Cowboy said.

"You mind your own business. Nathan and I will be just fine." There was a hint of feline rumble in her voice. "Won't we, Nathan?"

"Just fine."

A few seconds later, the Cessna coughed to life. The engine was still turning over when Active drifted off to sleep, as far as he could get from Helen Mercer without unzipping his side of the bag and curling up on the floor in the cold.

CHAPTER EIGHT

Sunday, April 13

THREE TIMES IN the night, the Cessna rumbled Active awake for a few seconds. Then his brain identified the sound and he drifted off again.

The next time Cowboy started the plane, twilight suffused the tent. Active realized this must be what passed for dawn in the foggy bottomlands of the Isignaq. He pulled on his Sorels and parka while Mercer slept.

He crawled out to find Pudu at work over Cowboy's camp stove as Two-Five-Sierra idled nearby, fanning snow across the slough behind it. Steam wafted up from a coffee pot, smelling as only coffee could on a cold morning. A saucepan simmered on the burner next to it.

Active poured himself a cup of coffee the color of crude oil and pointed at the saucepan. "Is that oatmeal?"

"*Arii*, that Cowboy, no Eskimo food in his plane," Pudu said with a dour look. "This kinda weather, you need *quaq* and seal oil, but I put in some of that caribou."

"That sounds good."

"Build a fire in your belly, all right."

Active headed into the brush for a few minutes. He returned as Mercer crawled out of the Arctic Oven. She yawned, stretched, and peered about, parka still open over the black snowgo suit.

"What's that, Mom?" Pudu pointed at Mercer's throat. Then Active saw them, too, a pair of angry red welts down the side of her neck. One showed a few beads of blood.

"What?" Mercer touched the place. "Ouch! How did that happen?"

Pudu drew the parka aside and studied the welts. "I dunno, look like maybe on the zipper of your sleeping bag when you're getting out?"

"I am such a klutz!" Mercer inspected the damage in her selfie camera. "But as long as they're there, let's get some video for Facebook and YouTube—further proof you never know what'll happen in the Alaskan Bush!"

Pudu went to the plane for his video camera. Active passed Mercer his handkerchief. She started to dab at the scratches, then seemed to think better of it.

Active gave up the attempt to figure her out, scooped caribou oatmeal into a bowl and spooned it down. Caribou did punch up a clump of amorphous gray mush. He had to admit that.

As Pudu shoot footage of the scratches on the First Neck, it occurred to Active that Mercer might well have scratched herself on purpose, just to get the video. What would Tundrabunny make of it when it hit the Internet?

Cowboy shut down the plane, covered the engine, crunched over to the stove, and filled a bowl with the caribou oatmeal. "The Air Guard's got a C-130 overhead," he said in a tone of wonder. "All the way from Anchorage. I was just on the radio with 'em. Apparently they've been up there a couple hours now waiting for us to get up and turn on the radio."

"A C-130?" Active said. A C-130 was a giant four-engine transport plane about as capable of landing on the Isignaq as a space shuttle. Active craned his neck and squinted up at the fog. Maybe he heard engines in the sky, maybe not. "I thought you said it would be snowgos from Walker or Isignaq."

Cowboy mumbled something that never made it past the oatmeal in his mouth, then swallowed. "Apparently there's a TV crew on board."

"Ah," Active said.

"That's my Air Guard." Mercer grinned as she dabbed the welts with Active's handkerchief. "Always got my back."

Then Active remembered that Mercer had appointed her sister's husband commander of the Alaska Air Guard.

Cowboy, his mouth now clear of oatmeal, reminded them that, as of yesterday's landing, he had expected to be able to fly out this morning. "But now I'm guessing we could have another twenty-four hours of this stuff." He jerked a thumb at the Cessna that popped and rang as it cooled down behind him. "Looks like Two-Five-Sierra ain't goin' nowhere today."

"*Arigaa!*" Pudu said. "Maybe I'll catch some caribou, all right."

"What!" Mercer said. "I'm not staying here another day. Cowboy, you do something!"

"It's already being done, ma'am. A bunch of guys on snowgos left Isignaq a couple hours ago. They should be here any time now."

"They can find us in this stuff?" Mercer waved a hand at the fog around them. "Really?"

"Of course," Cowboy said. "They know this slough. They know everything in this country."

"Of course, yeah." From Mercer's expression, Active sensed Cowboy might pay a price for suggesting she had lost touch with how things worked in the Bush.

Active picked up the faint whine of snowgo engines through the fog. He, Mercer, and Pudu turned as one to look down the slough.

"Is that them?" Mercer asked.

"Is that who?" Cowboy cocked his head, then turned to look as even his damaged ears caught the sound. "Yeah, must be. We probably oughta get you packed up."

"But wait," Mercer said. "Snowgos? All the way back to Chukchi? I mean, nothing's flying, right? I don't want to ride a snowgo all that way."

"No problem, Governor. Roland Sweetsir's with 'em. He'll wait out on the main river while the snowgos get you off of this slough, then he'll drive you back to Chukchi."

Mercer beamed. "Homin' home to home in Chukchi with Isignaq Ready-Ride! What could be more perfect?" Then she paused in thought. "Will the TV people be there when we arrive? Is Alaska Airlines getting into Chukchi in this stuff? Or the Air Guard?"

"Not even the Air Guard, ma'am. Chukchi's still flat on its back. They've got the same fog as us, plus a hellacious crosswind."

"No matter," Mercer said. "Pudu can always get some tape of it. Right, Pudu?"

Pudu raised his eyebrows, yes.

The snowgos buzzed closer as Mercer, Active, and Pudu packed up for the trip to Chukchi. Cowboy struck the Arctic Oven, stuffed it into its bag, and threw it into the back of the Cessna as two snowgos swam out of the fog, dogsleds behind, and pulled up at the plane.

"You better get your stuff into one of the sleds," Active told Cowboy as Mercer walked over to where drivers stretched and stamped to un-kink muscles and warm up.

"Nah, I'm gonna wait it out here." He pointed at a half-dozen red jerry jugs on one of the sleds. "See that avgas? Our agent in Isignaq sent it up. Somebody's gotta keep Two-Five-Sierra warm or it'll take most of a day to get her thawed out and started by the time this stuff does move out and I can get back up here from Chukchi to take her back. So I might as well stay."

Cowboy moved the jerry jugs to the bank of the slough while the other three loaded their duffle and the governor's caribou kill into the sleds. Active and Pudu each took a seat in the basket of a sled, where the riders from Isignaq had stashed the customary caribou hides and sleeping bags for cross-country travel by snowgo. Mercer hopped on the seat behind the best-dressed of the drivers and insisted Pudu get out and unpack his camera once more to get video as she started down the slough.

As Active bounced along in the dogsled behind the snowgo carrying Mercer, he looked back. Cowboy sat on one of Two-Five-Sierra's wheels, a Marlboro at his lips, and watched them go.

CHAPTER NINE

Sunday, April 13

TWO MILES DOWN the slough, the snowgos pulled up at Roland Sweetsir's rusty yellow Suburban, a plume of steam rising from the tailpipe to dissipate in the fog. The rig had "Isignaq Ready-Ride" painted in big red letters on the doors, and "Rut-Rider" in little black ones on the front fenders.

Roland himself was a 50-something Inupiaq with silver hair, a black Native Pride ball cap, and—even on this cold day—a windbreaker.

"Roland," Active said as they exchanged a single-pump handshake. "Been a while."

Roland raised his eyebrows. "Ever since that bootlegging case, ah?"

Active nodded back. "And you know the governor, I understand?"

Roland and Mercer bobbed heads in unison. "Roland took my basketball team back to Chukchi once when the weather went down. Remember that, Roland?"

"Ah-hah," Roland said. "Safe and sound." He swept an arm downriver toward the village named for the Isignaq. "It ain't a nice road, but it's an ice road! It's gone when it's hot, but it's here when it's not!"

Active and Mercer chuckled at Roland's ancient joke. Even Pudu, who had brought out his camera without a prod from his mother, grinned a little, sucked into the driver's whirlwind of affability.

"All right," Roland said. "Everybody ready for a little rut-ride?"

He swung open the Suburban's cargo doors and they threw their duffle into the back, then climbed in. As in Two-Five Sierra, Pudu took the front passenger seat so he could get video of the governor on her ride down the Isignaq. She took the left seat in back and Active the right.

Active shrugged off his parka in the heat of the interior and started to toss it on the duffle in the rear. Then he realized what their road was made of, and what was under it, and rolled the parka into a ball and set it on his lap. If they went through, maybe it would keep him afloat long enough to matter. After a little more thought, he loosened the laces of his Sorels so they'd be easy to kick off.

Soon they were rocking along at sixty in the fog. Occasionally, the line of trail markers made of spruce saplings bent around a patch of slush or new ice that meant the Isignaq was frozen almost to the bottom and that the water, in its relentless fashion, had found its way out along the edges and spread over the top of safe, solid ice. The problem was, sometimes what looked like overflow was instead a hole in that ice, with the cold, hungry, green-black Isignaq waiting below to swallow up a snowgo or a Suburban. Active remembered two Trooper searches, both futile, for travelers who had gone through the ice on the Isignaq, though he had never heard of one that involved Isignaq Ready-Ride.

Roland passed around a thermos of coffee and tuned in Kay-Chuck just in time for Gospel Hour. After "I Saw the Light" and "I'll Fly Away," they listened to a news report about Alaska's governor being forced down in the wilderness with only her son, a Bush pilot, and a Bush cop for company.

"But the Alaska Air Guard reports the party is safe," Roger Kennelly said. "The Isignaq village rescue team left just before dawn this morning to pick the party up from Shelukshuk Canyon. They'll be riding back to Chukchi with Isignaq Ready-Ride so, with any luck, the governor should make it here for the musher's banquet tomorrow night and personally present the trophy to the first-place finisher. Speaking of which, the report from Isignaq village is, Bunky Ivanoff was out first, with Brad Mercer hot on his heels. So perhaps the governor will be presenting that trophy to her very own husband!"

The travelers erupted in cheers and Gospel Hour resumed with "Prettiest Flowers" as rendered by a couple of devout Inupiat sisters named Suelene and Rae-Anne Williams.

"Maybe Dad's gonna pull it out, ah, Mom?" Pudu said.

"That would be super," Mercer said.

After that, no one said anything, and the Williams sisters filled the Ready-Ride, their strong, plaintive voices a perfect match for the yearning tone of the lyrics. The Williamses were famous around Chukchi for accompanying themselves on the accordion, which was Active's favorite thing about "Prettiest Flowers." That, and the third verse with its reference to "eternal morning in the sky, where we will never say goodbye."

He leaned his head on the backrest and closed his eyes for a nap in the warm cocoon of the Suburban and was pondering the eternal question of whether he and Grace would ever get their eternal morning when Pudu shouted from the front seat. "*Arii*, Roland, you're gonna hit it."

Active jerked up, saw a pond of green slush across the trail, and put his hand on the door handle. Roland had his cup to his lips as Pudu cried out. Roland lowered the cup, cut his wheel, fishtailed around the overflow, and resumed his progress downstream, all with no coffee spilled. He looked over at Pudu with a grin.

"You thought we was going in, ah?"

"I never," Pudu said.

"Maybe somebody's been down there at Juneau with them *naluaqmiuts* too much, ah?

"Maybe so, I guess." Pudu raised his camera and focused on the governor as she gazed into the fog. "Ah, Mom?"

"How's trapping this winter, Roland?" Mercer asked.

Active leaned his head back again and drifted off as the driver and the governor fell deep into a discussion of the unfair and unfathomable process by which fur buyers set prices.

CHAPTER TEN

Sunday, April 13

ROLAND'S RUT-RIDER GOT them safely into Isignaq at mid-morning on Sunday, but Cowboy was still waiting out the fog in Shelukshuk Canyon when night fell.

The governor and Pudu spent the rest of the morning following the Isignaq 400 via Kay-Chuck's live coverage from the finish line.

Brad Mercer indeed led the pack down Beach Street, which prompted a call of congratulation from the governor on a phone in the principal's office at the school, as Isignaq, like the rest of the villages along the river, was without cell service.

Active waited with Pudu at a desk in the administrative area outside the principal's office as Mercer went through the ritual with her husband and promised to call Kay-Chuck for an interview about the race.

Then she was silent as, Active gathered, the First Mate asked a question. When she answered, her voice had a slight edge. "Don't be ridiculous," she said. "I'll be there when I get there. I am not taking a snowgo."

More silence.

"I'm sure this will break up by tomorrow and..." She noticed Active and Pudu outside, eased up to the office door, winked, and closed it.

Active smiled. Every marriage had its secrets, he supposed. If it weren't for the universal compulsion to keep up appearances, civilization would no doubt collapse like a snowhouse in the sun.

Mercer spent the rest of the day squeezing in as

many of the things from her original village schedule as time allowed. She made it to the school Inupiat Spirit assembly, cut the ribbon on the new village health clinic, and bade Active farewell at the door to the home of Reverend Waldron, where she and Pudu were to savor a *muktuk*-based dinner and spend the night.

With the First Body safe in the care of the reverend and his family, Active made it to the village store just before closing. He picked up some pilot bread, squeeze cheese, beef jerky, plastic cutlery, and bottled water, as you never knew about a village water system. Then he made his way to the new clinic, downed his plastic-wrapped banquet and stretched himself out on an examination table in his snowgo suit with his parka for a blanket.

By dawn Monday, the sky was starting to thin, and by mid-morning was clear, as if the ice fog of two days earlier had never happened. Rodney Hamilton, Lienhofer's Isignaq agent, caught up with them at the village store to let them know that Cowboy was on his way.

Mercer wrapped up her purchase of a set of nesting birch bark baskets made in the village—no politician would dare pass through without doing so—and the agent hauled them to the runway in his pickup. Mercer rode in front, while Active and Pudu took the bed with the luggage and the birch baskets.

"*Arii*, my mom, ah?" Pudu lifted his eyebrows.

Active gave this some thought. "I work for her," he said finally.

"Ah-hah," Pudu said.

"At the moment," Active said after more thought.

Cowboy pulled up to the Lienhofer hut and shut down the ladies' model. He helped them in with their stuff, they climbed in, and were in sight of Chukchi in its lambent bed of snow and sea ice by ten-thirty.

They touched down and Mercer nudged him as Cowboy stopped the 207 at the Lienhofer hanger. "Thanks, Nathan. Quite a trip, huh?"

"Goes with, I guess. This is the Arctic."

"Indeed."

"So, ah, will you be—"

"Needing you again today? I don't think so, not till the musher's banquet tonight. I'm sure my folks and the girls have all been terrified, so I think we need some family time, plus I really should get on the phone to Juneau to make sure all's quiet on the political front, plus Brad and I have some business to take care of this afternoon, plus Fox News wants a Skype interview, plus I have to keep an eye on Pudu while he edits our video, and...oh, I won't drag you through it all. But no doubt you also...?"

"Yep, I'm sure there's something between a three-alarm fire and a train wreck on my desk by now, so I should probably shovel away the top few layers today if at all possible. And Lucy Brophy's supposed to take me through the accounting system. Oh, yeah, and I have to look at the applications to replace her while she's on maternity leave. So, I, yeah, definitely—"

"Good, then, let's both go take care of business and I'll see you at the banquet."

CHAPTER ELEVEN

Tuesday, April 15

ACTIVE DID A mental head count as he rolled up to the Mercer home on Beach Street the next morning. Just Suka and the First Mate if the kids were at her parents' place. Otherwise, Pudu and the three daughters he hadn't yet met would also be climbing in or on. Six Mercers in all for the ride the airport.

But he could take only four in the cab with him—three in the back seat and one in front. That left the truck bed for the other two, who presumably would be Pudu and the First Mate.

Not legal, strictly speaking, but who was going to arrest him? He was the law south of the Brooks Range and north of the Yukon River, pretty much. Plus he would have the governor on board.

But, when the Mercers marched out with their duffle, the head count was only two.

"No kids?" Active asked the First Mate as they tossed bags into the bed. He was burly for an Inupiaq, probably from the white half of his genes. He had an agreeable face, lightly stubbled and a little weathered from his time on the trail. Ruggedly handsome, the celebrity magazines usually called him. Tundrabunny had even once offered to let the First Mate "ride my runners anytime."

"Nope," he said. "This way they're not switching schools all the time. And they can be around their friends. That kinda stuff is really important to girls, I guess. Especially the friends. For Pudu, it's huntin', fishin', and basketball. I had to fight Helen on it because she always wants them around her—especially Pudu—but I knew Juneau wouldn't work for them."

"But you yourself don't mind it much?"

The First Mate shot a glance at the governor and grinned a little. "She's got something I need. Even after all these years."

Active let it pass. "So what do you do with yourself down there in Juneau?"

"Handle constituent calls for Helen if they're from Natives, sometimes, but mostly I just wish we were up here. Not much country for an Eskimo with the big trees and all that rain. But I'm back and forth a lot, what with doing my two weeks on and two off at the mine. So I spend a few days here at either end of my shift. I can keep in touch with the kids and run the dogs some and do a little huntin' and fishin' myself."

Active headed for the driver's door, then noticed the governor still at the front passenger door. She frowned and shot him a glance from the corner of her eye. Once again, he had forgotten the chauffeur part of his bodyguard duties.

"Sorry, Suka," he said as he assisted her into the cab. "Where are my manners?"

"You've probably been in Chukchi too long. Don't forget, I have an opening in Anchorage."

He said nothing, but went to his side of the truck and climbed in.

"Grace feeling better this morning?" the governor asked as he switched on the engine.

"I haven't had a chance to talk to her. She was still in bed when I left."

Mercer lifted her chin and touched the bandages on her neck. "I hope it wasn't these."

"I'm sure it wasn't, Suka. Grace knows better than to

believe gossip. Especially from the Internet."

"I hope so. We'll need to get Pudu at my folks' place. I want to get some more video before I leave."

He headed for the house and the morning sun hit the cab for the first time. It picked out a bruise over one of Mercer's eyes, with maybe trace of dried blood on it.

Come to think of it, the First Mate had looked a little haggard as they hoisted in the bags. Maybe the Mercers had done some catching up? Maybe they liked it rough?

He checked himself and shook his head. Why did his thoughts always drift that way in Mercer's presence?

But mention the injury or not? She was a woman, so she undoubtedly knew about it already. If not, if she'd dressed in a hurry or something, she'd show up for her flight with a bruise and a scab. People would notice and somebody would get a video then it would be all over the Internet, just like the scratches. What if the poster mentioned he was with her at the airport?

"Um, Suka?"

She turned his way. He touched the same spot over his own eye. "Do you—"

"Oh, crap, I forgot!" She twisted the rear view mirror around for a look, then got out her phone to use the selfie camera and fished in her purse for makeup and a tissue. "I am such a klutz! But you knew that, right?"

She talked as she dabbed the blood spot and worked with her makeup kit. "I was pulling bags out of the closet this morning while I was talking on this damn thing and one of them fell off the shelf and hit me right in the face which I hope will teach me I should never multitask but I doubt it!"

Faster than Active would have thought possible, the bruise vanished. She put away the phone and makeup. "Unlike the heroic scratches I got in Cowboy's tent in the line of duty, this was just plain stupid. Which is why

God made concealer, right?"

"Right," he said, though he had never heard of concealer before.

Pudu came out when he pulled up in front of the grandparents' house. Helen moved to the left rear seat as usual, and Pudu took right front to capture her in profile as she rolled through the streets of her home town.

Active saw the Mercers through security, returned Pudu to his grandparents, and was tempted to put in a couple of hours at the office to postpone the inevitable. Then he decided it was pointless.

Helen Mercer might be gone, but not so the problem of Grace Palmer. The same Grace Palmer who had refused to attend last night's Isignaq 400 Musher's Banquet with him, so furious over the scratches on the First Neck that he had elected to hole up at their new place for the night in hopes she'd cool off after sleeping on it. The question was, had she? She wasn't answering the phone.

When he pulled the crew cab to a stop in front of her house, empty paint cans on the front steps were the only evidence of the whirlwind of renovation that had swept through in in the past few days. The conversion to the Chukchi Regional Women's Shelter must be almost done.

Active let himself in and wrinkled his nose at the paint fumes.

"Grace?"

"Up here," she shouted from the second floor.

"Be there in a sec. I'm going to open a window and air the place out a little." The house was quieter than usual, he noticed. "Nita at school?"

"Yep. And eating at the cafeteria, not here—they're having fish sticks and tater tots, her all-time favorite.

We've got the place to ourselves today."

Place to themselves? Why would she mention that, he wondered as he wrenched at the window over the kitchen sink. He was about to shout the question upstairs when he heard Grace's footsteps coming down. She brushed past on her way to the refrigerator, leaving him lost in the scent of lavender. Then he noticed she was wearing one of his old Trooper uniform shirts, unbuttoned, and not much else. So that was what the Nita thing was all about. Maybe they would make it work this time? Daytime, nighttime, any time was fine with him. But how about Grace?

He moved to the refrigerator and had just laid hands on that wonderful swell of hips when the work phone in his pocket went off. He pulled it out to dismiss the call, then saw the number, rolled his eyes, and stepped back, a hand raised in supplication.

"Hello, Governor, I'm fine, thanks, everything OK? Oh, sorry. Of course, I remember, ah, Suka, is everything OK?"

Now Grace rolled her eyes. She bent over to retrieve a can of Diet Pepsi from the refrigerator and he realized that "not much else" didn't quite capture her state of undress. Grace was wearing the old Trooper shirt and nothing else. He averted his eyes so as to be able track what the governor was saying.

"I'm sorry, what?...Actually, it was kind of an adventure...yes, you're right, cell service would have been nice up there...what? Cell towers?...I'm sure it could be done, but the cost of those remote tow—run it through the public safety budget? So, yeah, there'll be some administrative overhead, of course. What?... OK, a supplemental appropriation would be great...OK, sure, and thanks, uh, Suka."

Grace eased up behind him and slipped her hands

into his trouser pockets. He jumped.

"Uh, listen, Suka." His throat tightened and it was hard to get words out. "Can I call you back? Dispatch is calling. Apparently something has come up...yes, thanks again, all right, sure, call me when you land in Juneau."

"So it's 'Suka' now?" Grace was in front of him, an eyebrow cocked. The work shirt had swung open, but not far enough, not yet.

Active grinned. "Her choice, not mine. And she wants to put cell towers along the Isignaq."

"Seriously."

He nodded. "No doubt so she can tweet live and direct from the wilderness the next time her plane goes down. I'm sure the cost of remote towers will be astronomical, but she's gonna say it's a public safety issue and run it through my budget, so all's well. She even suggested we bump up our cut for administrative overhead by a couple points and put the gravy into the village crisis centers. All good, right?"

"Very good." She didn't sound sincere.

"She's a woman of boundless energy," he said in a cautious tone. "Like a bouncing football, sometimes."

"Sounds like a case of *pibloktoq* to me."

He frowned. "*Pibloktoq*, that's, ah...what is that?"

"Arctic hysteria." The quicksilver eyes sparkled, then paused in concentration. "Let's see, I believe the exact wording is, a dissociative episode characterized by extreme excitement of up to thirty minutes, followed by convulsive seizures and coma lasting up to half a day."

He grinned, not surprised something so obscure should have stuck to that brain of hers. "Frenzy, convulsions, and half-day comas? This would be observed primarily in the female of the species, I'm guessing?"

She grinned back. "Exactly. Especially gorgeous female governors who fly around the Arctic wilderness with hunky young cops."

"This particular governor has a hunky young husband who races sled dogs and is very large and fit. So I doubt she'd be interested. And you know I wouldn't, long as she doesn't mess with my budget."

"The hell I do." The quicksilver in her eyes was gone, replaced by fire.

What switch had he flipped, and how?

"You spend the night in a tent with her, guarding that so-called body of hers, she comes out with scratches on her neck, and Tundrabunny is all over the Internet about how you—what was it she said?—canoodled with America's most gorgeous governor in a tent actually called the Arctic Oven."

"What was I supposed to do? She scratched herself and she made Pudu tape it and put it on YouTube and now—"

"And now I walk down here all tarted up like this and the next thing I know you're on the phone with her and it's 'Suka' this and 'Suka' that? What is she, in your contacts now?"

"She is the gov—"

"Yes, she is, and it seems like she's got you on a mighty short leash."

"She controls over half my budget, not to mention the appropriation for your crisis shelters. What am I supp—"

"Maybe that's what you like, huh? The woman on top? Handcuffs and a blindfold?"

"What's gotten into you? You're not—" He leaned over to check her breath. She pushed him back so hard he stumbled against the sink.

"No, I'm not drinking. I just can't give you what

you need, so you're out collecting it from our hot little governor with benefits. I hear there's nothing she likes better than serving her male constituents!"

"You know I'm not like that."

"You're a normal man with normal appetites. Of course you're tired of hand jobs." He winced at the desperation in her voice. "Let's get this over with."

She pulled open the shirt and pushed out her breasts and they were too much for him. He brushed the nipples with his palms, felt them swell, then pulled her to him and crushed his lips against hers. She reached up and sank her nails into his scalp. He groaned and slid his tongue into her warm, wet mouth. She responded for a second and the word "Finally!" came into his head and he boosted her onto the counter and fumbled with his belt buckle. Then it was over. She went rigid in his arms. He let her go and eased back a little.

"Just do it. I have to get past this."

"I can't, not like this. It's not in me."

"Just take me! Get me drunk. Something, anything. Help me undo what Jason did. Pretend I'm her if you have to."

Pretend she was Helen Mercer? My God, was it possible she could read his mind?

He shook off the picture of Mercer in the Trooper shirt and pulled Grace in and wrapped her in a bear hug. "Stop that." He softened his voice. "Stop it now."

Somehow, that un-flipped the switch. She relaxed like a swaddled infant.

"Sorry, baby," she sobbed into his neck. "I'm scared I'm never going to get there. It's like I'm out on an ice floe and I can see the shore but I just can't make the jump to normal. Go. Find someone else. A man can't live without sex."

"Come on, let's talk. Please?"

"No!" Her tone softened. "No."

She kissed him long and deep. "At least sit back and relax and let these hands work their magic." She give him an exploratory grope. "See? Little Nathan's interested."

She led him into the living room, pushed him into an armchair, knelt between his knees and opened his fly.

His phone marimbaed again. Her look dared him to answer it. His eyes dropped to the screen.

"Yes, it's Chief Active. Sorry, Governor, I'm still tied up. All right, Suka. But, I have to go. OK, sure, I'll call when your plane lands in Anchorage, I promise." He ended the call while she was still talking.

Grace was already on the stairs. She stalked into her father's bedroom and slammed the door.

His phone marimbaed again. Did he dare let Mercer go to voicemail after hanging up on her? But it wasn't "Governor" he saw when he checked the caller ID. It was the dispatch line at public safety. What now?

"Chief Active," he said.

He listened as the dispatcher reported a drunk passed out on the Isignaq trail a half mile east of the airport. "Why didn't the guy bring the drunk in himself?"

"That's not in my notes," said the dispatcher, a man named Winkler whom Active had inherited with the new job. "Mr. Sundown's pretty deaf, so it was kind of hard to ask him any questions, Chief."

Asking questions in English of an older Inupiaq with hearing damaged by snowgos, outboards, rifles, and shotguns wasn't so difficult when you got used to it. You just had to speak loud and clear, then wait out the long pauses that were part of any conversation with an elder. That was how old Inupiat talked. But Winkler was white and pretty new to Chukchi, like everybody on the force except himself and Alan Long. Winkler didn't speak Bush yet.

"OK," Active said. "Find Alan Long and send him out to retrieve the guy. Tell him to take his EMT kit, a sled, some sleeping bags—the usual, all right? The guy's probably hypothermic."

"Got it, Chief."

Winkler rang off while Active pondered the oddness of being called 'Chief.' Should he ask his people to call him something else? If so, what?

Then reality kicked back in and he headed upstairs for the apology. Maybe Grace would be charmed by the drunk passed out on the tundra. It was pure Chukchi. At least she'd know it wasn't another call from Helen Mercer.

CHAPTER TWELVE

Tuesday, April 15

Tundra Kill

ACTIVE SWIVELED TO survey the terrain around them and shook his head as Helen Mercer's flight faded into the haze. "So, again, what was he doing out here? Did he fall off somebody's snowgo and they didn't notice?"

"Yeah, and then he started walking and they finally came back to get him and ran him over by mistake," Long said. "You know how those drunks are."

"Let's see if we can figure out who he was."

He knelt beside the victim. Should he cut away the mask to see if one of them would recognize the man, or search his clothes for ID first?

No need to touch the mangled face if it could be avoided, he decided. He went through the parka pockets. Nothing. Then the cargo pockets of the snowgo suit. Nothing but a couple of the nylon booties mushers used to keep ice from balling up between their dogs' toes and cutting up the pads. He showed Long the red booties.

"He's a musher, ah?" Long said.

"Looks like it. Check around for dog tracks, eh?"

Long crunched away. Active put the booties back in the parka. Now he'd eliminated everything except the pockets of the dead man's jeans.

He dropped to his knees and folded up the tail of the parka, then sliced through the shoulder straps in back. He pulled the rear bib down until the jeans were exposed. One hip pocket had a prominent bulge.

He flipped off his gloves and fished out the wallet, then flipped through it until he found a driver's license. The photograph matched what he'd seen of the dead man's face.

Long crunched back up. "No dog tracks over here by the body, but maybe some over there on the trail. Hard to tell if they're new or even dog tracks for sure, the trail is so beat up from wind and snowgo traffic."

Active showed him the driver's license. "You know a Peter Wise?"

Recognition spread over Long's face. "Oh, yeah, Pete Wise. He was a couple years ahead of me in school. And he was on the basketball team."

Active nodded. The name was familiar but he couldn't place it. "He run dogs?"

"I think so, yeah," Long said.

"But he wasn't in the 400, right?"

"Not this year. He won it a couple times before, all right, then he quit."

"Got tired of it, did he?"

"I dunno, he said it was time for someone else to win," Long said. "After that he just did it for fun."

"He have a job?

Long thought about it for a few seconds.

"Let's see, I think he's—oh, yeah—he was the alcoholism counselor at Natchiq Association, remember?" Long said.

Now it clicked. Natchiq Association was the non-profit corporation that ran the Chukchi hospital and most of the social services in the area. "Yeah, sure, now I do," Active said. "His office takes counseling referrals from the court system when people get sentenced on something alcohol-related."

Long lifted his eyebrows. "And he was a volunteer

basketball coach at Natchiq's summer camp, usually."

"He ever have a drinking problem himself?"

Long squinted the Eskimo no. "Not that I ever heard of. He was pretty much a straight arrow. Even though he was a basketball star and could have had all the girls and booze he wanted."

Active turned a full circle, scanning the folds of tundra around them. "So, again..."

"Yeah," Long said. "Out here with no dogs and no snowgo. Not even skis. This is pretty far from town to be walking."

There was a lull in the breeze and silence fell over the tundra. First Long, then Active, cocked an ear toward a brushy little draw that dropped away from the ridge where the Isignaq trail ran.

"Is that...?" Long said.

"Has to be. Let's get him loaded in the ahkio, then we'll check."

Long started his snowgo and pulled the ahkio alongside the body. They flexed the corpse's shoulders until the muscles loosened up, then bent the arms down along his sides.

Active took the armpits and Long the boots and they heaved. The corpse's left leg folded at mid-thigh and the boot started to slide out of the snowgo suit. They lost their grip and dropped the body back onto the snow.

"Jesus!" Active knelt to examine the red-black stain where the thigh had been, then rolled the corpse onto its side and pulled apart the tatters of the parka, snowgo suit and jeans to check the damaged leg. He sat back on his heels and gazed at the mess. "It's actually severed. The impact cut off his leg. One of the skis, maybe."

"What a way to die," Long said. "Bleeding out on the tundra."

"Although with that head injury...," Active said. They

looked at each other, then at the corpse, then at the snow around them. Finally Active grunted. "All right, let's get him on the sled."

This time, they slid him sideways across the snow to the ahkio, then rolled him on. Wisps of goose down floated up from the ripped parka and wafted away on the breeze.

"You cover him up and follow me, OK?" Active mounted his Yamaha, hit the starter, and accelerated off the ridge and into the draw.

A quarter mile downhill he found the sled snagged in the willows. Seven huskies, still in their traces, erupted in hysteria as he circled the scene for a look and shut down the snowgo. A few seconds later, Long pulled up on his Arctic Cat with the remains of Pete Wise wrapped in a blue tarp on the ahkio.

"I guess we know how he got here," Long said.

Active raised his eyebrows. "Call animal control to come get them. And put an announcement on Kay-Chuck asking anyone spotting a snowgo with front-end damage and maybe blood on it to get in touch."

ACTIVE, LONG AND Carnaby waited in pointed silence as Lucy made a production of bringing in a carafe of coffee and setting around cups and condiments for the three of them.

Finally, she looked at Carnaby and asked, "You take yours black, right?"

"Ahem," Active said.

Lucy put on a look of mystified innocence. "What?"

"We can pour it ourselves, thank you."

"*Arii*, I'm just trying to help."

"Of course."

"Humph." She turned and waddled out.

"I called our village safety officer up in—" Long stopped at a look from Active.

"And shut the door," Active said.

The door closed with an indignant 'thunk'.

"And that'll be all now."

"I'm just waiting in case you need something," came Lucy's voice from outside.

"We're fine, thanks."

"*Arii*, I don't know why I work so hard," the voice said. Footsteps receded down the hallway.

"Maybe you should make her a detective." Carnaby poured himself a cup of the coffee, which he left black. "Officer Brophy. It has a ring. Plus, she usually knows more than the rest of us put together."

"Let's try to focus here," Active said. "To what do we owe the honor of this visit from the Alaska State

Troopers?"

"I'm just here to listen and advise," Carnaby said. "So far it's a borough case, but you never know when we Troopers will get pulled in."

"I don't recall us doing any sit-ins when I worked for you," Active said.

"Me, neither," Long said. "The Troopers never came in on a city case unless we asked for it."

Carnaby waved a dismissive hand. "No biggie. Something new the governor has asked us to do. Kind of facilitate local law enforcement, make sure you've got all the resources you need, partnership kind of thing. That's good, right?"

Active frowned. "The governor asked you to sit in on this?"

"Posilutely, Helen Wheels herownself. I'm from the state of Alaska and I'm here to help! You know how she likes you."

"But how does she even know about it? It can't possibly be news in Juneau."

Carnaby shrugged. "I dunno. From her family up here maybe?"

"Maybe," Active said. "And now that I think of it, she said she streams Kay-Chuck. Maybe she heard Roger Kennelly's story. Or our notice about the snowgo."

"She streams Kay-Chuck? What is that?"

"Never mind. Just Internet technojabber." Active studied the Trooper captain. "I guess we would have ended up bouncing it off you anyway."

"And so...?" Carnaby turned up his palms.

"And so...what do we have? Alan? You check with the victim's family in Walker?"

Long raised his eyebrows. "I called the village safety officer up there and he talked to them and they didn't know anybody that would have had it in for Pete. But his mom said they never heard much from him once he moved down here to Chukchi for high school. Sounds like he was a real private guy."

Active nodded.

"They think it was an accident probably."

Active frowned. "You didn't tell them what we found at the scene?"

Long stiffened a little. "Of course not."

"You go to his house?"

"Yeah, it's just a regular house," Long said. "Everything was pretty normal. Place was locked, nothing broken, messed up, spilled, turned over inside, from what I could see through the windows. Nothing funny-looking outside. I put up some crime scene tape."

"You didn't go in?"

Long stiffened again. "Of course not. Not without a warrant."

Active grunted. "Which we don't have any basis for getting that I can see. Our patrol guys see a newly banged-up snowgo anywhere? Especially with blood on it?"

Long squinted the no.

Active looked at his notebook. "I checked with the hospital. They didn't get anybody in the ER last night or this morning who looked to have been in a snowgo wreck. And Pete didn't turn up in our computer. If he was ever in trouble, it apparently never crossed a police blotter."

He turned his gaze on Carnaby. "You guys got any history with a Peter Aqpattuq Wise? I don't remember anything but the alcoholism referrals when I was at the troopers."

Carnaby shrugged. "Me neither. He was clean, far as I know."

"There's gotta be something somewhere," Active

said. "You can't just kill somebody and vanish. Not around here."

"*Arii*," Long said. "What if we never figure it out?"

Carnaby shifted in his chair. "So what exactly did you find out there on the tundra?"

"A bloody mess, basically." Active sketched the scene for him.

"Whew," Carnaby said a few minutes later. "Skull split open, face ripped up, leg cut off, and nothing but snowgo tracks?"

Active frowned. "Yeah. It sucks."

"Better you than us," Carnaby said as he rose from his chair. "But seriously. Let me know if we can kick in on this one."

Long and Active looked at each other as Carnaby slipped out the door.

"What now, boss?"

Active tented his fingers and looked across them at the sea ice beyond his window. Kay-Chuck had reported a temperature of five above a few minutes earlier. Why was he inside on a day like this? Why didn't Arctic police work involve more riding around on snowgos or in Cessnas, as long as it wasn't with Helen Mercer and the plane didn't ice up and fall out of the sky?

He turned his gaze back to Long. "No reports of a stolen snowgo, right?"

Long squinted the no.

"Nothing from our Kay-Chuck message?"

Another no. Then, "Maybe we should offer a reward?"

Active frowned. "Reward? What have we got for a reward?"

Long shrugged. "Free nights in jail, maybe?"

"Free nights in jail."

Long raised his eyebrows.

"Who'd want to be in our jail if they didn't have to?"

"We used to do it sometimes when Jim Silver was chief. You'd be surprised how popular it was."

"Jim Silver did it?"

Another yes from Long.

Active frowned in sudden suspicion. "Your sister wants another conjugal visit with Clevis Trafford, doesn't she?"

"They're engaged. They need to be together. It'll give Clevis a reason to straighten up when he gets out from the bootlegging charge."

"Yeah, all right. If Edna can find that snowgo for us, I'll authorize a conjugal visit."

"Three nights?"

"A conjugal visit is one night."

"Two nights maybe?" Long asked. "This is a big case, all right. And she hasn't seen him in a while. She says they need to catch up."

"All right, two nights. If she finds the snowgo."

"How about one night before she finds it and one after?"

"None before and two after. That's it."

Long grinned. "I'll tell her."

Active studied the deputy, still suspicious. "I don't suppose there's any chance she already found it?"

"No, but she's got really sharp eyes. And she knows lotta people, all right, especially the *aanas*. Them old ladies know everything and they always talk to each other about it."

"In other words, Edna's been bugging you to get her another conjugal visit and you're using this to get her off your back."

"*Arii*, I love my sister."

"Sure you do."

"So I should put the reward in our message?"

Active conducted a mental inventory of their jail

population, which totaled three at the moment, counting Clevis. "Is there somebody else interested in spending a couple nights in our jail?"

"The competition might make Edna work harder. You never know."

"You're right, Alan. You never do know. I don't, that's for sure. So, yeah, two free nights in jail for whoever finds the snowgo." He stood up and headed for the door.

"What you gonna do, boss?" Long asked.

"Talk to somebody who actually knows something," Active said. "I hope."

Lucy looked up in surprise and, Active thought, some apprehension as he knocked at the open door to her office. She made a quick movement with her computer mouse that he guessed was to close her Facebook page, on which she had attained some renown for the Eskimo recipes she posted in Inupiaq and English, and on which she spent a considerable part of her official workday at Chukchi Public Safety. Active had declined to take formal cognizance of this. It was his experience that knowing what not to notice was critical to success in any job, this one in particular. As long as she got her work done.

"You guys all done up there?" Lucy asked. "You want me to clean up your coffee stuff?"

"No hurry."

Lucy relaxed a little.

"I was just wondering what you might have heard about Pete Wise, especially lately."

"Oh, yeah, isn't it awful?"

"You ever know him?"

"He was, let's see, I think a couple years ahead of me in school, but he was already a senior when he moved down here, so we weren't there at the same time much."

"He ever have girlfriends? buddies? enemies?"

Lucy frowned over it for a few seconds. "Not that I heard of. He always keep to himself, seem like. He was a big basketball star and really cute, so of course there was always girls trying to, you know, but I never heard of him getting together with nobody."

"Really. A basketball star? And he didn't you-know?"

Lucy shook her head. "Some girls said it was a broken heart. Some of them said he maybe didn't like girls at all."

Active paused to think whether this would fit any square pegs into round holes. "Pete Wise was gay?"

"I probably shouldn't have said that. All I know is, he never try with me!"

"Of course you should have told me. Whoever killed him...no matter why...So, he didn't have any real buddies, either"

"Not that I ever heard of.

"If he was gay, that would make sense. I mean in a town this little, how many guys like that can there be?"

"I could go see *Aana* Pauline, maybe."

"How is it I always end up having you talk to *Aana* Pauline?"

Lucy grinned. "Same like always. She's an old lady. Them old ladies know everything that happens. I'll call her." She picked up her phone, then dropped it and pointed at the clock on the wall. "She's over at the senior center playing snerts with them other old ladies. I bet she knows everything about Pete Wise already. You wanna go talk to her?"

Active shook his head.

"You're still afraid of her, ah?"

"Of course not. I have other leads to pursue. And I think you could get more out of her. My Inupiaq's still not very good."

"Her English is."

"I'm your boss and I'm directing you to go."

"You're afraid of *Aana* Pauline because you know she'll say you should be with me instead of Gracie. That's why you don't want to go."

Active was silent.

"Ah-hah." Lucy paused a little longer to see if he would muster a rejoinder. He didn't. "All right, I'll talk to her, Mister Big Brave Chief of Public Safety. She'll probably want a ride in your police truck if she has any information. If you're not too scared to let her in the truck."

"I'm not scared. I told you."

"With the flasher and siren on."

Active groaned. "Whatever she wants. If she can tell us something useful about Pete Wise."

Lucy rose and pulled on her parka. "What you gonna do anyway? What other leads you pursuing?"

"I'm going to try to find somebody who actually knows something and won't ask me for a ride or a night in jail."

CHAPTER FOURTEEN

Tuesday, April 15

ACTIVE HAD JUST started his truck when the radio scratched to life.

"Hey, boss," said the voice of Alan Long. "We just got a call somebody might have found our snowgo."

"Huh. Anybody we know?"

"Anthony Childers?" Long said.

"Anthony wants two nights in jail? Usually he just wants one of our patches when he brings in a tip. Which is usually worthless."

"I dunno," Long said.

"All right, where is it?"

"Bottom of the bluff under the new cemetery."

"I'll meet you there."

Active switched to his Yamaha and drove across the lagoon back of Chukchi to the foot of the bluff, where Long and Childers waited on the seats of their own snowgos.

Active killed his engine and Anthony pointed out his find. Only handlebars and the remains of a shattered windshield were visible.

"*Arii*, Anthony, you're wasting my time. Look at the snow on it. I bet this snowgo was here all winter. Maybe a lot of winters."

"I dunno," Anthony said. "It could be from blow-in today."

Anthony was a chipmunk-cheeked kid possessed of buck teeth, an amiable goofiness, and a great enthusiasm for all things police-related. Active almost asked why he wanted the nights in jail, but decided he lacked the time for the story, which, like most Chukchi stories, no doubt had more meanders, cutoffs, and eddies than the Isignaq, but, unlike the river, never came to an end.

Active dismounted and thrashed through the willows and drifts to the snowgo. There he kicked and brushed away enough snow to determine the machine was ancient, rusted, and devoid of front skis. He turned on Anthony.

Anthony shrugged.

"Shouldn't you be in school?" Active asked.

"*Arii*, I dunno," Anthony said. "I was just—"

"Get going or I'll put you in my jail for a week, not two nights," Active said.

"But that Kay-Chuck say—"

Active glared and pulled the handcuffs from his belt.

"*Arii*," Anthony said again as he mounted his snowgo. "Nobody ever thank me when I try help." He cranked up and zoomed off.

MARTHA ACTIVE JOHNSON looked up and that familiar sunrise of a smile spread across her face when he knocked on the frame of the open door to the office from which she ran the teacher's aide program for the Chukchi Borough School District.

"Nathan! My baby! Come in here!"

But she didn't wait for him to come in. She jumped up, swept across the office and threw a major hug on him before he could twist away.

Not that he tried too hard. He liked Martha's hugs now. "Good to see you, *aaka*."

She pushed back to arm's length and gave him the eye. "You look pretty good. That Gracie must be feeding you right, ah?"

"Well enough, I suppose."

Martha's expression darkened a little. "What's this I hear about you and the governor? You scratch her neck in that tent up there on the Isignaq? You better watch out for her. She is not a nice woman." Martha shot a quick glance into the hallway. "But don't tell her I said that, ah? She controls a lot of our school budget."

"Everybody's budget," Active said. "But, no, I didn't scratch her neck. She—"

"But your brother showed me that Internet video. Everybody's talking about it."

"Don't believe everything on the Internet. In fact, you shouldn't believe anything on the Internet unless it comes from an official source."

"Like what?"

"Like the chief of the Chukchi Borough Public Safety Department, for example. That's me and I'm telling you I did not scratch the governor's neck. She did it herself getting out of her sleeping bag."

"Ah-hah." Martha waited in silence.

Did a smile play at the corners of her mouth? "*Aaka*."

"She's pretty, ah? And you're a man."

"Yes, but not a stupid man. A careful man. You don't have to tell me she's trouble." He shot a quick glance over his shoulder to see if anyone in the hallway had heard, then stepped inside and closed the door. "Besides, I've got Grace. What man would ask for more?"

"How's Gracie doing? I haven't seen her for a couple weeks, maybe."

"Same as ever." He waved a hand with a gesture intended to sweep in Grace Palmer's past, present, and future. "You know, she's working on her program for the women's shelters, she's getting ready to move over to my place, she's—"

"She's still seeing that Nelda Qivits?"

"Yes, she's still seeing Nelda Qivits."

Martha smiled. "That's good. Early days ago, that Nelda would be an *angatquq*, but the good kind. Try help everybody."

"Grace likes their talks a lot. I think they really help."

Martha paused. Active braced himself.

"And the *quiyuk*? You two—"

"*Aaka*."

"*Arii*. Early days ago, Eskimo boys talk to their *aakas* about everything."

"Not *quiyuk*, I'm pretty sure."

Martha grinned. "Maybe not." Then she paused with a look that signaled it was time to say what he wanted.

"So what do you know about Pete Wise?"

"Oh, yeah, what a terrible accident." She caught his expression and tilted her head. "Ah?"

He shrugged. "We're pretty sure."

"Humph. Not all sure?"

"I never say nothing." He grinned.

"Now you sound like you're from here."

"Maybe I am a little bit, now. But what about Pete Wise? He was in school here in Chukchi for a while, ah? After he came down from Walker?"

Martha's gaze drifted towards the street outside as she reflected. "I never hear too much about Pete, I guess. Me and my teacher aides, we mostly work with the littler kids and he was already in high school when he came down here. So we never have him in our classes." She wouldn't meet his eyes.

"But?"

"Ah, I don't want to say nothing I don't know. Let me get somebody." She picked up her phone and punched a button. "Could you send Arlene to my office for a minute?"

They waited for Arlene. Martha caught Active up on the chances that Sonny would make the basketball team next year, which, in Martha's opinion, would be all right if he stuck with his computer classes, in which he seemed to be some kind of genius and actually mentored the other kids.

"I know," Active said. "He works on our computers and he helps Grace with hers all the time."

Martha beamed. "Yeah, lotta other places around here let him do it, too."

"Maybe he'll even start charging them for it someday."

"Nah, he just like to do it and he get credit at school, that's enough for now. I'm just glad he's gettin' away from them snowgos a little bit. We don't need no sledneck in this family. All they do is, they wreck up their machines racing and waste a lotta money and go deaf from the noise. Maybe break their neck, too." She shook her head.

They waited some more.

Active studied the framed five-by-seven on her desk showing a teenage Martha, smiling gamely and holding a bundle of blankets, beside a beaming Ed and Carmen Wilhite, on the day she passed him over to his adoptive parents. Why did she display that picture? he wondered. It had to be painful for her, and she was always apologizing for giving him up. He had tried to tell her it was OK, now, it had worked out fine, and here he was back in Chukchi for the foreseeable future. But she kept apologizing and kept the picture out, alongside another of her with current family.

Active focused on what Martha was saying, which was a report on the latest hunting adventures of Sonny's father and Active's stepfather, Leroy Johnson. He had, it seemed, knocked over a dozen or so caribou on the Katonak Flats north of Chukchi, where the animals coming through in spring migration were lots and fat. But his snowgo had broken down and he was camped on the trail awaiting the parts he had ordered by a passerby.

"Oh, yeah, Leroy send down a caribou for us with that Henry Walter this morning. You and Gracie and Nita should come over for caribou stew tonight, ah?"

"Actually, we're going out to Leroy's sheefish camp tonight."

Martha opened her mouth.

"But don't ask me if there's any *quiyuk* involved."

"*Arii*," Martha said. Her gaze shifted to the doorway. He turned to see a middle-aged Eskimo woman in cafeteria whites. She had braids, good cheekbones and a kindly look.

Martha waved her into a chair near the desk. "Nathan, this Arlene. Arlene, you know my son Nathan, ah?"

"Pretty much everybody know your little *naluaqmiiyaaq* baby, all right." She grinned. Martha grinned.

Active grinned back, having resolved to bear with good grace his Eskimo name, which meant "almost white." In Chukchi, where teasing was as much a part of life as wind, ice, snow, and forty below, he would forever be *naluaqmiiyaaq* because of his time in Anchorage and his urban ways.

Martha's expression turned serious. "Nathan, he, ah, he's trying to find out about Pete Wise because..." She turned to Active, a plea in her eyes.

"It's for our investigation of the hit-and-run

accident," Active said. "We need a little background on him."

"And you're from Walker like Pete, ah?" Martha said.

Arlene shot Active a look, then gazed at Martha, who raised her eyebrows.

"What kinda background?"

"What did they say about him up there in Walker?"

"I always never like to talk about gossip, all right." Arlene adopted a pious expression and studied her hands.

There was a silence. Active pulled out his notebook and pen, so as to put on a little pressure, but not too much, while he pondered the likelihood that any female, anywhere, at any time in the history of the human race, had ever not been interested in gossip. Or male, for that matter.

"Some people said he had a married girlfriend maybe," Arlene said. "But mostly there was talk he didn't like girls at all. But I never listen to either one." The expression reappeared.

"I might have heard something about that," Active said. Arlene relaxed a little. "And this is official police business."

"Ah-hah."

"So, what else did they say about him up there?"

"Well, Pete Wise seem kinda normal, even fool around with girls maybe a little, till he's about tenth grade, then he pull inside himself, never talk to nobody hardly. His parents start to worry he's on that trail to *qiviktuq* and..."

Arlene's story stumbled to a halt. He puzzled over the word. Arlene pulled out a Kleenex.

"Suicide," Martha said. "Arlene's brother went on that trail and she don't like to talk about it."

Arlene dabbed her eyes.

"We don't have to," Active said. "Because Pete Wise obviously didn't—"

Arlene coughed and cleared her throat. "No, he never go that way. He leave Walker, come down here for basketball and live with his grandparents, finish high school, go down to the university at Kenai by Anchorage, play basketball there, too, get his degree, come back up here and pretty soon he's got that alcoholism job."

"Does he—did he still live with his grandparents?"

"No, they get too old and move back up to Walker to live with their kids. Pete was live by himself down here."

"You ever see him much, since you're from Walker like him?"

"*Arii*, I try all right. His *aaka* ask me. But he still keep to himself down here, won't even come over to have *muktuk* with my family and me when we get it from my cousin up in Cape Goodwin."

"Not even for *muktuk*," Active marveled.

The two women looked at each other and shook their heads in astonishment at the idea of an Inupiaq man passing up a nice chunk of boiled bowhead whale skin with an inch or two of fat still on. "Not even if it's fresh!" Arlene said.

"Did you ever hear of him having a, um, a special friend here in Chukchi?"

Arlene squinted the Eskimo no. "I never hear of him going around with nobody, never see him with nobody, hardly. Live by himself, hunt by himself, run dogs by himself, do everything by himself." She paused to dab her eyes again. "Maybe he's the loneliest man in Chukchi, ah?"

"Maybe so." Active looked at his notebook, then wrote "lonely" in it.

Arlene shot a burst of Inupiaq at Martha, too fast for

him to catch more than a word or two, maybe "rabbit" and "sick."

Martha raised her eyebrows at Arlene, then turned to Active. "Maybe you need a haircut, ah?"

What was this about? "Nita usually cuts it. She likes to do it."

"Maybe you should try that Arctic Hair, ah?"

"The Arctic Hair? You mean the..." He made the connection and folded his notebook. "Chukchi has a gay hairdresser?"

"Aren't they all like that if they're men?" Martha said. "Otherwise they call theirselfs a barber, ah?"

"But Chukchi has a gay hairdresser? How do I not know this?"

"Maybe because Milton Sipary never get in no trouble? He probably have to be pretty careful. Some of these slednecks we got now, they don't like no *agnauraq*, what they call it if a man don't want women. Early days ago, them old-timers never get in other people's business so much."

Arlene seconded the proposition with a vigorous nod. "Ah-hah. And that Milton is a pretty good boy anyway. Remember, he was in the Army, then he work at Anchorage long time, come back here to take care of his mother when she get real sick?"

"Oh, yeah," Martha said. "*Arii*, I forgot about that. And then she die but he get sick himself, now he's still here."

"I heard he got that lung cancer," Arlene said.

Active brushed his hand over his scalp and tried to get the conversation back on track. "I don't need a haircut. I could just go talk to Milton."

The two women looked at each other and frowned. "Maybe not," Martha said.

"Maybe too scare," Arlene said.

"But I'll say it's police business."

The women turned looks of pity on him. "Then he's really scare," Arlene said. "Never say nothing."

"OK, OK, I'll get a haircut."

"Wait, I don't know if Milton's open any more," Martha said. "He's been pretty sick, all right."

"Well, should I—"

"You could try check if he'll give you a haircut," Arlene said. "Maybe he will."

"Thanks, Arlene. *Quyaana*."

Arlene lifted her eyebrows with a nod.

Active rose and moved toward the door. "And thank you, *aaka*. *Arigaa*."

He was out the door too fast for Martha to hug him, and with a "We'll bring you some sheefish."

CHAPTER FIFTEEN

Tuesday, April 15

IN THE CHEVY, Active pulled a scrawny Chukchi phone book from the console, looked up the number, and dialed his cell phone.

"Arctic Hair," said an exhausted voice.

"I was wondering if I could get a haircut today?"

"I was just about to close up—"

"Maybe just a trim?"

"You could come over, I guess. Maybe I could do a trim."

The connection went dead before Active could ask how to get there. Should he call back? Maybe not. He barely had his foot in the door, judging from the sound of Milton Sipary's voice.

But where was Arctic Hair? He'd driven past it a hundred times, he could see it in his mind's eye, but it was sunk in his memory as part of the Chukchiscape, undifferentiated as the rest of it. Maybe he'd been around too long. Maybe he'd missed too many planes to ever get out now.

He opened the phone book again. "Third Avenue," the listing said. No number, just the street, but that was enough. His memory brought it up—a little old cottage, the kind of place some people still called an Eskimo house.

He drove to the spot, parked the Chevy in front, and studied Arctic Hair. It was well kept for a Chukchi house. No broken windows, no missing shingles, no dead snowgos in front, and the paint was still a deep red, not blasted down to a dull rust by wind and snow. Two rooms, he guessed, with a tiny *kunnichuk* in front. A wooden sign on the front identified it as the Arctic Hair, illustrated by a painting of an Arctic hare stretched out in full sprint.

Active smiled a little at the pun as he noticed another thing: Arctic Hair had trees in front—two spruces, two cottonwoods, all healthy and tall by Arctic standards. He couldn't recall ever seeing anything bigger than alders and dwarf willows on the spit of gravel and tundra where Chukchi stood. How had Milton Sipary coaxed trees to grow so large in front of his house?

He went through the *kunnichuk* and knocked on the inner door. There was a stir inside, then the door opened to reveal a lean Inupiaq with an angular face.

"I'm Milton," he said. "Come on in."

He was in his late fifties, maybe, silver hair in a kind of crew cut, a ring in one ear. He looked healthier than Active had expected. Also straighter, which made Active wonder what he thought a gay man should look like, and why?

"Nathan Active."

"I know who you are." The hairdresser studied him without offering a hand. "Your hair's not that long."

Active took off his parka and hung it on a hook by the door. "It's kind of a special occasion."

"And you're the new police chief. And you've never been here before."

He brushed a hand over his hair again. "I could use a trim."

"You said that on the phone. Am I in trouble?"

"Of course not."

Sipary tipped his head toward the barber chair in the middle of the room. Active settled in and noticed a slight smell of cat box mixed with the aroma of hair spray. Little dishes of food and water were set against a wall. There was no sign of the cat, though. All Things Considered played from a radio that shared a shelf with a cigar box, spray bottles, gel tubes, and hairdressing gear. Next to it were framed certificates that looked military, including one with a medal on a ribbon.

Sipary spotted him checking out the lineup on the shelf. "I guessing you won't be wanting any product?"

"Probably not."

"Mm-hmm." Sipary draped the cape around Active's shoulders. "Just a trim?"

"Just a trim."

Sipary took scissors from the shelf and Active watched him work in the mirror above it. His hand was light and sure, the same delicate touch as a house dog sniffing the cuffs of a new arrival. Sipary seemed to relax, and hummed little snatches of melody as he worked.

How to get into it? "They say people tell hair stylists everything," Active said at last.

"That's somewhat true," Sipary said. "At least I find out how the kids are doing and who's sleeping with who, if it's women."

"And if it's men?"

"How's fishin', how's huntin', how's the weather?" Sipary said with a little chuckle. "I like the women better."

"Who doesn't?" Active said.

Sipary seemed to tense a little, and Active wondered how to walk back what he'd said. But it was Sipary who eased the moment.

"I'm sick, you know."

"I heard that."

"Mm-hmm. But not what you might be thinking. It's nothing you can catch."

"I wasn't worried."

"Mm-hmm. That's why I didn't want to cut your hair. I'm tired all the time. I'm only going to cut hair one more month."

"Are you on chemo or anything?"

In the mirror, Sipary shook his head. "I was and it went away. But it came back. So now I'm done with all that."

"You'll stay in Chukchi after you quit cutting hair?"

Sipary lifted his eyebrows in the mirror. "Mm-hmm. I've got relatives in Anchorage, all right, but most of my family and friends are here, so this is more home."

"I'm sorry for your trouble, Mr. Sipary."

"I don't complain. My life's been all right."

Sipary snipped away as Active tried again to come at his question.

"I like your trees," he said finally. "Nobody else in Chukchi has trees in front of their house."

Sipary smiled in the mirror. "My mother had a secret."

Active lifted his eyebrows in the Anchorage expression of inquiry.

"You plant them on the east wall. That way, they're protected from the west wind, and they get the light of the rising sun in the coldest part of the day. It bounces off the wall and they get it twice."

"Ah," Active said. "I think my house has a pretty good east wall, all right."

"Then you should plant some trees over there." Sipary pulled the cape off Active's shoulders and shook it free of clippings. "But that's not why you're here, ah?"

"No, it's not," Active said.

"And you're not like me."

"Ah, no, that's not it. I'm...I'm with Grace Palmer."

"A beautiful woman. If I wasn't like me, I'd like to be

with her, I think."

"I'm very lucky," Active said.

"So why are you here, then?"

"Did you know Pete Wise?"

"The guy who was run over? A little, not very well."

"Was he, ah..."

"Like me? No."

"You sound sure."

"Pretty sure, all right. My *naluaqmiut* friends call it gaydar. It's almost always right."

"And Pete didn't trip yours or anyone else's?"

"Not that I ever heard of." Sipary paused. "But I could check around. People tell their stylists everything, all right."

"Thank you." Active handed him a business card. "How much for the trim?"

"It's twenty-five."

Active found two twenties in his wallet and passed them over. Sipary put them in the cigar box and returned with a ten and a five.

"No, you keep it."

"I probably won't need it," Sipary said. "But it can't hurt." He put the bills back in the box.

Active put out his hand. Sipary hesitated, then took it.

"Good luck on your journey," Active said.

Sipary lifted his eyebrows, yes, and studied the business card. "I'll call you if I hear something."

CHAPTER SIXTEEN

Tuesday, April 15

THE SUN WAS sliding toward the northwest horizon as Active pulled his crew-cab to a stop at Grace's house. Nita burst out, threw an armful of sleeping bags into the dog sled hitched behind his snowgo, and started to lash them in place with yellow polypropylene line.

He studied her in the slanting light. She was coltish now, all energy and enthusiasm and drama, her body a little ahead of her coordination, and starting to look enough like Grace to spook him sometimes.

She straightened, examined her lashings, then spotted him with his arm out the window of the Chevy and his official cop mirror sunglasses down over his eyes.

"Uncle Nathan! You ready? I got all our stuffs on the sled. Me and Christina are gonna win the sheefish derby!"

"Both of you? How is that possible? I thought there was only one first place."

"We made a pact. We're both gonna win, like first place and second place or something, then we're gonna share the prizes equally. There's, like, an iPhone, some mukluks, a beaver hat—I'll give you the beaver hat—a caribou parky."

Active frowned as he walked over to the sled. "You two are gonna share an iPhone maybe? How's that gonna work?"

"It'll be so cool. Each of us will have it for a week and we'll tell all our friends. And we're gonna record the voicemail message together—like a duet?—and it'll say you can leave a message or you can call either one of us at home and then we're gonna put our home phones on it. Cool, ah?"

"Pretty cool, all right. But what if I try to call you and Christina answers?"

"Duh! She'll say, 'It's Christina, Nathan. You could call Nita at home.'"

Active grinned. "That's a great plan. What could possibly go wrong."

"*Arii*, you always do that. You're a—what is it Mom says?"

"Curmudgeon?"

"That's right, a great big curmudgeon. You should learn to be happy. It's not that hard."

"The world needs curmudgeons," he said. "We take care of the worrying so regular people can be happy. Like you."

Active put his agnosticism on hold long enough to send up a small prayer that the girl would never have to unlearn happiness, as her mother had done. In that space, Nita dashed over, mounted the running board, and put her cheek against his.

"Poor Uncle Nathan. Such an old soul."

"What?" he said as she sprinted for the door. "Where did you hear that?"

"Nelda Qivits told me," she shouted as she raced inside. "It's the same as a curmudgeon, but more lonely."

He stared after her, then pondered the words as he checked the load on the sled. What else did Nita and the tribal healer talk about?

He shook his head in resignation—no man could understand women, even little ones—and followed Nita inside. He found Grace in the kitchen with a red Igloo cooler abrim with supplies, plus two wooden jockey boxes, one topped off, the other almost so.

"Think you got enough stuffs there?"

Grace dropped a package of Oreos into the not-quite-full box. "Shut up if you want these with your milk tonight."

She waved the Oreos at him. His mouth watered.

"Yes, ma'am," he said. "But it's only one night and Leroy's ice camp is just up by the Point. We could drive back to the Arctic Dragon if we get hungry."

"Nuh-uh, no way," Grace said. "Fish camp is fish camp. You don't break the experience in the middle. You come back when you come back, and that's that."

An hour later, Active cut his engine and coasted the Yamaha to a stop at Leroy's ice camp. It consisted of a white canvas wall tent with a stovepipe that poked out a rear corner of the roof. The west wall—the one against the wind—was stacked with firewood scavenged off the beaches or cut from the scrub spruce that started a mile or two inland. A rusty bow saw lay atop the pile.

He swung off the seat, stamped a few times to loosen his joints, unzipped his parka, threw back his hood, and pulled off his goggles and neoprene mask. He turned to his womenfolk, as he found he thought of Grace and Nita these days.

Just their noses and goggles showed amid the cocoon of sleeping bags and caribou hides they'd used for cover on the way out. They shook their way free. Nita raced to the tent and began to unlace the front door. Grace came to stand beside him.

"Looks good, ah?"

He nodded. "The wood rack's still squared up, no sign anybody's borrowed any, door flaps still tied in place till Hurricane Nita hit."

Nita poked her head out. "Well, come on in. We gotta light the lantern and the halfagascan."

"I'll do the halfagascan," Grace told Active. "You do the Coleman. Those things scare me."

Active had to admit, lighting a pressurized lamp full of camp fuel—white gas, as it was called in the Bush—was not for the faint of heart. First you used a little plunger to pump air into the gas tank to create pressure. Then you turned on the gas valve for a couple seconds to get fuel into the mantle. Then you lit a match and put it though the access hole under the mantle. The mantle caught with a whoosh—hopefully soft, not a boom—you turned the gas on again, and then you were in business. Lots of light and quite a bit of heat, enough in mild weather that you didn't need a halfagascan. And, as Active also had to admit, it was rare to hear of a tent or cabin blown up by a Coleman lantern, despite the lethal-seeming proximity of gas, pressurized air, sulfur matches, and human fallibility.

And this time the lighting did go well. He put the match in at the right moment, the whoosh was soft, not percussive, and the tent filled with the homey hiss and buttery glow of a reliable old Coleman on camp duty.

The other essential in a cold-weather Bush camp was the halfagascan, so-called for a couple of reasons. One was, it consisted of half an oil drum with a door in front and a stovepipe that came out the top and ran up through the cabin roof.

The second was, the thing's official name, other than

barrel stove, was Athabascan stove. As far as anyone knew, that was because it was so much used by the Athabascans of Alaska's vast interior after British and Russian fur traders came into the country.

Somewhere in the migration of "Athabascan" to "halfagascan," Active sensed, lay a sly Inupiat joke, though he wasn't quite sure what it was. There were tales of actual warfare and woman-stealing between the Athabascans and Inupiat in the old days before the white man arrived. Maybe enough of the old rivalry still lingered that, by calling the stove "halfagascan," the Inupiat insinuated the Athabascans were half-men, especially below the belt? Active wouldn't put it past them.

At any rate, the halfagascan was perfect technology for its operating environment in the Alaska Bush. Crude, simple, easy to make from scrap materials, and almost idiot-proof. Plus, the halfagascan would burn pretty much anything you threw in it—wood, whale blubber, seal fat, even waste engine oil. You could use it to cook food, boil water, heat the tent, or dry clothes and mukluks—nearly any process that involved the transfer of thermal energy.

Grace, he saw, was just about set with the halfagascan. Leroy—or whoever had borrowed his camp last—had, as Arctic protocol dictated, left a stack of wood and scrap paper in a box beside the stove. Grace had crumpled some paper, thrown on four or five logs, and poured on a little white gas. Now she struck a match, it flared, she tossed it in, and whoosh!

She turned and gave him that smile. "Heat from the halfagascan, light from the Coleman, what could make a camp more perfect?"

He shrugged. "I dunno? Some dinner?"

She grinned, hands on hips. "Just like a man. Expecting the woman to do all the cooking."

He grinned back. "Would you eat a dinner I made? Or

feed it to your child?"

"Mom, don't let him make dinner." Nita, out of Grace's line of sight, winked at Active. "Ple-e-e-ase?"

Active had to admit, it was maybe the most expert wheedle he'd ever heard out of a kid. He wanted to give the girl a fist-pump, but he was within eyeshot of Grace.

The audience for their little charade shook her head in disgust. "All right, you two, enough. I know, I know, it'll be dark before long, it might be too dark already, but you just gotta get your rigs in the water right now in case there's one or two last really stupid sheefish down there. Don't even say it, just get out there."

They raced out before she could reconsider, pulling on winter gear as they went, and rifled through the jockey box at the back of the sled for the sheefish hooks.

Like the halfagascan and the white canvas wall tent, sheefish hooks were perfectly suited to their environment. A "hook" actually consisted of the entire rig, not just the hook itself: a boomerang-shaped stick about a foot from tip to tip with a line attached at one tip, a notch at each end to catch the line as you wound it on or off the rig, and a few yards of clear monofilament with a big silver spoon and treble hook.

But it didn't look like they would catch any sheefish tonight. They patrolled around the camp looking for an open hole. They found plenty of holes, but all had layered over with several inches of new ice since their last use. Active went back to the sled for the long-handled ice chisel known as a *tuuq*, picked a hole, and began testing. Impervious to the *tuuq*. He moved on. He was on number three and thinking of breaking out Leroy's gas-powered ice auger when Grace yelled from the tent door.

"*Bunnik*, phone—it's Christina."

So ended the sheefishing for that night. Nita dashed away. Active gathered up the gear and trudged back to dump it into the sled.

As he stepped into the tent, Grace had the phone and was saying, "Great, I'll bring her right down."

Active cocked an eyebrow at the two of them.

"I'm gonna stay with Christina tonight and we're gonna watch the whale movie on her iPad!"

"Nice! How many times is this?"

"Only, um, seven, I think." She looked at her mother.

"Or eight," Grace said. "Maybe nine."

"Whatever." Nita gathered up enough stuffs to get her through the night and dashed out to lash it onto the sled.

They grinned after her.

"The whale movie," Active said. "I forget, is that the inspiring one or the uplifting one? Or heartwarming?"

"Shut up," Grace said. "Especially if you want to get lucky." She waggled her fingers like a masseuse limbering up.

"Ah-hah. Servile silence it is, then. "

"Just wait till I get back. We'll see how silent."

She suited up and followed Nita out to the snowgo and soon the machine sputtered away into the distance as he contemplated the prospect of an evening at the mercy of Grace Palmer's magic hands.

Maybe it wasn't real sex, but it was really good sex, especially when it worked right, which it usually did. He just hoped it wouldn't go sideways from the Pete Wise case and Helen Mercer's calls.

WHEN HE HEARD the snowgo returning, he realized with regret he was going to have to play watchdog for one last round. Maybe he wouldn't get lucky tonight after all. Well, he had emotional intelligence, Carnaby had said. Maybe it would get him through.

The machine sputtered into silence and in a moment there she was in the doorway, pulling off the helmet, hair tumbling out, face flushed from the ride, rubbing wind-tears from the corners of her eyes.

"So," he said. "All good over there at Christina's folks' camp?"

He didn't see her tense up, but he could feel it.

"Of course."

"Really all good? No men in camp? No liquor?"

"Seriously," she said. "You're asking ask me if Nita's safe? Me?"

He shrugged. "I'm just—"

She put her fingers across his lips. "Not all men are like my father, you know."

"Enough are. Too many."

"You're not."

"I hope so."

"Trust me," she said. "You'd know by now."

He nodded and she drew back to study him.

"But, for the record, no. No men in camp, no booze. Just a mother with a .30-30 and an *aana* with an *ulu*." Her face softened. Her eyes brimmed in the Coleman light. "You're so Nathan sometimes."

"That's a good thing, right?"

"Very. Don't ever change. Now, where were we?"

She moved into his arms for a kiss, several of them, then eased away a little. This, he knew from experience, was where the magic hands would come into play. Their first stop would be at his belt buckle. To make sure it was accessible, he unzipped the down vest he wore under his parka when he was outdoors or in camp this time of year.

But, no, she moved to one of the boxes, rummaged for a few seconds, and came back with a Marlboro carton. She pulled out a baggie with four fat hand-rolled cigarettes in it.

"Oh, no," Active said. "Tell me that's not what it looks like."

"Yep." Grace nodded. "*Qaaq.*"

She tossed the baggie and he caught it by reflex. "My God, these are big."

She nodded. "There was a name for them on Four Street, what was it? Boffo, that's it. No, it was boffo plus something else."

She shook her head. "But boffo is good enough for Chukchi. You are now in possession of four prime boffos."

"But why?"

"Strictly medicinal."

"Eh?"

"Nelda Qivits says it's just the thing for girls like me, too screwed up by sexual abuse to do the deed even when they do find their soul mate. I went and had a special session with her after I behaved like I did this morning."

He studied her eyes and narrowed his own. "Is this one of Nelda's old *aana* jokes? I mean, *qaaq*, it's pronounced like—"

Grace nodded. "Like cock, pretty much. Joke or not, I'm gonna try it if Nelda says there's a chance." She sobered for a moment. "And we can't go on like this. I really want to be sexual and when I talk to old Nelda, I really think I could. And, you, Nathan, you want to go through life on hand jobs? Come on, you got a right."

"I'm happy."

"Well, let's try to make us both even happier. Now, light up." She pulled two joints out of the baggie and passed him one.

He thought it over and passed it back. "I don't think so. One thing, I never smoked anything in my life. I'll cough up a lung. Another thing, maybe one of us oughta keep a clear head. You know, in case it doesn't go, er, quite right?"

"For me, you mean?" Her eyes softened again. "Poor Nathan, always my guardian angel."

"And you gotta know all too well by now, seeing you naked is all I need to achieve, um..."

"Liftoff?"

He grinned and winked. She struck a match on the halfagascan and lit a boffo.

CHAPTER SEVENTEEN

Tuesday evening, April 15

SHE TOOK TWO hits, coughed a little, and parked the boffo on the cooler, then stood and turned down the Coleman. The tent filled with a sourceless glow in the mingled light of the lamp and the low sun outside. She slid out of the wool shirt she'd worn on the trail and dropped it over his head where he sat on a cot.

He breathed in the scent of lavender for a moment, then flipped the shirt onto the cot beside him. The Coleman, he noticed, seemed to be as fascinated by her bra as he was, setting it agleam almost as if lit from within. She reached behind her to unfasten it—then she stopped and bent, presenting him her denim-clad rump, grabbed a chunk of wood from the box, and threw it into the halfagascan.

"Jesus," he said. "Is this strip tease really necessary?"

"Wouldn't want the tent cooling off on us, now, would we?"

"I doubt that'll be a problem."

She unhooked her bra and let it dangle from her shoulders as she gazed at him with the quicksilver eyes. "No," she said, "I'm not ready for a full unveiling yet. It's still a little cold in here."

She leaned over and retrieved the boffo. In the process, he got a brief flash of one perfect breast from the side. The nipple was at least half erect, he judged. A good sign—unless it was only the cold.

She shot him a smirk. "How ya doing, there, officer? Enjoying the show?"

He reached out to show her how much, but she wagged a finger and looked serious. "Uh-uh-uh, you know the rule. I can touch, but you can't till I say so. Not unless you want your tundra bunny turning into an ice maiden."

"Even with the"—he struggled to say it with a straight face—"with the *qaaq*?"

She nodded. "So far."

She put the boffo in her mouth and wriggled her jeans over her hips and down her thighs. She made as if to throw them at him, too, but shook her head and put the boffo back on the cooler.

Then she made a show of turning sideways and, while the Coleman lit up her panties and the dangling bra with its occasional flash of breast, folded the jeans and set them on the cot beside him, too.

She looked at him. He rolled his eyes. "How long is this gonna go on?"

Without a word, she shed the bra and panties, dived onto the other cot, rolled onto her side, grabbed the boffo and put it between her lips, and put her hands behind her head.

"Jesus," he said again as he stood and slid out of his own clothes. "You look like that painting. *The Naked*, um..."

"*Maja*." She grinned. "*With Qaaq*, right?"

He could only stare. She returned it for a moment. "What are you waiting for? Come on over." She patted the narrow space left on the cot.

He eased down beside her, and brushed one palm over a nipple. It stiffened and he raised his eyebrows in inquiry as he stroked the side of her breast.

"Not quite yet," she murmured. He pulled his hand away. She dragged on the *qaaq* with a thoughtful look. "How about I distract you while we let this stuff work its magic?"

She fumbled in the jockey box, came up with a little bottle of baby oil, squirted some on one hand, and clenched her fist to warm it up. "On your back, officer."

He complied and she straddled his thighs.

"You're magnificent in this light," he said.

"So's this." She grabbed him in a warm slippery hand and set to work.

"Jeez," he said. "Take it slow or we're gonna—" He tried to roll free but she had him in a death grip. And his struggles didn't help.

"Nice work," he said about sixty seconds later. "Now what? Grab me a towel or Kleenex or something, eh?"

She didn't move, just sat over him with a triumphant grin and took another hit from the boffo. She took it out of her mouth and studied it. It was about down to her fingers. She parked it, threw herself flat on top of him and rustled around in the jockey box, grunted in mild frustration, then rattled through a couple of trash bags where more of their supplies for the night were stashed. Finally she sat up with a box of Kleenex and resumed her position on his thighs.

He reached for the tissues but she shook her head.

"No, slide up and sit and I'll clean up the mess. I made it, right?"

He complied again and closed his eyes to let events take their course on this strange night. *Qaaq* had put Grace in charge and it seemed to be good for her.

She bent to her work, which soon slowed to a stop, even though his skin told him she hadn't finished the job. He opened his eyes for a look. Only the top of her head was visible. She was studying him up close. "Hmm," she said in a tone of wonder. "Maybe I could."

"Uh-huh." He whispered for fear of breaking whatever spell this was.

"You know I've always wanted you inside me, but,

you know, what with my father, I've never been able, ever, with any man, not the regular way, not even you, the only man I've ever loved, except I loved my father until he started, how could he..."

He waited for her to return from that awful maze of back trails that led from her childhood bedroom in Chukchi to alcoholic homelessness on Anchorage's Four Street and iron-willed self-exile in the Aleutian remoteness of Dutch Harbor and back to Chukchi for her father's murder by her mother. One day, he was afraid, she'd enter the labyrinth and never come out.

Then she shook her head and was back.

"Don't worry about it," he said. "What just happened is fine for now. The time will come when it comes."

She raised her head and shot him a wicked grin. "You're not gonna believe this, but I think it's now. The *qaaq*, being out on the ice like this, I don't know what, but hang on. I used to be pretty good at this on Four Street. I couldn't do the other thing, but I could to this for the next bottle if I was drunk enough."

She grabbed a caribou hide from Nita's cot, threw it onto the ice floor of the tent, swung him around to a sitting position, and dropped to her knees on the hide. She took him in one hand and held him immobile as she engulfed him in the wettest, warmest mouth he had ever known and he felt himself respond, already, the nails of her other hand were scratching him in that place underneath. She was mumbling past him in her mouth, somehow, and he thought he heard "OhGodOhGodOhGod" and he sensed her other hand was between her own legs. Then he was sucked into the vortex of lust and fulfillment she created and he couldn't remember anything for a while.

When he came back, she was astride his thigh, riding it to her own finish, moaning and crying now, loud and unrestrained, sobbing, "Oh, God, you were inside me, God, I love you so much."

Without a word, he grabbed her waist, reversed their positions on the cot, and touched her sex. She was hot and impossibly wet as he put his head between those smooth thighs.

"I'm not sure, baby, what if..."

But this wasn't like before. Her voice didn't mean it, she didn't stiffen. He took her in his mouth, and used his own tongue until she went over the cliff again and collapsed into a fetal curl on the cot, cheeks still wet.

He spooned in behind her, pulled a sleeping bag over them, and wrapped his arms around her.

"Thank you, thank you, thank you," she murmured. "I was afraid I'd never be...be...like that. I thought he killed it in me."

She moved against him to adjust her position and cupped one of his hands over a breast and jiggled it some, as if to demonstrate how she could bear his touch now.

The nipple under his palm, the smooth friction of her skin on his loins and thighs brought him alive again.

"What!" she said. "Already? well, my, my, my."

"I know, me, too."

She wiggled her rump against him, experimentally.

"Eh?" he said.

"I don't know, baby. Maybe. We could try."

He touched himself to the luscious heat of her entrance and paused.

She went rigid in his arms.

"Too soon?" he asked.

"Sorry, baby."

He eased away from her and she relaxed. "It's definitely progress."

"Oh, God, I'll say. A little more practice, a little more

qaaq, and I'm pretty sure you're gonna be carving another notch on your gun belt, there, officer."

"Here's hoping I need a lot bigger belt real soon now," he said.

She chuckled and reached behind herself to feel between his legs. "The sooner the better. But for the here and now—well, one of these is a terrible thing to waste and—God, I loved having you in me." She rolled off the cot and dropped to her knees on the hide, then swung his legs off the cot, parted them, and buried her head again.

This time was the sweetest yet. Not the hottest, not the hardest, not the craziest, just the sweetest. He rested on his elbows, barely erect at first, and she raised her head as she worked so they could maintain eye contact, and they watched it build and build and build in each other's faces.

When they were done, Grace got them a bottle of water and they snuggled on the cot and gave each other drinks.

"Splibo," she said.

"Splibo? Is that another Inupiaq word for sex? It doesn't sound Inupiaq."

"It goes with boffo. A big fat joint is a boffo splibo."

"Excellent," he said. "And I think I know what it means on Zerpalon or whatever planet that language came from."

"What's that?"

"Viagra for girls!"

"This girl, anyway." She giggled, he chuckled, and they cuddled for another minute or two.

She sat bolt upright and said, "Oh, my God."

"What?"

"How far is the next tent?"

"I doubt it matters," he said. "They probably heard you back in Chukchi."

"How loud was I?"

"Like this." He imitated.

"I was not."

"You were."

"I was?"

"Repeatedly. And in a prolonged manner. I'm surprised my cell didn't ring from somebody reporting an assault to the cops. No, actually, I'm not surprised. You invoked the name of the deity so many times and in so many forms, they probably thought you were experiencing a religious epiphany."

He thought she blushed, but it was difficult to be sure in the tent light.

"I'm mortified," she said. She thought for a moment. "No, I'm not. I'm proud. I thought I'd never see the skyrockets you read about."

"Apparently, it's not a problem."

"So where were we?"

"About done, I'd say. I know you're a girl and I'm told girls are pretty much inexhaustible in this department once they get going. But I'm a boy, and three in one night, well, it's a bit draining."

She shook her head. "I don't know who I am all of a sudden, but somehow I'm ready again. I don't want to let this moment go."

"Have we created a monster?"

"I hope so! This is great. I love having you—"

"I know, you love having me inside you."

"No, you don't know. No man can."

"I guess not. But I do know one thing. It was pretty nice being in there."

"Look. You drink some water and chew some of that beef jerky we brought and think dirty thoughts. I'll smoke a little more of this stuff and think filthy thoughts. Then we'll see what we see."

"No promises. But if anything will bring Little

Nathan to attention, it's a beautiful naked woman with a filthy mind."

He took another swallow from the water bottle and bent over the food box for the jerky.

Active's phone marimbaed from somewhere in the clothes he had shucked onto the other cot. He grinned at Grace as he fished it out of the heap. "Apparently someone does want to report rape and murder at Leroy Johnson's sheefish camp." He looked at the display and handed her the phone. "You better tell Alan you're OK."

A look of horror spread across her face and she pushed the radio away. "No!"

"What's up, Alan? What? Really. Dammit, OK, give me a few minutes to pack up and I'll call you back before I head over."

"What?"

"Some guy may have found that snowgo we're looking for in the Pete Wise case. I gotta—"

"It's not the same guy that found the old dead one in the brush, is it?" Grace asked.

He nodded with a shrug.

"You'd leave a beautiful naked woman for Anthony Childers?"

"I was skeptical, too, but Alan Long says the it's only a couple miles from here. Apparently there's an open spot in the ice and you can see a machine under the water."

"Come on, it'll be dark soon and that snowgo will still be there in the morning. And look what you got right here in this tent." She turned to give him a three-quarters view and waggled her shoulders to give her breasts a stripper's jiggle. "Dirty thoughts, Nathan." She raised one knee and rested her heel on the edge of the cot to show him her sex. "Filthy, dirty thoughts."

Active admired the view for a few seconds, then

sighed and shook his head. "Look how light it is." He jerked a thumb at the north and west tent walls, dimly aglow in the sun. "It's maybe an hour yet till sundown, then couple more hours after that before it's really dark. We gotta get that thing out of the water tonight, or at least get it tied off to some floats. We get a wind from the southwest, it could cause enough of a surge to move it. Or we get a real storm and it'll be gone for sure. Or a late cold snap freezes it in solid and it'll take us a week to get it out."

"I know something else that's gonna freeze solid if you leave."

He returned the grin. "Maybe we can figure a way to thaw it out when I get back."

"Something tells me," she said. "Seriously, baby, go ahead and be you. I'm good here."

"You sure? I could call somebody from town to come get you. Or I could take you down to Christina's family's camp, maybe."

"You kidding? I want to stay right here in this tent with this moment and this smell of sex and sweat and you all over me." She pulled him in for a long kiss. "I'll work something out tomorrow if you don't make it back tonight. Call me when you're done. If my cell's off, just stay in town."

CHAPTER EIGHTEEN

"I HAVE TO admit," Active said. "I'm impressed."

"Thanks, boss," Alan Long said. "I got 'em out here right away and Gabe's getting it figured out pretty good, all right."

Active surveyed the scene before them—two of his officers from public safety, the chief and two members from the Chukchi fire department, all bundled up in Carhartts, parkas and Sorels and looking as if nothing could be more gratifying than to stand around on the ice near sunset and figure out how to drag a sunken snowgo out of icy water. There was even a portable emergency light on a stand with its own generator.

They had already snagged the snowgo—one of the skis, Active gathered—with a grappling hook when he pulled up. By the time he walked over to stand beside Long at the hole, they had a hook on the other ski and were horsing the machine up to the edge.

"Maybe I could help," came a voice from behind them.

Active turned to see Anthony Childers.

"You sure can help," said Gabe Reeder, the fire chief. He had a big belly, hair that was mostly gray, a big beard that was still red except for a brown streak from tobacco juice down the middle, and an air of immense competence about all things practical. Like most whites who settled in Chukchi, he was married to an Inupiaq. "You go over by the light there and make sure it doesn't go out, OK?"

A look of alarm and suspicion spread over Anthony's face. "But I still get the night in jail, right?"

"Yes, Anthony, if this is the right snowgo, you still get your night in jail."

Anthony grinned and headed for his snowgo. Gabe shook his head. "Good kid, but..."

"Yeah, not the smoothest rock in the river." Active watched Anthony walk away. His involvement in the case looked weirder and weirder. First, anyone who took undue interest in a criminal investigation automatically topped the list of suspects. And, second, how likely was it that anybody could spot a snowgo under the water unless he already knew it was there?

But, then, why would Anthony lead them to the abandoned snowgo in the brush near the cemetery? Was he capable of dragging such a red herring across the trail? Anthony was a Chukchi kid, so he would know about the perennial open spot near the mouth of the Katonak and figure it was a good place to look. And Anthony did act like all he wanted out of the matter was two nights in jail. Plus, he had been on a snowgo when he led them to his first find and looked to be sitting on the same one tonight as he watched the proceedings. Could he have stolen the snowgo now under water, hit Pete Wise with it, brought out it here to ditch, walked back to town, and then led them on this wild goose chase on his own snowgo to find it again? Had he cooked it up with an accomplice? Why?

Active's head hurt to think about it, so he filed it away with a mental note to interview Anthony the next day.

Unless Anthony suddenly disappeared, say upcountry on a caribou hunt. Active walked over to Anthony at his station by the emergency light.

"I'm pretty sure this is the snowgo, so I think you got your night in jail, Anthony," Active said. "How about we start tonight?"

Anthony beamed. "*Arigaa!*"

Active raised his eyebrows in assent. "In fact, we can even handcuff you to a sled right now if you want."

"Really? Maybe you could take a picture for my Facebook."

With an inward "Aha!" Active realized now what Anthony's motive for the nights in jail must be: to share with the hive mind of the Internet one slightly less humdrum moment in a humdrum existence. Anthony Childers wanted to be famous.

They marched over to Active's dog sled and Anthony was cuffed and photographed.

Active sat down beside him. "So how did you find that snowgo, Anthony? That's pretty amazing."

"I can do soul travel like them old *angatquqs* so I just fly around till I find it. You know I always try help."

"I do know that. But even with the soul travel, it's still pretty amazing. How did you know where to fly to?"

Anthony chewed his lip for a moment. Finally he grinned.

"Everybody know about this hole in the ice the current always make in the spring. Everybody except *naluaqmiiyaaq*, maybe?"

Active pulled out his handcuff key. "If it's that easy, maybe you don't deserve those nights in jail after all."

"*Arii*, I jokes," Anthony said. "You're learning not to be a *naluaqmiiyaaq* so much, all right."

"Uh-huh." Active got up and returned to the patch of open water.

Just as Active wondered how Gabe's crew would get a five- or six-hundred pound snowgo up and over the edge of the hole, one of the men went to a flat cargo sled parked several yards back and dragged over a wooden ladder.

Soon the ladder was levered out over the edge, rungs up, then angled down to form a ramp. A pair of snowgos was roped to the sunken machine's skis and the tow began. The machine hit the ladder and caught on the rungs. The ladder tried to climb over the edge on its rails but broke through thin ice for a few yards. Then the ladder hit solid ice, skidded out of the hole on its rails, and whomped down flat with the snowgo on top, dripping seawater.

The tow continued another few yards for safety, then the snowgos shut down and everybody walked over for a look.

"There ya go, Chief," Gabe said as they watched the rest of the crew hoist the snowgo—a black Arctic Cat—onto the cargo sled and strap it down.

"Nice work," Active said. "Never saw anybody do that before."

"We don't do it much," Gabe said. "Usually, one goes into salt water, it's not worth pulling out because it'll never run right again. We'll yank one outta fresh water for somebody once in a while, that's about it."

"Mm-hm," Active said, his mind already on the possibility of getting back to sheefish camp that night.

Gabe waved at the snowgo. "Where do you want to put it?"

"Oh, yeah." The blood returned to Active's work brain and he realized the snowgo would have to be locked up for the night. It was evidence. "I'll take it back to public safety. We'll put it in the garage bay at the jail."

He walked over and kicked the snowgo on the sled. "What do you make of it?"

"'Bout like my Cat." Gabe pointed to a machine a few yards off. "Four-five years old maybe."

"Borrow your light?" Active asked.

Gabe handed it over and Active took a tour around

the machine. There was a dent in the aluminum bumper that could be from hitting a man in the legs at high speed, a kind of cracked furrow up the cowl that could be from his body crashing into it, and a vertical split in the windshield that could be the body sliding up it after the impact.

Or not. Most Chukchi snowgos more than a month old had dents and cracks and there was no way to tell by flashlight if these had trapped any blood, flesh or fiber. That would have to be checked back in Chukchi, or perhaps at the crime lab in Anchorage.

So would the machine's drive track. Judging from the state of Pete Wise's face, scalp, and severed leg, the track of whatever had run him over was highly likely to hold minute pieces of him.

Active squatted and ran the light over the aluminum drive tunnel beneath the driver's seat. That's where the state registration decal would appear if, contrary to Chukchi custom, the owner had bothered to register it. This one hadn't.

He shook his head and rose. "Anybody recognize it?"

He looked around at Gabe and the rest. Head-shakes, shrugs, the Inupiat squints for "no".

"My brother-in-law could probably figure it out for you," Gabe said. "He works for the Cat dealer."

"You get back to town, call and ask him to meet us at the jail, OK?" Active asked. "And bring whatever invoices they've got from three-four-five years ago?"

Gabe grunted assent, flipped up his hood, and pulled on the heavy mittens dangling from lanyards braided from colored yarn. He straddled his own Cat and took off.

Long hitched Anthony's snowgo behind his machine, then Active hitched his own dogsled with Anthony still cuffed to it behind Anthony's snowgo, and instructed

Long to pull the whole train to the borough jail.

Then Active hitched the cargo sled with the Arctic Cat on it to his own machine and pulled away.

A few minutes later, he passed within a couple of hundred yards of Leroy's tent. It was almost full dark now, so it was easy to see the glow of the Coleman inside. He resisted the temptation to imagine he saw Grace's silhouette on the canvas and kept his focus on the lights of Chukchi as they grew on the horizon.

An hour later, he stopped with his load behind the jail and punched in the code to open the big garage door. Soon enough the Cat was safe in the garage and Anthony was happily ensconced in his cell and photographed there with his own phone. They even let him keep the phone, since nothing he could photograph from behind the bars seemed likely to be a threat to security. As they left him, he was trying to upload the photo to Facebook over Chukchi's snail-like data network and grumbling about the jail's lack of wi-fi.

Active and Long returned to the garage and went through the machine, checking the storage compartments and flipping up the cowling for any sign of the owner's identity, without success. Nor did a closer inspection of the damage give any clue about what caused it. Perhaps the driver had cleaned it before dumping it. Or maybe anything left in the cracks in the plastic and the crevices of the track had been washed away by the Katonak.

Active was contemplating turning the machine on its side to examine the drive track when the dispatcher ushered in an Inupiaq of about forty with bristling black hair and black-framed glasses that gave him a studious look. He had a clipboard under his arm with a sheaf of papers attached.

He came down the steps from the jail into the garage

and Long introduced him as Reggie Garfield. Active nodded, remembering now that he already knew Garfield slightly from having visited the Cat dealer before ordering his own Yamaha.

Garfield copied down a number stamped into the side of the metal drive tunnel, then flipped through his papers for a minute or two as Active and Long watched.

"Oh, yeah," Garfield said. "Now I remember. We sold this one about four years ago."

"Yeah?" Active pulled out his notebook. "Who to?"

CHAPTER NINETEEN

Wednesday, April 16

"BRAD MERCER," THERESA Procopio said.

Active nodded.

"No shit."

He nodded again.

Procopio rattled her nails on her desk and gazed out her office window. Active looked, too. So much for the golden April weather and oral sex, maybe more, in sheefish camp. Today was pure Chukchi—a hard wind from the west that had come up in the night, snow falling sideways, more being kicked up by the blow.

Procopio was curly-haired, intense, possessed of a law degree from Stanford, and had been around the village for years, much longer than Active. When he'd first crossed trails with her, she'd been a public defender. In fact, she had defended Grace Palmer against charges of murdering her father.

Now she was the a state prosecutor, which Active supposed was a step up. But Chukchi, he thought, had started to get to her. She'd been presentable enough when he had arrived, but now—well, she was getting close to what Cowboy Decker would call a widebody, her horizontal dimension approaching parity with the vertical. Manless—or womanless, as the case might be—and stuck in a town hard enough on couples from outside, much less singles. As far as Active knew, she didn't do much off duty except volunteer at the senior center and watch talent shows on TV. She was in over her head in every aspect of life except the courtroom.

But there, he was just glad they were on the same side.

"Let me see if I got this straight," she said. "You pull a snowgo out of the water and it was bought by the governor's husband four years ago. It has damage consistent with the hit-and-run that killed Pete Wise."

"Or not," Active said. "Anyway, it's on its way to the crime lab in Anchorage. Maybe they can tell us. And if there's any fiber or human remains on it."

Procopio rattled her nails some more. "He got a rap sheet? I don't remember him ever winding up in my crosshairs here."

"Nothing in the crime computer. But Lucy Brophy remembered a 911 call from their house a few years ago, when she was still in Dispatch. She dug out the old logs and actually found it, amazingly enough."

"And?"

"Dispatch gets the call one night, they hear a lot of yelling and screaming, then the line goes dead. They call back and Helen comes on and says it was just one of the kids goofing around on the phone and she'll make sure it doesn't happen again."

"Hmm," Procopio said. "Did Dispatch send somebody over?"

"Not that Lucy could remember. She was referred to as 'Mayor Mercer' in the report."

"Ah. That would explain it. And that's all?"

"Not quite. She had a bruise and a little cut over one eyebrow when I dropped her off at the airport yesterday."

"Hmm," Procopio said.

"Hmm, indeed."

"She say how it got there?"

"Ubetcha. Said she was pulling luggage off a closet shelf with her cell phone to her ear and the bag got away from her and hit her in the face. Blamed it on innate klutziness, just like with the scratches on her throat after our night in the tent."

"Plausible," Procopio said. "Or, Brad Mercer could have beat up the governor of Alaska and killed Pete Wise with a snowgo."

"Yeah, right."

Procopio chuckled. "Anything else?"

"That's it," Active said. "No arrests, no charges, no nada. The First Mate's as clean as a hound's tooth, officially speaking. So what now? We still gotta talk to him, right?"

Procopio nodded. "It was his snowgo under the water and said snowgo's our best candidate to be the one that hit Wise."

"Do we, um, need to Mirandize him?"

"You kidding? A, he's the governor's husband. B, he's not in custody. C, somebody could have bought that snowgo from him years ago. D, whoever owns it now, how many snowgos get stolen around here? Wouldn't surprise me if we find some drunk's body under the ice at breakup. So, E, no, Brad Mercer is not a suspect and we do not need to Mirandize him."

"How much of this do we ask him about? Just the snowgo? Or all of it?"

The prosecutor rattled her nails again. "Let's stick with the snowgo. Let the old 911 call and the bruise over her eye lie for now unless he says something that leads that way."

He pulled out his cell phone and found the voice memo app. "We'll record this, eh?"

"Absolutely," Procopio said. "You'll email me a copy?"

"Posilutely. Let's just do it on speaker and we're good to go."

She pushed her phone across the desk to him. "That button right there. Dial 9 for an outside line."

He pulled out his cell phone. "I've done this before,

thanks." He found Mercer's listing in his contacts and punched in the number on Procopio's phone, then started the recorder app on his cell.

Maybe they'd get lucky and he could leave a voicemail. But what would he say, exactly? Then she was on the line.

"Nathan! What a pleasure! What's new in the pearl of the Arctic? How's sheefishing?"

"Oh, fine, Suka, all good here. Except we're investigating a fatal snowgo hit-and-run—"

"I heard about that. Too bad, huh? From all I hear, Pete Wise was a solid member of our community and—"

"Yes, and thanks for asking the Troopers to help. But I'm here with Theresa Procopio from the district attorney's office and we need to talk to your husband. It looks like his snowgo may have been used in the hit-and-run and—"

"Brad's snowgo? You're kidding. That Cat he bought a few years ago, how long was it?"

"Four years, according to the dealer."

"Mm-hmm, that sounds about right. But how awful. Let me get him. I'm home with some Taco Bell for lunch, he's around somewhere. Oh, and hi, Theresa, we've met, right?"

"Yes, ma'am," Procopio said. "When you toured the state building."

"Of course, well, thanks for the good work you do for the entire Chukchi region. But you two hang on, OK?"

The line went silent. Active muted his line and looked at Procopio, eyebrows raised. "Well?"

She grimaced.

Active nodded.

After a long wait, the governor's line came back to life and Active punched his off mute. "Hi, this is Brad. Helen says somebody ran over Pete Wise with my snowgo?"

"Our best guess at the moment. We pulled it out of Chukchi Bay last night and the front end is banged up in the right places to match what we found at the death scene. We sent it and Pete's dogsled and clothes down to the crime lab in Anchorage to see what they can figure out."

"You say it was in the water? How the hell did you find it?"

"We didn't. A guy named Anthony Childers did."

The First Mate snorted. "Anthony? I'd be surprised if he could find his butt with both hands. But how did he find my snowgo?"

"It went in up near the mouth of the Katonak in a spot that opens up early, apparently. Something about the currents thinning out the ice right there?"

"Yeah, there's places like that around the bay, all right. Whoever took my snowgo would probably know where to dump it if they're from Chukchi."

"So Anthony's your suspect, I suppose?" the governor said.

"Not exactly, no."

"No?" Was there some frost in her voice now?

"We can't see why he'd essentially turn himself in if he used Brad's snowgo for the hit-and-run."

"Maybe to throw you off the trail? What do you guys call that, a red halibut?"

Active decided against correcting her attempt at cop-speak. "I suppose Anthony could be a criminal mastermind," he said. "But we think he probably just wants—"

"Oh, yeah," the governor said. "The night in jail. I heard about that on Kay-Chuck. That still a big draw up there?"

"Big as ever, ma'am," said Procopio.

"Yet another reason I love my Chukchi," the governor

said. "So who is your suspect, if you can tell me?"

"Actually, we don't have one yet. Brad's snowgo is the only lead we've got so far. Other than the basics—happened a half-mile east of the airport sometime early yesterday morning. So..."

"Let's see," Brad Mercer said. "When was the last time we used it? I did some running around on it a couple days before the race started, all right, then I parked it behind the house under a cover. I don't think I took it out at all after the race. I was busy getting the dogs squared away, so I used my dog truck, then there was the banquet Monday night and we left for Juneau yesterday morning."

"I didn't use it," Helen Mercer said. "I only used my old Expedition. I think my snowgo days are over now that I gotta run our nation's largest state."

"Mm-hmm," Active said. "And Pudu?"

"He better not have," the First Mate said. "He's got his own machine and he knows that one's mine. It's hands-off other than me and Helen."

"Anyway, once we got back, Pudu spent the whole time editing video, except for going to the banquet," the governor said.

"And did you check on the snowgo after you got back from the race?" Active asked.

"Hmm," the First Mate said. "I can't say that I did. Like I said, I was running around to get the dogs squared away and lining my brother up to watch them till I get back up there again, then we went to the banquet and I came down here yesterday."

Active scanned his notes. "So, if I'm hearing you right, the machine could have been stolen any time from a couple days before the race up through yesterday morning when it hit Pete Wise, assuming the state lab confirms your machine was in fact the one that hit him?"

"Sounds right to me," the First Mate said.

"Me, too," said the governor. "Do we need to file a police report about it being stolen, or can this be it?"

"This can be it," Active said. "It's all in my notes here."

"Thanks, Nathan. And you'll keep us posted if you find out who took it?"

"When we can, yes."

They disconnected and Active pushed the phone back across the desk. "Well?" Procopio said."

Active shook his head as he emailed the recording to Procopio. "Back to square one, I guess."

"Alan went to the house again, right? Maybe he came up with something."

"Ah," Active said. He tapped Alan Long's contact in his cell phone.

"Hey, Chief," Long said in a few seconds.

"Anything so far?"

"Not really. Found an Arctic Cat cover blown up against the wall of the house and kinda snowed under."

"Brad Mercer just told us he parked his Cat behind the house under that cover a couple days before the race and it must have been stolen."

"Makes sense," Long said. "But I can't see any tracks from anybody doing that now. Too much blow-in and new snow."

Active thanked him and disconnected.

"Yup," Procopio said. "Square one."

"WHAT, OUR KOREANS are Vietnamese all of a sudden?" Grace grinned a little as she scanned the new menu at the Arctic Dragon.

Like almost every restaurant in town, the Dragon was run by a Korean named Kyung Kim. As long as Active had been in Chukchi, the Dragon had confined itself to burgers and Chinese food. The new menu had a page headed "Pho Saigon."

Active grinned back. "You think Kim knows anything about Saigon? Or pho?"

"I think it's 'fuh,' " Grace said.

"What?"

"It's 'fuh.' You said 'foe.' "

" 'Fuh' Saigon?"

Grace nodded.

"What is that, anyway? Pho." He said it right this time.

"Soup, I think."

Active ran his eye down the menu. "You must be right. Look at the phos. Pho this, pho that, pho everything, pho Pete's sake."

"How about a pho seafood superbowl? We could split it."

"I was thinking a bacon cheesebur—" Active stopped at the sight of an arched eyebrow. "a bacon cheeseburger would play hell with my cholesterol, so a seafood superbowl would be perfect!"

Grace grinned.

He grinned. "Did you pass a pleasant night in Leroy's tent?"

She leaned in and he knew she was up for a little dirty talk.

"You kidding?" she said. "You're gonna pay for leaving me in that state."

"Happily," he said. "I never welshed on a debt in

my life. Plus, I always dreamed I'd die from having my skull crushed between a woman's thighs. Did I ever tell you that?"

She grinned. "You did not, and I'll thank you not to do so again. A lady does not care to hear such talk. Well, not more than a dozen times a day or so."

"No hope of a rematch tonight, looks like." He pointed out at the blow.

"Getting pretty thick out there, all right," she said. "Darn it. But we've got a few weeks before the ice goes out, so fish camp will keep."

"How'd you guys finally get home?"

"With Christina and her mom, like we talked about. We jumped outta bed at the crack of ten-thirty and loaded up and made it into town, what, about an hour ago?"

"Mm-hmm. Sounds very fish-campy, all right. No trouble finding the trail in this weather?"

"Christina's mom must have a GPS in her head." She paused as if she expected him to speak. "So. You found your snowgo last night?"

He nodded.

She tilted her head and narrowed the silver eyes. "And?"

"It's police business. You know. Fifty shades of secret."

She snorted, but in a ladylike way. "In Chukchi? Stand and deliver, Chief Active."

He chewed his lip for a moment, then told her who owned the sunken Arctic Cat.

"Brad Mercer? You're kidding."

He shrugged and explained the Mercers' explanation of how the First Mate's snowgo might have come to kill Pete Wise.

"You believe it?"

"Why not? This is Chukchi. My guys spend half their time chasing stolen snowgos. A ten-year-old could hotwire one. And anybody in the mood for a little joyride could figure that one wouldn't be missed for a while, what with the Mercers heading back to Juneau and all."

"Uh-huh." Grace nodded and pursed her lips.

"What?"

"It's just that I talked to the governor this morning, too."

"What?"

"The phone at the house was ringing when I got in from camp."

He took a moment to line it up in his mind. "So this would be a couple hours after Theresa and I called her about the snowgo?"

Grace raised her eyebrows.

Active was about to say, "What the hell did she want?" when a Korean kid with bleached hair and a ring in his lip came to the table. Active kept silent as his mind cycled through the possibilities and Grace ordered the superbowl, plus tea for herself and a Diet Pepsi for him. She passed their menus to the waiter and he left.

"What the hell did she want?"

"To apologize."

"Helen Mercer apologized? Seriously? For what?"

"For those rumors about the scratches on her neck. She assured me they were self-inflicted and that your behavior in that tent was strictly honorable."

"It was."

"I hope so," Grace said. "I think so. But her call coming when it did...."

"Yeah. The timing."

"She went on to say she hoped the rumors hadn't caused problems between us and then she asked how the women's shelter project was coming. And she said to let her know if I needed anything. I almost said, 'Posilutely.' "

"Almost?"

"What I did say was, 'Thanks, Suka.' "

"Very prudent." Active relaxed a little. "She apologized and she offered to help. That's it?"

"Not quite. Then she asked me how Nita was."

"Huh."

Grace gazed out the Dragon's window, across Beach Street into the semi-blizzard brooming snow across the ice. Then she read his face.

"What?"

"Remember when she came in last week and shanghaied me to play bodyguard?"

Grace raised her eyebrows, yes.

"There was some of that conversation I didn't tell you about."

"Didn't tell me—wait, she mentioned Nita then?"

He nodded. "She called her your little girl."

"My little girl. Oh, God. She knows that? How could she?"

"Maybe she just assumed it. I said Nita was your cousin you adopted after her mother's death and she seemed to accept it."

Grace studied his face and narrowed her eyes again. "What else?"

"She said her people looked into the records of your father's death."

"His death? No."

He nodded. "But—

"Oh, Jesus."

"But she said it was only due diligence so she could offer me the Trooper job."

"The woman scares me to death."

"My point is, that was long before I called her today about the snowgo or Pete Wise was even killed. So how could it be connected?"

Grace didn't speak. Her lips took on a stubborn set.

"And she did offer to fund your crisis centers," Active said. "And to run money through my public safety budget for the cell towers on the Isignaq. And she is coming back up from Juneau just to cut the ribbon at your center on Friday."

The marimba ring tone sounded from Active's shirt pocket.

"Jesus," Grace said. "That better not be her."

"If it is, I'll let it go to voicemail." He looked at the caller ID and felt the tension drain from his shoulders. "Nah, it's a Chukchi number." He moved the slider to answer.

"Chief Active."

"I have a friend in the court system," the tired voice said. "She says, you want to know about Pete Wise's sex life, you should go to the courthouse."

"The courthouse? Why?"

"Just don't get my friend in trouble, OK? She shouldn't have told me."

Active disconnected with a frown and tapped Procopio's contact on his phone.

"What's in court?" Grace asked as the prosecutor answered.

Active held up a finger. "Theresa? We need to look Pete Wise up in court."

"What?" Procopio said. "Why? How do you know?"

"A source, that's all. Can you do it?"

"Call you right back."

He punched off and looked at Grace.

"Pete Wise was in court?"

"Supposedly. We'll see."

"And your source is?"

"Sorry, this one really does need to be secret."

She frowned for a moment, then nodded.

"So where were we?" he asked.

"Discussing Helen Mercer." She shrugged. "As usual lately."

"Well, again—it did start long before there was a Pete Wise case. Last week, remember? The only thing that's happened since we found him on the tundra is, she called to apologize about the scratches and wish you and Nita well. And maybe that's because she figured out why you skipped the musher's banquet and she wants to help patch things up between us. How is that scary?"

"I don't know. It just is. Call it woman's intuition."

He paused as the waiter delivered their order.

"Look," he said when they were alone again. "Maybe we should take this all at face value. She does want to help us, she was doing due diligence for the Trooper job, she is sorry about the rumors, she does wish you and Nita well. It's just her way. An idea a minute, popping out unfiltered. That gerbil wheel of a brain in overdrive, as usual."

Her chin unwrinkled a bit. "I guess."

But she didn't look very convinced as she dipped into the pho seafood.

Active was dipping his own spoon into the superbowl when his phone marimbaed again. He checked the caller ID, then his watch as he put the phone to his ear. "Theresa. You went to the courthouse already? That was quick."

"Modern times, Nathan," she said. "We lawyers got our own computer system, too."

"Ah. I forgot about CourtView for a minute. Whatcha got?

"Just get over here. You have to see this for yourself."

"How about the short version?" he said. "What is it?" She was already gone.

"Pete Wise was in court?" Grace asked. "What about?"

He took a last spoonful of pho and pulled on his parka. "I'm about to find out."

CHAPTER TWENTY

Wednesday, April 16

"PETE WISE FILED a child custody petition against the governor of Alaska?" Active looked over Procopio's shoulder at her computer screen again. "Holy shit, but what does it mean?"

"It's what we call a putative father case. It means Pete Wise thought he was the biological father of at least one of the governor's kids. He probably wanted a DNA test to prove it so he could get shared custody."

"At least one? Good grief, she's got four."

"Maybe it's all of them, who knows." Procopio pointed at the screen. "CourtView doesn't show that kind of detail."

"I see Pete named both Mercers as defendants? Not just Helen?"

Procopio shook her head. "They're called respondents in this kind of case. But, yeah, both of them. That's because the First Mate is legally the father if they were married at the time of birth, no matter who she did the actual deed with. Or deeds."

Active dropped into a chair beside her. "I suppose you caught the date Pete filed this thing?"

"Yep," Procopio said. "Monday of last week, three days before Helen hit town for the Isignaq 400."

"Huh. Whereas Brad had already been here a while gearing up for the race," Active said. Procopio nodded. "So, assuming he got served reasonably fast, he had a couple days to stew about it before he got a chance to confront her."

"Must have been a fun conversation," Procopio said.

"And then three days on the trail to brood some more

about Pete Wise in bed with his wife."

"Maybe even giving her a warm welcome-home while he was staring at four hundred miles of dog butts," Procopio said. "A guy could work up a pretty good head of steam picturing that out there on the trail all by himself."

"And by Tuesday morning, maybe he decides to settle up with Pete before they go back to Juneau."

"Highly plausible, given my limited understanding of the male brain."

"Huh," Active said again. "So this CourtView summary. I don't see anything about a hearing while the Mercers were here?"

"You wouldn't expect one so soon after the case was filed. There wasn't even one scheduled by the time Pete died."

"Who's listed as Pete's attorney? Maybe he'll give us a copy of the file."

"Nobody's listed."

"He was representing himself?"

Procopio shrugged. "I hope not, for his sake. Not against the governor of Alaska. But that's kind of what it looks like. People sure do stupid things sometimes."

"So it's off to court we go?"

"You go," Procopio said. "I got some paperwork on your honeybucket murder. Just ask the clerk to copy the file. Bring it back here and we'll go over it."

Active shrugged into his parka and started for the door.

"No peeksies!"

"Ha!"

BUT GETTING TO the courthouse was not simple, as things in Chukchi tended not to be. A Honda four-wheeler, it seemed, had driven into the side of a city garbage truck. The Honda sustained much damage, the garbage truck none, and the fourteen-year-old driver of the Honda a bruised, perhaps fractured, left forearm. She denied texting while driving, despite the "LMFAO" still present on the screen of her phone when Active arrived to investigate. While the passenger, uninjured, recorded the encounter on her own phone, no doubt for Facebook, he ticketed the driver for texting and underage driving before the EMTs rolled up to haul her to the emergency room.

By the time Active reached the clerk's office, it was past two. He didn't recognize the lumpish gray-haired white woman at the counter, but that wasn't unusual. Turnover and absenteeism both ran high in the court clerk's office, particularly when spring or fall hit and the sheefish or caribou passed through. The court system often had to send in temporary help from Fairbanks. This one was dome-shaped and her name was Doris, according to her nametag.

"Sorry," Doris said when Active asked for the Wise-Mercer file. "It's sealed."

"Sealed?" He touched his badge and looked at hers. "Doris, I don't think we've met. I'm Nathan Active, the borough public safety chief here, and this is for a criminal investigation."

Doris shook her head. "Judge Stein sealed it about thirty minutes ago."

"But—"

"Talk to the judge. His ruling."

Active swore to himself and started down the hall.

The front desk in Stein's office was vacant. Active walked into Stein's chambers, where the judge was scrawling notes in the margins of a sheaf of legal papers.

Stein had arrived in Chukchi as a lawyer representing poor people with Alaska Legal Services a couple of years before Active himself showed up. No doubt Stein had also planned to rack up some experience in the Bush, then move on to Anchorage for a bigger job with a bigger title and bigger money.

Instead, like Active, here he still was in Chukchi. Active supposed Stein had missed too many planes. But he had made a better job of it than Theresa Procopio. He was now a full-on Bush rat, complete with boats, snowgos, a wife from a Chukchi family, and a fish camp on her Native allotment up the Katonak River. He'd been clean-shaven with a decent head of black hair when Active first met him. Now the hair had started to go, but he had grown a full beard, perhaps to compensate.

Stein put down the brief and pulled off his glasses. "Nathan! Sit, sit. So good to see one of Chukchi's finest. To what do I owe the pleasure?"

Active nodded. "It's business, actually. You sealed Pete Wise's custody case against the governor and her husband? What—"

Stein shrugged. "The governor's lawyer moved to dismiss and seal it on the grounds it's moot now that Wise is dead, so I did seal it. Probably dismiss it, too, in another day or two. Pretty routine, actually."

Stein saw the look on Active's face and cocked his head. "Or maybe not?"

Active chewed his lip for a moment, then plunged. "Brad Mercer is a, er, person of interest in Pete Wise's death."

"Come again?"

Active told him about the sunken snowgo and its ownership.

Stein massaged his chin for a few seconds. "Any

chance it's just a coincidence?"

"Of course," Active said. "Pete Wise files this putative father action claiming he had a kid with Brad Mercer's wife and a week later he's killed by Brad Mercer's snowgo. And the day after that, they come in and get the file sealed. Sure, that could all be just a coincidence. Anything's possible."

"Something tells me I'm gonna wish I never heard this." Stein rubbed his eyes and put his glasses back on. "We should probably get Theresa Procopio on the phone."

He studied the buttons on his desk phone for a moment, then pushed one, and in another moment Procopio was on the speaker. He let her know Active was in on the call.

"Hi, guys." Her voice was tight and cautious. "All good at the temple of truth and justice?"

"Not exactly," Active said. "Maybe Judge Stein can explain it better than me."

Stein took Procopio through the story, though with more legalese than when he and Active had discussed it.

"Your honor, this is a criminal matter," she said when Stein was finished. "We need to look at that file."

"Yeah," Stein said. "Nathan here explained a little about that. I understand your situation, but, now that it's sealed, I can't just flip a switch and unseal it. It's gonna take a motion from your side and a hearing, at minimum. I guess I don't need to remind you, we're talking about the governor of Alaska here. We leave one i undotted or t uncrossed and we do so at our peril."

"Loud and clear, your honor. It's been an age since I did any civil work—what's that motion you file to get in on a putative father case?"

"Ahem."

"Right," Procopio said. "You have to stay above the fray."

"Right, "Stein said. "Law school just let out for spring break and it's gonna stay out till this is over. You'll have to figure it out for yourself."

"Yeah, yeah," Procopio said. "I'll have something to you by closing time."

"10-4," Stein said. "Hang on a minute and I'll get you the contact info for the Mercers' lawyer. Email it to us and him and that'll cover it. You can bring the paperwork over tomorrow."

Stein rifled through some papers on his desk then read off a name, a telephone number, and an email address. "You get that OK?"

"Can I ask a question?" Active said.

Stein raised his eyebrows. "You can try, Nathan."

"Can you tell me which child or children Wise thought he fathered?"

"Sorry. We're done here."

"DON'T WORRY, THEY can't keep it closed," Procopio said. "It's a murder investigation, for chrissakes."

"You figure out what that motion is?"

Procopio nodded. "There's this civil rule on something called Intervention of Right." She sprayed out some legalese.

"And in English that means?"

"If you can show what your interest is and the judge thinks it's legitimate, then you can get into the file. Ours is, so we will."

"You couldn't just say that? This type of thing is why Shakespeare said all you people should be killed."

Procopio chuckled. "He was right, mostly."

"You know this guy that's representing the Mercers?" Active asked. "Frank McConnell, was that what Stein said?"

"Criminal defense attorney in Anchorage. Pretty well known, actually."

"Criminal defense? In a putative father case? Why would that be?"

Procopio shrugged.

"Think maybe they hired him after our call this morning?"

"Reasonable guess," Procopio said. "CourtView doesn't even show him as counsel yet. But who knows why they did it and who cares? Let's kill one snake at a time and the first one is this motion to intervene. Which I gotta finish tout de suite if we want to get it in by deadline today, thank you very much."

"All right, but one more thing. You think there's DNA tests from Pete and the kid or kids in evidence?"

"You never know, but probably not," Procopio said. "Too early in the case. And how would he get samples from the Mercer progeny?"

"Good question," Active said. "Copy me on the email when you file that motion, eh? I'd like to see it for myself."

Active returned to his office, plowed through his email inbox, then deliberated for a few minutes, thought of checking with Procopio first, decided against it, and called the medical examiner in Anchorage to add a DNA test to his wish list for the Pete Wise case.

He had just rung off with the examiner when his email notification ponged and there was Procopio's motion. He checked the clock in bottom corner of the computer screen. It read 4:13. They had beaten the court closing hour by seventeen minutes. Then he checked the addressees to make sure McConnell was included.

He was.

ACTIVE SLIPPED INTO Grace's house like a movie hit man, eased the door shut and savored the normalcy for a few moments. Mukluk Messenger on Kay-Chuck coming from the kitchen, something about an urgent request for baby formula in Ebrulik, where the store had run out. Grace and Nita talking in the kitchen, something about homework from the sound of it. And a heavenly smell from the oven. God, it was good to be in from the storms of the day. He braced himself as Grace appeared in the kitchen doorway.

"I thought I sensed your presence, Chief Active."

"Would that be sheefish I smell?"

She nodded. "You likee?"

"You know I doee. But it smells fresh. Where'd we get it? We got skunked last night, if I remember."

"Leroy brought it over this afternoon," she said. "He finally got his snowgo fixed and stopped on the way in and absolutely killed 'em."

Active jerked a thumb at the blow outside the window. "With that still going on?"

"You know Leroy. Less competition in bad weather, he says, plus the sheefish come in when it's like this." She waved him into the kitchen and led the way. "And how was your day?" she said over her shoulder.

"Could hardly have been worse, to tell the truth."

"Eh? Oh, the Pete Wise thing in court? What was that about?"

"I'm not sure I can tell you, what with our investigation—"

"Oh, come on. I know from my job anybody can look somebody up on the computer—what's that system?"

"CourtView?"

"That's it, like when we need to find out a baby daddy's history and if he's supposed to be paying child support, and so on. If they've ever been in court, they'll be in CourtView. Do not make me look Pete Wise up myself, Chief Active."

He cut his eyes at Nita, who was doing homework with earbuds in.

"I don't think she can hear us, with her music on."

"Still."

"*Bunnik*," Grace said. "Nita!"

Nita looked up and unplugged the earbuds. "Oh, hi, Uncle Nathan! When we going back to sheefish camp?"

He pointed out the window again. "When that lets up, I guess."

"Nita, honey," Grace said. "Weren't we gonna watch the Barrow vampire movie with Christina after dinner? You want to go find the DVD and get it set up?"

"Sure. Maybe I'll watch just a little bit of it while the sheefish finishes cooking?"

"Sure," Grace said.

"The Barrow zombie movie?" Active sighed. "Again?

I think I'm more burned out on that one than even the whale movie."

"I could probably talk her into *Notting Hill* if you prefer."

"Zombies will be just fine, thanks."

"So, stop stalling. What's so serious about the Pete Wise thing I had to exile my daughter to the land of the undead?"

"Well, it turns out to be a custody suit."

"Really? I don't recall Pete ever being married or having a sweetheart. And there were always those rumors about him being...well, so much for rumors, I guess. Anyway, who's the lucky girl, allegedly?"

"Helen Mercer."

Grace's face froze. She dropped into a chair and gripped the edge of the dining table as if she might topple over. "Helen Mercer?"

He nodded.

"Jesus."

"Yeah."

"How? Which kid?"

"We don't know how or which. Technically speaking, we don't even know it's just one."

"What? Wouldn't all that be in the file?"

"The file's sealed."

"Oh?"

He nodded. "As of this afternoon. The Mercers' lawyer got it sealed on the grounds the custody issue is moot now that Pete's dead."

She was silent. She had that look she got when she was doing life math in her head. "You mean a few hours after you and Theresa called her?"

He nodded again.

"And after she called me."

Another nod.

"Still think this is all coincidence?"

He shrugged. "Theresa says it doesn't matter. We just have to kill one snake at a time, as she puts it."

"What's the next snake?"

"She filed a motion to get us into the file, just before the courthouse closed this afternoon. Stein says it'll take a hearing."

A buzzer sounded from the oven. Grace got up and went over. "Just before the courthouse closed? Meaning the governor will know about it by morning, if she doesn't already."

He nodded again.

"Nathan, you have to get that file."

"I know, baby, I know."

She pulled out the sheefish and lifted the foil. "It's done," she said in a shaky voice. "Shall we eat? Or at least try?"

CHAPTER TWENTY-ONE

Thursday, April 17

ACTIVE STUDIED THE application on his blotter, then arched an eyebrow at Lucy Brophy, who sat before his desk with a steno pad on her belly.

"Jeremy Generous? Your cousin."

"He might be. It's hard to keep track around here."

"He might be."

Lucy arched both eyebrows in the Eskimo yes. "He'll do real good job, and my maternity leave is only three months anyway."

"If he's so good, why would he take a three-month job?"

Lucy gave him a look of pity. "*Arii, naluaqmiiyaaq.* This job will end the same time commercial fishing start, remember? That's what he like to do, hunt and fish, but he like to work sometimes, too."

Active pondered. Jeremy's references were good, including a year as dispatcher when the department was still run by the city. And Lucy was right, the job should be over well before the Chukchi Bay chum salmon run, in plenty of time for Jeremy to get his gear ready for the season. "If he messes up, you'll straighten him out?"

"My *Aana* Pauline will. She's his *aana*, too. And I can come in sometimes if you need me here."

"All right," Active said. "Call him and set up an interview."

"When you want to talk to him?"

"How about three this afternoon?"

"I'll call him." Lucy trundled out as he tapped Jeremy's appointment into the calendar.

He filed away the applications for temporary office manager and with dread pulled over the other stack of paper on his desk and the jump drive that lay atop it. This, Lucy had informed him, was his briefing on the borough finance system, as prepared by the Anchorage accounting firm that had installed the system and somehow ran it remotely.

His assignment, she had said, was to go over the executive summary in the printout, then review the PowerPoint presentation on the jump drive. Then she'd come in and explain how, with Sonny's help, they got around the *naluaqmiut* in Anchorage to make the thing work in Chukchi, where the exception always ruled.

He pushed the flash drive into a port on his computer and started it up. Ninety-six slides! Who did a ninety-six slide PowerPoint?

He was up to slide eighteen, in the section on depreciation, when the line from Lucy's office lit up.

Thank God. Anything was better than PowerPoint.

"There's a gentleman from the Alaska Bureau of Investigation here to see you. OK to send him up?"

Active looked at the clock on his wall as he tapped open the calendar on his phone. "The ABI? What about? Did I forget an appointment?"

"Not unless you made it without telling me."

"Of course not. Send him up. What's his name?"

WHERE DID HE know the guy from? Active tried to pull it up as he shook hands with Trooper Stuart Stewart and ushered him to a chair. Stewart was forty-ish and Native, maybe Yup'ik, with a jet-black flat top, but after a couple of sentences of pleasantries, Active gave up.

"Have we met? You look awfully familiar."

"Maybe from the Trooper TV show?"

"Ah," Active said. "The famous Trooper Stuart Stewart. Two-Stu, is that what they called you?"

Stewart nodded with a grin. "The same. That was back when I was on patrol in Mat-Su. Meth cookers, Bible-thumpers, baby-bangers, wife-beaters—happy hunting ground for a rookie cop, I have to say. Now that I'm an investigator, it seems like a dream."

"Well, you made us all look good. Nice work."

"You're probably wondering what brings the ABI to town," Stewart said.

"Absolutely. And how can we help? Chukchi Public Safety about to be famous, too?"

"You're already kind of famous, thanks to your camping trip with the governor."

Active grimaced. "But not in a good way. Craziest episode of my entire law enforcement career."

Stewart nodded. "That's kind of what brings me to town. I gather you're interested in being director of the Troopers?"

"God, no. I told the governor that a dozen times. Apparently I didn't get through."

Stewart grinned and nodded and pulled out a note pad, then a recorder. "OK if I tape this?"

With an effort, Active maintained. Not thirty seconds since Helen Mercer had entered the conversation and already he could feel it sliding out from under him. "Tape away." He waved at the recorder. "But why? I already said I don't want the job."

"That's not it," Stewart said. "Not exactly. Apparently there was a tangential matter that turned up during the due-diligence review the governor requested and now that matter has landed on my boss's desk. And he's dropped it on mine. We both know where shit rolls, right?"

Stewart passed over a card. Active studied it. Stewart was not only with the ABI. He was part of the Cold Case Unit. "We've got a cold case here in Chukchi? I just took over this job, but I don't remember anything major still being open."

"It's the murder of Jason Palmer."

"Jason Palmer."

Stewart nodded.

"I remember it, of course. It was pretty famous at the time. But it's been closed for quite a while."

"Well, it's been reopened and the Office of Special Prosecutions has passed it on to us. I took a quick pass through the files at your court house yesterday afternoon and this morning. Fascinating stuff."

"Uh-huh."

"For you especially, I'd guess."

Active nodded. "I was in the Troopers at the time, as the files probably show. It was a city case, so we didn't have much of a role."

"I was just about to get to that. I don't think we need to go through the whole thing in detail, but let me just make sure I captured the high points."

"OK, but why is it being reopened?"

"There seem have been a few holes in the original investigation." Stewart waved a hand, as if to dismiss a small matter. "I gather your predecessor when this was still the city police department could be a little casual about procedure?"

"Jim Silver was a really good man," Active said. "He

died in an arson fire and we should show respect."

"Of course," Stewart said. "I meant no offense."

Active raised his eyebrows, then realized he didn't know if Yup'iks did that for 'yes.'

"No problem," he said.

Stewart paused for a decent interval.

"So the Jason Palmer case starts when he asks you to track down his daughter, Grace, who's been missing, or at least out of contact with the family, for something like ten years. He tells you Grace's mother is dying and wants to see her daughter one last time."

Active's direct line rang. He shot a glance at the caller ID and snagged the phone, holding up a just-a-moment forefinger to Stewart.

"Hey, Theresa, can I—what, that soon? OK, can I get back to you in a few? Sure, thanks."

"Sorry," he said. "Prosecutor's office. We've got a hearing tomorrow."

Stewart nodded.

"As I was saying, Jason Palmer asks you to track down his daughter so her dying mother can see her one last time. "You tell him it's not a Trooper matter and you'll pass it along to the Anchorage Police Department, but he shouldn't expect much after so long."

Active nodded and tried to focus on what Stewart was saying. But the Jason Palmer case reopened yesterday and a hearing scheduled for tomorrow on the Pete Wise files?

"But in fact," Stewart continued, "you do go look for her and you do find her, all on your own time and at your own expense. All the way down in Dutch Harbor. Why would you do that?"

"Her father showed me her picture, a big mural on the wall at Chukchi High from when she was Miss North World." Active deliberated for a long time. "And

I fell in love with her."

"From a picture."

Active nodded again.

"You want that on the record?"

Active didn't speak.

"This the picture here?" Stewart pointed at the eight-by-ten of the Miss North World portrait amid the clutter on Active's desk.

"They took the big one in the high school down last year when they remodeled."

Stewart picked it up for a closer look. "I guess I see what you mean. She look like this now?"

"Pretty much. Better maybe. Less haunted."

"It's sure not how she looked in the mug shots at the court house."

"She'd been on Four Street a while when those were taken."

"Ah," Stewart said. "I guess I didn't get that deep into the files over there. Anyway, I'll be seeing for myself in a bit. She's next on my interview list, followed by her daughter. Nita?"

"Nita's her cousin, actually," Active said. "Grace adopted her after the death of her mother, Grace's aunt." Then it dawned on him. "You want to talk to Nita?"

"Sure," Stewart said. "That's what I was saying about the previous investigation. The girl was in the house at the time of Mr. Palmer's death, but it's not clear she was ever considered as a suspect or even interviewed in depth. We have to cover all the bases." Again he waved the dismissive hand.

Active sat in silence, stomach knotted, as Stewart looked at his notebook.

"But, to get back to your piece of this. You go to Dutch Harbor and find Ms. Palmer and bring her back to Chukchi to be reunited with her parents?"

"Partly true." Active took a breath and went on, trying to limit how much his voice shook. "I had to go to Anchorage on Trooper business, so I nosed around a little after hours with the help of a buddy on the Anchorage force. I found out she'd been a Four Street drunk for several years."

Stewart winced.

"Yeah, you should have seen her mug shots from that era, when she was busted for disorderly conduct and assaulting cops. They...well, they were even worse than the ones taken here when she was arrested after Jason Palmer's murder. And they got worse as time went on. Like a time-lapse movie of a face slowly...dissolving."

Active studied the eight-by-ten on his desk, while Stewart waited another decent interval.

"From Anchorage," Active said at last, "the trail led to Dutch Harbor and I followed it and found she'd somehow pulled herself together and straightened out. She was working a slime line down there. But she wouldn't come back to Chukchi."

"Why not?"

"I think it's all in the court record that developed later," Active said. "But she told me her father had raped her from an early age and had raped her sister until he got her pregnant and she committed suicide. Grace finally had to get away."

Stewart penned something into his notebook. "If that was true, why would he ask you to bring her home?"

Active shrugged. "I don't know. Neither did she. She thought maybe he had some crazy idea he could win her back. Or she'd forgive and forget because of her mother being sick. Or something. What she said was, 'Evil is opaque.'"

Stewart nodded. "She was right about that."

"I bear it always in mind."

Stewart flipped back in his notebook and checked something. "But she did come back to Chukchi, obviously. Why was that?"

"It was something I told her while I was down there."

"And that was?"

"I told her Nita was living with Grace's parents in Chukchi after the death of her mother in the plane crash. Grace couldn't stand the thought of Jason doing to Nita what he had done to her and her sister. She fell back onto Four Street for a while, then she came home."

"And Mr. Palmer ended up dead."

"Grace showed up at my office one day and said 'The son of a bitch is dead' and dropped a pistol on my desk. The murder weapon, it was determined to be."

"Whew," Stewart said. "Quite a story."

"That was just the start. There was a lot of evidence, fingerprints, gunshot residue, all pointing straight at Grace. But the defense—mostly Grace, I think—kept stalling. The state prosecutor couldn't get an actual confession and a plea, but neither could he get the case in front of a jury."

"I saw that in the record," Stewart said. "The pretrial stuff dragged on and on."

Active nodded. "Grace's PD once described it as a nightmare case with a nightmare defendant."

"And you—"

"Stayed out of it. It was a city case, not a Trooper case. Plus, this woman I loved appeared to be a killer. I couldn't process it."

"And then one day..."

"Yeah." Active shook his head at the memory. "And then one day."

"Grace's mother, pretty much terminal with the cancer by this point, comes in and testifies she's the one killed her husband."

"They still weren't at trial," Active said. "So they had a hearing and got her on videotape, complete with cross-examination. That way if she died they could use it later."

"Which they never did, as far as I can tell?"

"Uh-uh." Active shook his head. "They let Grace out and put the mother under house arrest. There was a sealed indictment against her, but it stayed sealed until she died and that was the end of it."

"And then you and Grace formed a domestic partner relationship, she adopted Nita, and here you are."

Active was silent.

Stewart studied his notebook and made a brief entry.

"So I watched that tape," he said. "Quite a story the mother told. Grace comes back from Dutch Harbor, tries again to convince her of what her husband did to Grace and her sister and is gonna do to Nita if he's not stopped. The mother gets mad like always and sends Grace away, only this time something tells her it's true. She catches her husband with the little girl, not really doing anything to her yet, but she realizes he will if he's not stopped, so she shoots him after Nita goes out. Grace comes back to the house, finds out what happened, and rigs the evidence to point at herself instead of her mother. Scrubs the residue off her mother's hands, wipes the gun down for fingerprints, then fires it into a wooden post in the basement to put her own fingerprints on it and get residue on her own hands. They tell the little girl Mr. Palmer shot himself by accident while cleaning the gun, and Ms. Palmer turns herself in to you. And then she stalls till it's time to bring her mother into court and make the magic videotape. Amazing, wouldn't you say?"

"Amazing Grace was what they called her on Four

Street," Active said.

"Chief Active?" Stewart said after another decent interval.

"Sorry, guess I got a little cobwebby there."

"I was just saying, the whole matter of the tape was pretty ama—pretty remarkable, eh?"

"It was remarkable," Active said. "But this is Chukchi. I've learned not to rule anything out."

"Especially when it's someone you love."

Active shrugged. What was there to say?

"Let's suppose it wasn't someone you love. Can you put your cop hat on for me?"

"I'll try."

"Would you believe that story? " Stewart said. "The mother is dying, she's got nothing to lose, so why wouldn't she lie to save her daughter? Mine would for me. And if the mother really did do it and Ms. Palmer really was innocent, why would she rig the evidence and run interference to protect her mother and take the risk it'd get away from her and she'd get convicted herself?"

Active chewed his lip. "Because she knew no Chukchi jury would convict her when that tape of her mother was played in court. Especially if the jury was full of women. Half of them have been where Grace was and the other half have a daughter or sister who has. Grace had to know she was pretty safe."

"Geez," Stewart said with a hint of admiration. "It's kinda like one of those corn mazes, huh? No wonder it never got to trial."

Active tented his fingers. "The mother's story's is either true, or it was a flawless piece of stagecraft by Grace. As I recall the evidence, when Grace was arrested, one bullet from the gun was found in Jason Palmer's heart, and an empty casing was found in the gun."

"Along with four live rounds."

"Uh-huh. The prosecutor initially concluded an empty cylinder was kept under the hammer for safety reasons, leaving five cylinders with live rounds till the one was fired at Jason Palmer."

"But what about the round that was found in the post downstairs after the mother came forward?"

"According to Grace, there were actually were six live rounds kept in the gun. When she fired that second one into the post, she drove a nail into the bullet hole and hung an old snowgo suit on it in case the house was searched. It was, but they didn't find anything in the basement. Once Grace and her mother told them about the post, they went back and dug out the bullet."

Stewart studied his notes and smiled a little. "And the casing? Did they find the casing from that basement shot?"

Active cleared his throat. "They did. In a cup on my desk. That pencil cup, as a matter of fact." He pointed. "Apparently she dropped it in at the same time she was dropping the pistol on my desk. I guess I was a little distracted."

"I guess you were." Stewart still wore his little grin. "Musta been kinda embarrassing."

"More than kinda. She has a flair for the dramatic."

"But, seriously," Stewart said. "It sounds like Ms. Palmer at a minimum confessed to evidence tampering and obstruction of justice. Know why that never went anywhere?"

Active shrugged. "I don't. But I have the impression the whole mess was so embarrassing for the prosecutor and the Chukchi police they just wanted it to go away. They had the mother's confession all tied up with a bow and why would they look that gift horse in the mouth? By that time, I think they were scared of Grace. She's frighteningly smart."

"Uh-huh. And your prosecutor then was—"

"Guy named Charlie Hughes. Got his fill of Chukchi not long after that and bailed for someplace warmer. Albuquerque, Amarillo? Something with an A."

Stewart made a note of it. "And your prosecutor now—"

"Is Theresa Procopio. At the time, she was the PD who defended Grace in the case. I'm sure she'll make Charlie's files available to you, but I imagine attorney-client privilege would prevent her from talking about the case in any detail."

"I'm sure," Stewart said. "Small world out here, eh?"

Active nodded. "Very small. Probably where you come from, too?"

"Aniak. And, yes, small world there, too." He closed his eyes and pinched the bridge of his nose. "Let's see, don't we have three possibilities here?"

Active waited, knowing.

"One, Ms. Palmer's mother killed her husband to protect Nita. Two, Ms. Palmer killed him for the same reason. And, three, Nita did it, for, well, for obvious reasons. Assuming Ms. Palmer's story of child abuse is true. In which case it could be argued to be self-defense in Nita's case, I guess, but that would be up to the grand jury."

"There is a fourth possibility," Active said.

Stewart looked at his notes, then at Active. "Yeah?"

"Maybe it's time the women of this family were left in peace."

Stewart raised his eyebrows. "Have you told me everything you can recall that would be relevant to our investigation?"

This, Active knew, was a cop trap. If the investigators found out later he'd omitted something material, sometimes even something trivial, they'd be back and back heavy. The next round would start with 'You said you told us everything' and go downhill from there.

His mind raced back through Grace Palmer's story. What had he left out and how would he explain it? He finally decided there was nothing and shook his head. "That's the case as I recall it. Talk to Lucy on the way out and she'll dig out the old city police files for you."

Stewart collected his things, shook hands and left.

CHAPTER TWENTY-TWO

Thursday, April 17

ACTIVE GRABBED THE phone as the elevator door closed on Stewart.

"Hey, baby," Grace said. "I'm on my way to your place now with my last load of stuffs. As of tonight, it'll be the three of us. Here's to cohabitation!"

The cheer in her voice was so painful to hear he had to pause a moment to collect himself.

"Baby?"

"Listen. I don't have much time. The state is reopening your father's murder case. They sent an investigator up from Anchorage this morning and he just left my office. He's on his way now to interview you and Nita."

"Are we suspects?"

"Yes. Maybe. Probably."

"Even Nita?"

"They're not ruling anything out."

"Nita? Helen Mercer is after my *bunnik*?"

"What? It's not the gov—"

"That bitch. I'll kill her."

"No, it's something called the Office of Special Prosecutions. It came out of the due diligence review for that stupid Trooper job."

"I don't care what it's called. It's Helen Mercer and that bitch is not getting Nita."

"We don't know she's behind it. Maybe it's random bad luck."

"Another coincidence? Ha!"

He said the only thing he could think of, which was

nothing. And then, suddenly she was sliding away.

"I have to get her out of here, Nathan. Maybe Dutch Harbor. I disappeared there before, I can do it again. I gotta pack, can you pick her up at school? When's the next Alaska Airlines flight? No, they might be watching already. Maybe I can charter Cowboy to Anchorage. You won't tell anybody, right? I have to round up—how much cash can you get your hands on? They might be watching my bank account too and there's—"

"Baby. Baby! Come back!"

With a click he could almost hear, she was with him again.

"Oh, Nathan. What do we do?"

"Absolutely do not talk to the investigator. His name is Stuart Stewart, Yup'ik guy from Aniak. Tell him you won't consent to any search and you're exercising your right to remain silent and not answer questions. And do not give consent for Nita to be interviewed. You're her legal mother and you can hold them off at least for a while."

"My God, I have to get a lawyer. We have to get a lawyer. Theresa was my lawyer before, maybe I'll—"

"Not Theresa. She's a prosecutor now. She's conflicted out. We'll have to find you another one. Let me check around. For now, all you have to do is not talk to the investigator. And don't tell him I called you. It's probably unethical."

"But what should I do now, right now this minute?"

He gave it a few seconds thought. "Like I said, forget about this call. Keep moving to my place. Let him find you the same as if you didn't know he was coming and act like you don't know anything till he tells you."

"I want to come see you."

"Probably not a good idea. Just follow your normal routine and gut it out. We'll see each other later."

"I'll try, baby. But—"

"Look, I gotta go. I'll see you tonight. I have to stick to my normal routine, too. In case he comes back."

Grace rang off. He cleared the line on his desk phone and punched the button for the prosecutor's office. It rang three times and he was about to try Procopio at home when she picked up.

"Eleven o'clock," she said.

"What?"

"The Pete Wise hearing. Eleven o'clock tomorrow."

"Oh, yeah. Gimme a minute." He put it in the calendar on his computer, which linked it to his phone thanks to more of Sonny's magic he only vaguely understood.

"All good?" Procopio said. "I've got work to do if we're gonna have a prayer at that hearing."

"Did you know ABI's in town?"

"I heard, yeah. Apparently that cute Two-Stew guy from the Trooper TV show was at the courthouse. You want me to poke around and find out what he's—"

"They're reopening the Jason Palmer case."

"What?"

"Yeah."

"Oh, shit."

"Yeah, he was just here."

Procopio was silent a few moments, then spoke in a somewhat relieved tone. "But I guess I'm out of it, right? I was Grace's lawyer at the time, so I can't talk to them about it even though I play for their team now."

Active gave her time to work through it.

"But if they're reopening it, that means they don't think Grace's mother did it. Which means they think Grace—"

"That's one theory they have, yes."

"One? They have another?"

"Yeah, they—"

"Nita?" Procopio said. "They don't think Nita might have done it!"

"They're not ruling anything out."

"Your girls need a lawyer," Procopio said. "Big time."

"Mm-hmm."

"Let me get back to you with some names."

"I kind of have someone in mind." He told her the name.

"That snake?".

"Yeah, I've crossed trails with him once or twice myself. He's the best."

"And the worst," Procopio said.

"Just what my girls need, eh?"

Procopio sucked in a breath. "I have to admit that."

She rang off and he stared at his phone for a minute or two. Then he went back to his PowerPoint on the accounting system. He slogged through another five slides, then gave it up. Lucy would just have to come up and explain it to him. He punched her button on the phone.

"Hi, Nathan, Jeremy's coming at three, like you said."

"Great, thanks."

"You need me for anything else?"

"I was gonna ask if you—hang on, I have a call coming in on my cell."

He punched her button offline, took out the silent cell, and stared at the blank screen for a moment. Then he pulled up his contacts and scrolled down to her number.

It took him another moment to summon the nerve to tap it.

"Nathan!" she said after two rings. "How are things in Chukchi? See you tomorrow, right?"

"Right, right, Suka."

"I'm looking forward to it. And what can I do forya? I'm kinda busy, but never too busy for my favorite cop."

He shuddered inside. Favorite cop. That was what Grace called him.

"Well, you said if I ever needed anything in Juneau, I should just ask. As one friend to another."

"Sure, anything."

"I don't know if you've heard, but the Law Department has reopened the Jason Palmer murder case. Grace's father? Apparently it grew out of the due diligence review before you offered me the Trooper job?"

Mercer was silent for several long seconds. "Oh, yes, I think I heard rumblings about that. I haven't really been briefed, but I seem to remember it being on the daily summary I get from my chief of staff."

"There's a cold-case investigator up here today. He just talked to me because it was a city case at the time and we inherited those files when the new borough public safety department was formed."

"Uh-huh."

"And now he's on his way to interview Grace and Nita. I think he actually considers them potential suspects."

"Really? Is that a possibility?"

"Of course not. Grace's mother confessed to shooting her father."

"Oh, yes, some of that is coming back to me now," Mercer said. "So, there's nothing to worry about?"

"I'm not so sure. I know this is going to freak Grace out. And Nita, too. They've already been through hell with that family history. They're both still seeing Nelda Qivits, the old tribal healer."

"Those poor women."

"Exactly. So..."

"So...?"

"I was wondering if you could ask the Law Department

to back off," he said. "It's time Grace and Nita were left in peace."

"Of course. Let me see what I can do. I'll talk to the Attorney General. As one friend for another. We can talk about it tomorrow after the hearing. Maybe we can get a moment together at Grace's ribbon-cutting. You'll be guarding my body anyway, right?"

At FIVE, HIS normal departure time, he called Grace on her cell.

"I'm at the new place," she said in a shaky voice. "Can you come? I really need you."

The moment he was in the door, she was on him, arms clamped so tight around his neck it hurt.

"Oh, Nathan, oh, Nathan."

He patted her back. "It's OK now. Go ahead."

She let the sobs out as he led her to the sofa. They sat down and she buried her face in his shoulder and sobbed some more. He gave her his handkerchief. Finally the sobs eased off. She wiped her eyes and blew her nose.

"Can you tell me about it?"

She looked up at him, red-eyed. "He, he...I, I...oh, Nathan."

She turned into his shoulder again. But this time she didn't sob or howl. She just let out a long breath into his uniform shirt. Then she straightened and a little of the old Grace showed through.

"He caught up with me at the house, my house, my old house, and as soon as he told me what it was about, I did what you said."

"No search, no questions, no interviews with Nita?"

She shook her head, then snuffled into the handkerchief.

He looked around the house, and listened.

"Um, where's Nita now?"

"She stayed after school. Volleyball."

"So, what did Stewart say after you went Fifth Amendment on him?"

"Did somebody tell me what to say."

"And you said—"

She grinned a little. "I went Fifth Amendment on him again. I don't think he liked that. And then he said they could get a search warrant for the house and have a guardian ad litem appointed for Nita." She frowned for a moment. "Our program has had to get guardians ad litem a couple times when a kid's mom was unfit, but how would that work in a criminal case? I am not unfit!"

He put his hand on her thigh and rubbed absently. "I don't see how it would work in a criminal case either. No matter what, if Nita's an actual or potential suspect, she's entitled to a lawyer and what the lawyer says goes. He—or she—might be able to be the guardian ad litem if there's any reason to appoint one."

They were both quiet for a moment.

"Obviously, we need—"

"—a lawyer," he finished. "And I have a name for you: Alex Fortune."

She frowned. "Do I know that—"

"You might. He's pretty famous in Alaska in criminal defense. He used to be in San Francisco, but he's had so much work up here over the years, he's finally based himself in Anchorage. At least most of the time. Remember the Dirty Rotten Scoundrels Club?"

"Ah," she said. "All the crooks in Juneau that went to jail a few years ago."

He shook his head. "Not the ones who hired Alex Fortune."

"Ah," she said again. "But I'm not a crook."

"No, but Stuart Stewart and his bosses may think so. In which case Alex Fortune's name may back them off a little. They'll know it. Trust me."

"You'll call him for me?"

He threw up his hands like he'd just touched a hot stove. "No can do. In theory, I'm on Stuart Stewart's side here. You're what we call a lovint, so he'll be watching me."

"Lovint?"

"Love interest." He grinned.

"That's what you guys call a lover?"

He nodded.

"Cops." She shook her head. "All right, lovint, you got a number for this Alex Fortune?"

"Certainly not. You have to google him yourself."

"All right, first thing tomorrow." She made a calendar note in her cell, then put her hand on his thigh. "You know, we've got a big date with Helen Mercer tomorrow. She's the star attraction at my ribbon-cutting."

"Two dates, actually, for me at least. Our hearing on the Pete Wise file is in the morning. Gonna be quite a day. Fight her in the morning, guard her in the afternoon."

"Poor baby. I'm thinking we could both use some relief." The hand on his thigh drifted higher.

"I don't follow," he said. He did, though. The question was, had Stewart Stuart flipped her switch and she'd held it in till now?

"Look at me, baby." She did. Direct eye contact, no hesitation, no hint of crazy. "You OK?"

"You mean other than having Stuart Stewart and governor of Alaska after me? Ubetcha." She grinned and he decided she probably was herself. "And I need the comfort. God, do I need the comfort."

With a mental shrug, he relaxed into it. If it blew up, he'd deal with it somehow. Like always. "We both do. And we'll explain to Nita that we're going upstairs before dinner how?"

"Hmm, good question." She looked at the time on her cell. "She'll be done with volleyball in a few. Why don't you go get her while I see what I can do for dinner with what I brought from the house and whatever moldy bachelor food you've got around here. Throw a big dinner with lotsa carbs into Nita after volleyball and she's out by eight."

"Frozen stuff doesn't mold," he said.

"You want some lovin' from your lovint tonight or not?"

"I'm going, I'm going."

IT WAS NINE o'clock by the time Nita crashed, but the anticipation only made it sweeter when they finally reached his bed.

They undressed, roamed hands over each other's bodies, then formed themselves into a sixty-nine and satisfied each other like they had in the tent on the ice.

Afterward they spooned on their sides, his front to her back. She reached down and pulled him up between her thighs, then nestled him in the lips of that warm, slippery opening and said, "Mmm."

"Mmm," he said. "Maybe another sheefishing trip and a boffo splibo this weekend?'

"Mmm," she said.

He drifted off, marveling for perhaps the millionth time at the emotional reserves that let her shove aside pressures that would crush any normal psyche.

CHAPTER TWENTY-THREE

Friday, April 18

JUDGE DAVID STEIN's chair squeaked as he leaned back, laced his fingers behind his head, and gazed unseeing at a photograph of Helen Mercer and her lieutenant governor on the wall opposite his desk. "You're right. This doesn't look like your ordinary snowgo accident."

"No, Your Honor," Procopio said. "It was at least manslaughter. And then leaving the scene? And that snowgo in the water? Obstruction of justice, destruction of evidence? All felonies with clear intent."

"That's how my department sees it, too, Your Honor," Active said.

"Mr. McConnell?"

There was a pause, then a cough of static from the speaker phone on the table in front of the Mercers as their lawyer un-muted himself and came on the line from Anchorage.

"We're not here to argue whether a crime was committed, Your Honor. Our only position is that the contents of Wise versus Mercer cannot possibly have any bearing on the matter, and therefore there is no earthly reason to unseal it. The governor is an innocent bystander here. First, somebody steals Mr. Mercer's snowmobile and now the state has launched this fishing expedition to drag Pete Wise's ridiculous lawsuit into it. Given the governor's position and what a target of lurid popular obsession she is, the ridicule, rumor, and speculation that will inundate her should this become public will be completely out of proportion to its investigative value, which we maintain is nil, in any event."

The Mercers nodded vigorously from their table.

Stein raised his eyebrows in acknowledgment and lifted the top off the candy jar on his bench. "Dark chocolate?" He pulled out a tiny Hershey bar and unwrapped it. "Guaranteed to increase life expectancy and libido." He slipped it into his mouth and held it there without chewing. "Though why you'd want more of either one in Chukchi is hard to imagine."

Active, Procopio, and the First Mate grinned. The governor frowned, then covered her mouth. Masking a smile, Active figured.

"Don't mind if I do," Procopio said. She took two of the judge's miniatures as his clerk Doris passed the jar around. The prosecutor swallowed and closed her eyes for a moment. "I don't know if dark chocolate really does make you live longer. But it sure makes life easier to bear. Especially in Chukchi."

Active and Brad Mercer declined the jar. The governor took a single miniature and Active found himself unable not to watch as she put it on her tongue and slid it between her lips. She caught his gaze and he jerked it away.

"Ms. Procopio? What say you? Why exactly is it you think you need to look at this file?" He tapped the folder on the bench before him.

"As you know your honor, investigative discretion is very broad in a felony like homicide. The fact that Pete Wise was killed by a snowmobile within days of suing Mr. Mercer is so strong a coincidence that we can't rule anything out at this juncture. We have to check off every item on our list that might remotely relate to the death, and this file is one of them. If it's not relevant, it's in the interest of all parties to establish that fact promptly so the investigation can focus elsewhere."

"Mr. McConnell?" Stein said.

Procopio cut a glance at the governor, who returned a glare of pure hatred. "You catch that push-up bra she's wearing?" the prosecutor muttered.

"Absolutely not," Active muttered back.

"The other testosterone-based units in the room did, trust me. Especially Stein."

"Your Honor," McConnell said over the phone. He, at least, would be immune by virtue of distance from the distractions of Mercer's attire. Knowing the governor as he did, Active was pretty sure chance had played no part in her choice today of a satiny, clingy scarlet blouse under her blazer and, architecturally assisted or not, a generous display of cleavage.

"My clients have already explained the snowmobile was stolen," McConnell was saying. "Is Ms. Procopio saying Brad Mercer is nonetheless suspected of Pete Wise's murder? If so, this smacks of a vendetta and we may need to invoke the Fifth Amendment here and suspend proceedings in this case while the investigation proceeds."

"Calm down, Mr. McConnell, calm down. Mr. Mercer can invoke his Fifth Amendment rights and keep silent if he wants to, but we're not asking him to talk in court today anyway. The sole purpose of this hearing is to determine if this file"—he tapped the folder again—"should be unsealed and made a public record again. There's a very strong presumption to that effect in Alaska, as I'm sure you know."

"We must object, Your Honor," McConnell said.

Procopio was on her feet. "Your Honor, Mr. McConnell, strictly speaking the state doesn't need the file made public. We just need it for investigative review. We'd be happy to take it under seal and stipulate—"

Now the governor was on her feet. "We object, Your Honor!"

"But I haven't even ruled." Stein pointed at the telephone on the Mercers' table. "And we usually let the lawyers do the talking at hearings like this."

"Your Honor," McConnell said. "May I confer with my clients?"

The governor looked questioningly at the judge, who shook his head with a resigned expression. "Sure, be the court's guest. Governor, Mr. Mercer, you can use my chambers to call Mr McConnell."

Doris led them out. Procopio doodled on her pad. Active checked email on his phone. Stein, he saw from the corner, was engaged in something on his computer that seemed to absorb his full attention. He doubted even a judge would have the nerve to watch porn in court, but what? Then he recognized the pattern of clicks and drags. His Honor was playing solitaire.

In another minute, the clerk and the Mercers were back.

"Your Honor, I want to a—"

"Please, Governor," Stein said. "Our clerk needs to call Mr. McConnell and we have to go back on the record before anybody can say anything."

Mercer fell silent and sat down. The clerk consulted her notepad, dialed, and put McConnell on speaker again.

"Your Honor," McConnell said, "Mrs. Mercer wishes to say something."

"Governor," Stein said.

"I'm sorry for interrupting. It won't happen again."

"Thank you, Governor. Now, if we may proceed?"

"The governor did in fact state our position," McConnell said. "With respect to releasing the file, we think it's either all or nothing in a small town like

Chukchi. Once the prosecutor's office takes it under seal, the chances are far too great that—"

Procopio was on her feet again. "Your honor, now we object. My office is not a Swiss cheese! We will not let the contents of that file—"

Stein rapped his gavel. "Good grief, people. This is an actual courtroom, not Judge Judy. Let's get a grip." He paused and cleared his throat.

"The fact is, I'm persuaded that the presumption of investigative discretion is sufficiently strong that the state should see the file. However, I'm doing so under the proviso that it remain closed to the public and the state take it under seal and hold it confidential absent further proceedings before this court." He raised his gavel again.

"Motion to reconsider, Your Honor," McConnell said from the phone.

"Say what? On what grounds?"

"Two grounds. One is, we're confident Your Honor is wrong on the matter of investigative discretion, which we will demonstrate by further briefing and argument, followed if necessary by appeal to the state Supreme Court."

Stein shook his head. "Threats of appeal never go out of style, I guess. And your second ground, Mr McConnell?"

"The Fifth Amendment, Your Honor. We need time to brief and argue our position that opening that file could compromise Mr. Mercer's protection against self-incrimination, also to be followed by appeal if necessary."

Stein put his head in his hands. "Ms. Procopio?"

"What can I say? The state thinks Mr. McConnell's arguments are specious and we want the file."

Stein sighed. "A reconsideration hearing it is."

He flipped through a binder—his calendar, Active figured—and put down his finger. "Same time a week from today. Work for everybody?"

The parties nodded.

"Anything else before we go?" Stein asked.

"Yes, Your Honor," the governor said.

"Ahem," Stein said.

"Sorry," McConnell and the governor said in unison.

"But my client is right," McConnell went on. "We're also filing to block any effort by the state for a search warrant on the victim's home."

"Say what?" Procopio and Stein asked in unison.

"That's correct, Your Honor. One thing flows from the other. It's fruit of the poisoned tree."

"I think I see where you're heading," Stein said.

"Yes, Your Honor," McConnell said. "We have little doubt there are copies of the files in printed or digital form at the house, as well as at his workplace and in any safe deposit box he may have. So our filing will cover those, as well."

"Ms. Procopio?" Stein said in a weary tone.

"Of course we want to search the victim's house. There could be evidence there related to his death but unrelated to the lawsuit at issue in this hearing, and the Mercers have no expectation of privacy in Pete Wise's home in any event. As for the fruit-of-the-poisoned-tree argument, that's easily dealt with. We'll stipulate to conducting the search jointly with Mr. McConnell and he can—"

"Your Honor, they've waited this long," McConnell said. "They can wait another week."

"Agreed. It's all on hold till our next hearing. Everybody get your motions in by Tuesday at four-thirty, responses by eight a.m. Thursday. And happy reading to all of you."

Roger Kennelly pounced outside the courtroom, microphone standing at attention. "Governor, Governor. Can we get an interview for Kay-Chuck?"

The station got its money from the state, Active knew, like practically every other organization in Chukchi. Kennelly had long gray hair and and a flowing beard that made him look a little like Buffalo Bill. He been in public radio a long time, long enough to know he couldn't push Mercer too hard. But at least he was giving it a shot.

"It's a non-story," Mercer said with a touch of asperity Active hadn't seen her show in public before. She seemed to realize it herself, and tugged the scarlet blouse into proper clinginess and lowness then touched Kennelly's wrist before continuing in a softer tone and with lots of eye contact. "This is just another of the crazy things that's been coming out of the woodwork ever since I came to national prominence. I don't know who or what's behind this, but it's nonsense and I wish my political enemies and the lamestream media would leave my family and me in peace"—here she paused just long enough to shoot Kennelly a blood-freezing stare without it becoming too obvious—"so I can get on with running this great state of ours." She touched Kennelly's arm and leaned forward as if to whisper into the mike. "Right, Roger?"

"Uh, right, governor, absolutely," Kennelly said, his eyes exactly where they shouldn't be and Mercer no doubt wanted them to be. "But what—"

The governor detached herself. "And I want to thank you for the great job your station does for our region. And you tell that station manager of yours, if there's anything more from the state she needs to run Kay-Chuck properly, all she has to do is give me a call, OK?"

"Sure, governor, I'll—"

"And call me Suka, how many times have I told you?" Kennelly nodded.

"Oh, and thank you for your great coverage of the new women's center. I hope you'll be there for the ribbon-cutting a little bit later?"

"Yes, ma'am."

"Roger...?"

"Yes, Suka. I'll be there."

"WHAT THE FUCK was that?" Procopio said a few minutes later as they flopped down in her office.

Active shrugged. "I don't know. A honey trap for the hapless Roger?"

"That bitch."

"Actually, she looked pretty hot in that blouse. You gotta admit."

"Fuck you. But seriously." Procopio tapped a pen on the brief she had filed in their effort to get into Wise versus Mercer. "Further briefs? Further argument? Appeals? What is this, the Pentagon Papers?"

"They're stalling."

"Well, yeah. But why? What's gonna happen in a week?"

"Look on the bright side," Active said. "Maybe we'll figure it out by then without the file."

"Yeah, right. Or maybe an asteroid will hit the earth and put us out of our misery."

CHAPTER TWENTY-FOUR

Friday, April 18

ACTIVE GAZED AROUND the steps and parking lot in front the Chukchi Women's Shelter at the smattering of people gathered to watch Helen Mercer officially cut the ribbon. "Not good, eh?"

Grace pursed her lips. "Not the crowd I was hoping for. If there's anything a narcissist hates, it's not being noticed."

Active did another quick scan. "We got Pudu here and his camera and your staff. And those guys over there are the carpenters doing the remodel? And the kids on the steps there are the entertainment, am I right?"

Grace nodded. "Yup, the Episcopal youth choir, they're usually a big draw around here, plus we've got pilot bread and caribou and sheefish and seal oil inside, and it was all over Kay-Chuck."

"No clients, though?"

She frowned. "Nope. Besides the offices, we've only got three of the residential units ready and the women in them are all afraid to come out, in case the boyfriend or husband shows up. Still, we got a few *aakas* and *aanas* and *aanagas*." She pointed at a little cluster of Inupiat ladies before the steps. Most were older, of bountiful displacement, and clad in flowered *atiqluks*.

"Maybe not too bad," Active admitted.

"Don't forget about me," Nita spoke up from Grace's side. "I'm here."

"I know, *bunnik*. And you're gonna meet the

governor. After that, you go back inside and wait for her like we talked about, OK? She's going to say some stuff for the camera that will probably be kinda boring, then we'll come inside and eat sheefish with her and she'll meet some clients and maybe you can talk to her there."

"I *know*, Mom," Nita said. She rolled her eyes in the ancient preteen gesture of disdain for adult fuddy-duddiness.

"How was the hearing?" she murmured as Nita left and they were alone for a moment.

"Still at a standoff," he said. "Re-run a week from today."

"She really doesn't want you in that file."

"Nope."

"And she really wants to keep the pressure on you and me."

For a few seconds, neither could think of anything to say. "Nice touch, the duct tape," Active mustered at last.

Grace turned to inspect the shelter's new double doors. The handles were duct-taped together and adorned with a bow to match. "What can I say? We couldn't find any of those giant ribbons they use everywhere else, much less giant scissors, so duct tape it is. One of our clients made it. But we do have a ceremonial Old Timer to cut it with." She pulled the knife from a pocket and waved it at him.

"Fingers crossed she likes it," Active said. "Actually, I think she will if we put some cute kids around her while the camera's rolling."

"Plus her favorite cop, I'm sure."

Active raised his eyebrows, thankful his bi-cultural background—born to a Chukchi mother, raised by white adoptive parents in Anchorage—meant the gesture could stand for either the Inupiat 'yes' or the *naluaqmiut* signal of ironic acknowledgment.

"Just make sure you don't stand too close when she doesn't need you in the shot." Grace waved the Old Timer again. "I'll be watching."

Finally, the governor pulled up in her Expedition, and Active moved over to report for duty as guardian of the First Body.

"Afternoon, Governor."

"It's Suka, Nathan. I thought we discussed that." She squeezed his arm as she stepped down from the SUV in the Naughty Monkeys. Her throat, he noticed now, still sported a pair of Band-Aids.

"How are the scratches?"

She touched one of the Band-Aids. "Oh, nothing a village girl can't handle. But it's good to be back in civilization, eh?"

"It is. No complaints about the company or accommodations in Shelukshuk Canyon, but a real bed and indoor plumbing are hard to beat."

"That's your Grace Palmer over there? I don't think we've ever met in person. Can you introduce me?"

They moved toward Grace. She was deep in discussion with Pudu as they squinted up at the April sun that had returned when the storm blew itself out late the day before. It appeared the subject was lighting and camera angles, for they teamed up to wrestle the lectern to a new position that, Active calculated, would allow the governor to be taped in dramatic, yet flattering, sunlight from the side and above.

Then he noticed with alarm that Mercer had not merely retained her grip on his arm as they made their way toward the lectern. She had linked elbows. From Grace's perspective, they would no doubt look like the closest of friends, perhaps with benefits. The question was, would Grace look up from her discussion with

Pudu in time to see it?

Grace did and her face froze. Mercer detached herself from his arm and put out her hand. Active thought he detected a slight thaw, but he could never be sure with Grace.

"Governor," he said, "this is Grace Palmer. And this is her daughter Nita."

"Governor," Grace said in a tone at least borderline civil. She took the governor's hand and gave it a shake of sufficient length to be, like her tone, just inside the bounds of civility. "Thanks for your help with our shelter. We couldn't have done it without you."

"Oh, call me Suka," Mercer said. "Everybody does. I've told that to your fella here at least a hundred times but I just can't seem to get it through that thick skull of his. Maybe you can help me talk some sense into him?"

Grace mustered another borderline smile. "I doubt it. I've never had much luck with that myself."

Mercer stepped back a pace and sized Grace up—that was the only term for it, Active thought—as she stood at the lectern in the sunlight where Mercer would be standing in a few minutes.

"My God," Mercer said, "you're even lovelier than they say. And you've already had a child? Amazing." Grace appeared dumbstruck as Mercer turned on Active. "And you're a lucky man, Nathan. Take good care of this one."

"Yes, ma'am, er, Suka," Active mumbled.

Grace started to speak but Mercer put her hand out to Nita. "And, hello, Nita, it's always great to meet a future voter! Especially one as pretty as her mother!"

Nita blushed. "Thank you, Governor."

"Now, you, too, young lady. You call me Suka, too!"

"OK, Suka."

"So what's your favorite class?"

"Oh, social studies, I guess." She cut a glance at her mother, who gave the slightest of eye rolls. Social studies, if Active recalled right, was the class with the cute boy. He made a mental note to run a background check on the kid's family.

"Social studies, huh?" Mercer said. "That's good. You'll be more prepared than most people when you get old enough to vote."

"*Bunnik*," Grace said, "Why don't you go on inside until we finish with the videotaping, then we'll come in and maybe you and the governor can talk some more."

"OK, Mom. It was nice to meet you, Suka."

"I think I have some pictures in my bag," Mercer said. "Would you like one, Nita?"

Nita nodded with a huge grin. Mercer produced a red Sharpie and an eight-by-ten color glossy from her bag. "May I borrow your back, Nathan?"

"What?"

"Your back. For a desk, like."

Active shot a glance at Grace, who looked as stunned as he felt. He turned away from Mercer and bent forward. There was a slight pressure as she spread the picture on his back and signed it.

"Here you go, Nita." The inscription read, "To my best friend in Chukchi," Active saw.

"Wow," Nita breathed. "You're so awesome, Suka!"

"Thank you, Nita," Mercer said as the girl raced away. "Your daughter is an absolute sweetheart, Grace. You are so lucky!"

"Actually, Governor, um, Suka, I was going to say that Nita is my adoptive daughter. We're first cousins, actually. I adopted her after her mother, my aunt, died in a plane crash."

"Yes, now that I think of it. Nathan mentioned that." Mercer smiled and did the arm touch with Grace. "I'm sorry if I stirred up painful memories."

For a moment, Mercer studied Grace and Active as they stood side by side at the lectern. "And, Grace, you are also lucky about this fella here. You better keep an eye on him or one of these Chukchi girls will snatch him right up, him with that sexy uniform and that badge and that great big gun and all. Not that many years ago, I might have been tempted myself!"

Mercer saw their expressions and patted Grace's arm with a smile. "Just making conversation, right? Shall we get the show on the road? Pudu?"

A snowgo coasted to a stop across the street. "Actually, guys, why don't we put things on hold for a minute. I need to talk to that guy." Active jerked a thumb at the snowgo's driver.

"Joe Penske," he said when he reached the machine. "How you doing today?"

"Oh, pretty good, I guess."

"You're still under that protective order, right?"

"I dunno."

"I do. So you need to be moving along, OK?"

"Is Ginny in there?"

"I don't know. But if she is, you're violating your order, OK?"

"I just want to talk to her."

Active put his hand on the Glock. "No, you just want to move along, OK?"

"Then I want to talk to the governor about it. A man should be able to see his wife."

"Not when he's got a protective order. Now you move along, or I'll have to handcuff you in the back of my truck and get somebody over here to take you to jail." Active pulled out his handcuffs and slapped them against his palm. "And we still got no Eskimo food in our jail. Just *naluaqmiu*."

Penske hesitated. His face was oily and his eyes were red.

"That's not liquor on your breath is it?"

"*Arii*, a man should be able to see his wife." But he started the snowgo and pulled away.

When Active got back to the lectern, Grace raised her eyebrows and smiled. "Thanks, my captain. His wife's in the shelter."

"Guessed as much," Active said. "He comes back, you know our number. Just so you know, Governor, he wanted to take it up with you, too."

"Aha! I was right. I do need a bodyguard in Chukchi!"

"You're welcome," Active said to himself. To the governor he said, "Absolutely. Chukchi Public Safety at your service." Over the governor's shoulder, Grace winked at him.

Pudu patted his camera, set up on a tripod. "Ready, Mom."

Grace backed away from the lectern. "Shall we, Governor?"

"Hold it a sec," Mercer said. "Grace, stay up there if you would. You're gonna be my lighting double! Pudu, frame a shot on her like you're gonna do with me."

Grace, the dumbstruck look on her face again, stepped back to the lectern as Mercer moved over to peer into Pudu's viewfinder.

"Lovely, just lovely. Nathan, come see how the camera loves your girl."

Active thought how to wiggle out of it, but Mercer was...well, she was Mercer. Helen Wheels. No filters, no boundaries, always at full throttle.

Besides, now he was back in the memory of how Grace's picture at Chukchi High had started him down that long trail to find her. Like somebody smart had said, the past was never dead, it wasn't even past.

He jerked himself back to the present and stepped up to Pudu's viewfinder and studied Grace in the sun for as long as he could bear it, then looked away. "Very nice," he mumbled.

"It's good for me," Mercer said. "Good for you, Pudu?"

"Good, Mom," Pudu said. "I told you that already."

Grace stepped aside and Mercer took the lectern as the youth choir arranged itself behind them. Active noted with gratitude that he seemed to have been overlooked and was allowed to stand a few feet in front of the lectern with Grace's staff and four or five people he guessed were aunts, mothers, and sisters of the clients afraid to come out for the ceremony.

The kids sang the Alaska Flag Song and then Mercer took the mike.

"Look," she said. "I know you're probably figuring I'll talk a long time because I'm a politician now. Well, yeah, but I'm still a village girl, so I'm going to keep it short and make my point, like when I played and coached basketball." She paused for the crowd's chuckle. "This network of shelters is something we've needed for a long time, because women in this region who were beaten by their men or who had children molested by those men, those women had no way out, nowhere to go. Now they will, thanks to the efforts of Grace Palmer, here"—she pointed to Grace, standing beside her—"with a little help from me down in Juneau on the funding. When we get the village crisis centers set up to do intake and get their clients on the plane to Chukchi and the shelter here, why, then, girls and women all over the region will have a place to go. And, now, Grace?"

Grace stepped up to the mike with a nod to Mercer. "Governor, what can I say? You're right, this region has needed something like our shelter for longer than anyone can remember, but it didn't happen till you came along. Which I guess answers my question. What can I say? What can the women of the whole Chukchi region say? We can say thank you, Governor, thank you from the bottoms of our hearts. And, now, if you would do the honors."

She made a show of handing Mercer the Old Timer with a flourish. Mercer stepped up to the duct-tape bow, made an equal show of unclasping the knife, and sawed through the tape, then swung open the *kunnichuk* doors with a curtsy of her own.

The little crowd broke into pretty hearty applause for its size. The choir closed with a hymn about being sheltered safe in the arms of God, and the choir director offered a prayer not only for the troubled women sheltered in the center, but also the angry, hurting men who had put them there.

Grace took the mike again.

"All right, everybody, we've got some great food inside, and we'll be giving tours of the main shelter and the annex next door. The offices are already set up and working, but the living areas are mostly still under construction, so you'll have to be ready for a little dust and debris."

As the crowd started in, Mercer put a hand on Active's elbow and held him back. Grace shot him a glance over her shoulder as she moved through the doors.

"About what we discussed the other day?"

"The Jason Palmer case?"

Mercer nodded. "I talked to the attorney general about it."

Active drew in a breath.

"Well, it's delicate, you know, for a governor to get involved in a criminal case. The Law Department tends to tell one and all to butt out at times like this. Even governors."

"I realize it would require all of your diplomatic expertise, of course, but maybe you could—"

"It's just that it's doubly sensitive right now, what with Pete Wise's ridiculous custody suit being caught up in your hit-and-run investigation."

"Of course. I understand. Still, there must be some—"

"Maybe after the Pete Wise matter is cleared up. It's obvious from today's hearing that will take a while, right? Until then I'm afraid I have to stay out of the Jason Palmer thing."

Active rocked back on his heels a little. "Even you."

"Even me. Shall we?"

She hooked elbows and led him inside.

Grace spotted them and hurried over. "We're about to start the tour, Suka. Do you want—"

"Is that sheefish and pilot bread I see? I want Pudu to get some video of me eating sheefish and pilot bread first. There's no *muktuk*, right? I don't dare eat *muktuk* any more—I'd have Greenpeace all over me in ten seconds. Don'tcha hate that political-correctness thing?"

Grace struggled for a moment to find an answer, and finally squeezed out, "No *muktuk* whatever, Suka, just all the sheefish and caribou and pilot bread you can eat!"

Mercer moved off to corral Pudu. Grace hooked Active's elbow, just like Mercer had done.

"The bitch, treating us like flunkies. And what the fuck was that about at the end?"

Active looked at her forehead just above her eyebrows. Grace didn't appear to notice the fake eye contact. "I asked her to see what she could do about

Stuart Stewart's investigation."

"And?"

"And she won't. Or can't, as long as our Pete Wise investigation is open."

"She linked the two?"

He raised his eyebrows. "I could make Pete Wise go away."

"You?"

"Mm-hmm."

"You'd do that for me?"

"And Nita." He shrugged.

She pushed him back a little and studied his face. "Not and still be you."

"She's not gonna let up until we back off. That's pretty clear."

"Fuck that. You and Theresa just get the file."

"We're trying, baby, we're trying."

CHAPTER TWENTY-FIVE

Saturday, April 19

THEY ARRIVED AT Leroy's sheefish camp at a more favorable hour than on their previous excursion—barely after three, by Active's phone. Sun still high in the sky with some wispy cirrus streaking up from the south, a nice breeze popping the white canvas of the tent, temperature maybe ten above but cooling.

Nita checked the sheefish holes near the tent while Active and Grace went inside to check things out. A couple of ice-encrusted silver tails poked out from under one of the cots.

"I guess somebody borrowed Leroy's tent, huh?"

"This must be the rent, all right," Active said. He pulled the fish from under the cot. "Nice of 'em. Not headed and gutted, though."

"They keep better if you freeze them whole, *naluaqmiiyaaq*."

"Yeah, yeah," he said. "Looks like we're gonna have to go old-school tonight and eat some *quaq*, ah?" He pronounced it the *naluaqmiut* way, which produced a grin from her.

"That's why I brought the seal oil," she said. "I see Leroy's got a hacksaw in the box by the halfagascan there. You saw off a steak and I'll shave it into strips while you help Nita find a hole and get set up. Then I'll come and we'll have some old-time Eskimo snacks out at the hole and I'll show you how it's done."

Nathan grunted assent and found the hacksaw in Leroy's everything box. Then he cleared some cartridges, a Coleman stove, a box of pilot bread, and a can of Spam from the top of a set of utility shelves Leroy had with his usual practicality thrown together from a pair of old wooden gas crates. Active laid one of the sheefish on some cardboard and newspaper from the everything box and went to work with the hacksaw at the narrow part between the body and the tail.

In a couple of minutes, he had shucked off his parka and the vest underneath and was down to the wool shirt and snowpants. Finally the tail came off and he went to work a couple of inches higher up. This time it went a little faster, or at least easier, as he hit the rhythm.

"There," he said. "One prime sheefish steak, as ordered"

"Except the guts are still in." She pointed.

"Oh, yeah." He found a tool box on the bottom shelf under the sheefish and a hammer inside that, then used it to tap out the medallion of frozen intestines at the center of the steak.

"Very good. We'll make a real Eskimo out of you yet." She pulled an *ulu* from a dishpan by the halfagascan. "Now you and Nita go find us a hole."

He pushed open the flaps of the tent and stepped outside. "Any of these look good?" He waved at the four or five craters in the ice nearby.

Nita wrinkled her nose and squinted. "I don't like them. They look fished out to me."

"You can tell?

She raised her eyebrows. "Ah-hah. I'm a real Eskimo."

"Ah-hah. And where do you suppose we might find a hole that's not fished out?"

"I dunno, maybe down by Christina's tent."

"By Christina's tent? That's pretty far to go back and forth."

"Maybe I should spend the night again."

"Hmm. I never thought of that. We better go ask your mom, huh?"

They did. Active made a "please!" sign with clasped hands behind Nita as Grace pretended to ponder.

"I don't know," she said. "We wouldn't want you to be a burden."

"I won't, Mom. I'll help Christina's mom cut fish or wash dishes or anything she wants, I promise."

"Well, let me give 'em a call, then."

Grace made the arrangements on her cell, Nita gathered her things for the night, and they set off for Christina's tent a half-mile down the ice while Grace stayed behind to shave the sheefish.

Christina bounced out as they came up and her mother, Fannie, followed.

The two girls hugged and Nita admired her friend's chin for a moment. "I sure like your tattoo." She looked at Fannie. "I sure like Christina's tattoo. You did really good with it."

Active studied the chin in question. The traditional lines of dark gray dots fanned down from the lip toward the chin. They were making a comeback among the young for some reason, though the tradition seemed to have skipped over most of the women in Grace's generation. Fannie, with her own chin tattoo, was one exception. Perhaps that was because she was from Katonak village, a hundred or so miles up the river from Chukchi. The old ways tended to hang on there.

"You know what your mom said, Nita," Fannie was telling the girl. "No tattoos till you're sixteen."

"*Arii*, I wish my mom was cool like you."

Fannie wagged a finger at her. "I told you, don't say nothing like that. Someday you'll be your mom and your little girl will be you and she'll say mean things to you and then you'll know what it's like to be a mother and you'll cry, lotta times."

Nita's face softened and Active thought this might be one of those times. But she turned to Christina. "We gonna go catch some sheefish?"

Christina pointed at a crater in the ice a few yards off with a stack of sheefish beside it. "Look at that hole we found." Nita dug her sheefish rig out of the jockey box and the two girls raced off.

"You wanna come in for some sheefish stew, Nathan? They're real fat and oily this year."

"I don't know, maybe later. I think we might take a nap."

Fannie tilted her head for a moment, then grinned. "Ah-hah."

"We're real tired." Active grinned back and mounted the Yamaha.

"You could come back later for dinner, in case you need to build up your strength after your nap."

"Maybe we will."

When he got back to camp, Grace had laid out the sheefish strips with pilot bread and a jar of seal oil. "*Arii*," he said. "I was thinking we might take a nap."

Grace chuckled. "The old-timers say seal oil and *quaq* will build a fire in your belly."

"That's been my experience on the trail, yes."

"So that's a good thing, right?"

"All for it." He dipped a strip of *quaq* in the seal oil, chewed it till it thawed enough to swallow, and chased it with a bite of pilot bread. The familiar warmth started in his belly almost as soon as the stuff hit. "Now I'm a real Eskimo, ah?"

"You're getting there." Grace had a boffo splibo going. She puffed on it, then got some *quaq* of her own and they crunched in silence for a while, side by side on the cot in the incense of the boffo.

"So," Active said. "About that nap...?"

Grace pointed at the sun coming through the tent flaps. "But it's full daylight, m'lord. Surely you can't mean...?"

"I can and I do, wench. Now peel off that Arctic insulation lest I do it for you."

"Just you try!"

He tackled her and threw her to the cot. She mock-fought back and he waited for some sign it would call up too many memories and turn real. But, no, she stayed in the moment and let him wrestle off her clothes.

And there she was.

"There's something sexy about being this naked when you're fully dressed," she said. "Or maybe it's the boffo."

She opened his snow pants, then his jeans, and slipped a hand down the front. "I see Little Nathan is perking up. But he feels so constricted, with all those zippers and things. Would m'lord like me to see what I can do?"

He nodded and she stripped him down and they crawled under the sleeping bag on the cot and tried the sixty-nine position.

"Poor baby," she said a few minutes later.

"Not my day, I guess," he said. "But I don't mind. I'm just glad you got there."

"It doesn't seem fair."

"Seriously. It's OK."

"Let's see what the magic hands can do."

He lay back in anticipation while Grace fished around her in backpack. The mouth usually worked. The hands, always.

"Crap," she said. "I think I forgot the baby oil."

"Meh," he said. "Next time."

"No, wait, try the missionary position. Maybe this'll be the one."

She rolled onto her back and wrapped her legs around

his waist and guided him to her entrance, then froze into that familiar rigidity at his touch. He felt himself wilt.

"Sorry, baby, I am so..." She didn't say any more.

"Are you crying?" He kissed salt on her cheeks and eyelashes. "Don't, it's OK, really."

"No, it is not OK! It means I'm a failure. A woman who cannot do this is not a real woman! She's—I don't know what. But not a woman."

"We're getting there."

"I wish. I hope. But I'm not sure we'll ever make it."

He was out of variations on "it's OK," so he just pulled her into the spoon position they always used at the end.

As usual, the contact brought him to life. She lifted her leg and bent her knees and pulled him between her thighs. She rubbed and rolled her thighs and he responded even more.

"Wow, baby," she said. "You're like a walrus tusk."

He realized he was witness to another of her uncanny emotional rebounds, and crossed his fingers it would get them through the rest of this.

"Tell me about it. Except for being kind of dry, that feels a lot like the real thing. I'm dying here."

"There's gotta be something we can do." She started to dive down for another try with her mouth, then snapped her fingers. "Let's do what the old-timers probably did."

"Say what?"

She stretched across to Leroy's shelving unit and grabbed the seal oil.

"Come on, seriously?"

She giggled. "Seal oil and cock? A match made in Inupiat heaven, right?"

She oiled her hands, slid them up and down his length, then oiled her thighs and slipped her fingers up and down the outer folds of her sex.

She pulled him back into position between her thighs,

bent her knees and squeezed and rolled him again, even rocked her hips so that her lips slid up and down his shaft. He grabbed her hip bones and drove back and forth.

"Oh, God, no, I don't I can't—oh, Jesus!"

She laughed and kept him in the divine grip. "That was quick."

He shook his head. "We oughta bottle and sell that stuff. I've never felt anything like it."

"Tell me about it." She put her hand between her legs. "Holy crap. See how swollen I am."

He slid his hand between her thighs and slid his fingers along her folds.

"What you waiting for? Do me again!"

He did, with his mouth, locking his arms round her thighs to hang on as her hips began to convulse. By the end, she was slapping the top of his head and screaming, "Stop, stop." He did.

"Don't stop, goddammit. What is wrong with you?"

He resumed and hung on again till it was finally over and she came down from wherever she was. "Wow, I'm not doing that again without a helmet. I was kidding about having my skull crushed between a woman's thighs."

She sighed.

THEY WERE PACKING the sled the next morning in jackets-open sunlight and preparing to retrieve Nita from

Fannie's tent when Christina pulled up on a snowgo with Nita riding behind. The snowgo stopped and the pair bounded off to stand side by side, like twins.

"Look, Mom," Nita said as Grace came through the tent flaps. "I got my tattoo." She pointed at her chin.

Active checked the chin—it did indeed have the lines fanning down from the lip, though the dots looked a little more bluish than Christina's. He stepped back and busied himself loading the sled to avoid the explosion, though not so far back as to miss another round in the long-running tattoo fight.

"Jesus Christ," Grace said. "What did I tell you?"

Nita's face set into a look of pure stubbornness. "You're not the boss of me."

"And what the hell is Fannie doing? I told her about this. I'm going to—"

She stamped into the tent and returned with her phone, tapping at the screen for Fannie's contact.

First Christina, then Nita, cracked, and burst into laughter.

"Look, Mom." Nita licked a finger and rubbed the tattoo until it smeared. "It's just ballpoint. We tricked you."

Grace glared at them, then tapped her phone off and shook her head. "All right, good one, you got me." She grinned finally. "Now load your stuffs into our sled and let's get going. I've got things to do back in town."

She caught Active's expression. "This is not funny," she hissed. "A daughter between princesses and puberty is an instrument of torture to her mother."

"Maybe just a little tattoo?" Active whispered.

"Children," Grace said with a look of disgust. "Men are children. The more so the older they get."

"Didn't Nelda Qivits say it might be good for her?"

"You leave Nelda out of this. This is family and I told

her so."

"Oh, yeah, Mom," Nita said from the sled hitched behind Christina's snowgo. "Look at this."

Active watched Grace steel herself for another tattoo but Nita unlashed a corner of the cover on the sled. "See what I caught?"

Active counted the sheefish. Six, all told.

"Wow," Grace said from his elbow. "Those are for us?"

Nita lifted her eyebrows. Then she wrinkled her nose and stared. "*Aaqaa* you guys! What you been doing?"

Active masked his grin and enjoyed the spectacle of Grace groping for a response.

"Oh, we spilled some seal oil," she said finally. "You know how hard it is to clean up. But you caught all these fish?"

The girl lifted her eyebrows again. "Aren't they awesome?"

"You're awesome," Grace said. "We'll take 'em back and get 'em weighed in for the sheefish derby in case any of them are big enough to make the top ten, then I'll cook one tonight."

"Can I help?" Nita said. Then she paused in thought for a moment. "With cooking the sheefish. Not with cleaning up the seal oil. *Aaqaa!*"

CHAPTER TWENTY-SIX

Monday, April 21

"It's gotta be one of 'em, right?" Procopio put her chin in her hand and regarded her files on the Pete Wise case with a glum look. "I don't believe that shit about a stolen snowgo for one minute."

"Nope."

"But which one, and how do we prove it? We got two suspects, one of which surely did it, the other of which surely aided and abetted, and neither of which can be compelled to testify against the other."

"Or themselves," Active said as he gazed out at the day. The cirrus streaks and lazy breeze from Saturday had developed into a moderate blow from the southwest with snow hurrying sideways through town. But it hadn't reached blizzard proportions yet and wouldn't, according to Kay-Chuck. Another day or two, and the April sun would be back. Fair enough weather, except when you were stuck on a case. "Unless they are innocent bystanders, like they claim."

Procopio snorted, and said nothing.

"You hearing anything about Jimmy Shaw?"

"Zip," Procopio said.

Jimmy Shaw was a six-year-old who'd been reported missing by his parents Saturday night when he failed to come back from "playing out," as letting kids, even little ones, roam the streets was called in Chukchi. A search had started the next morning when Jimmy still didn't show up and a quick canvass of his buddies' houses came up dry. Now it was Monday

Active shook his head. "Normally you can't sneeze around here without somebody putting a message on Kay-Chuck saying to watch out for pneumonia. But this time there's nothing, just nothing. It's like an alien abduction."

"Foul play?"

"You'd think. I mean, how does a six-year-old get lost in this town? My people have talked to his family, his friends and their families. We're getting no vibe whatever that somebody took him."

"I guess Gabe's on it?"

He nodded. "Yeah, his search-and-rescue guys are everywhere, they put up posters all over town, messages on Kay-Chuck, pictures on Facebook and the borough website, not a clue.

He opened his printout of the medical examiner's report on Pete Wise, which had arrived in the morning's email. Procopio saw what he was doing and unfolded the copy he had printed off for her

"M.E.'s office any help?"

"Not a bit," Active said. "Pete bled to death from the leg being cut off and probably would have died of the head injury if he hadn't. All consistent with being hit by a snowmobile, no evidence on him as to who was driving said snowmobile."

"The crime lab was equally unhelpful, I see."

Active thumbed further into his own copy. "Pretty much. Damage to snowgo consistent with running somebody down, blood smears matched the samples from Pete Wise. Big whoop." He looked at the blood work again. "Hmm."

"What?"

"When I picked the governor up to take her to the airport Tuesday, she had a cut over her eyebrow. Said she got it pulling luggage out of a closet, but it strikes me now that it was consistent, as our M.E. might say, with what could happen if you banged your face into the top of the windshield on a snowgo."

"Tuesday? Of last week? The same day Pete Wise was killed?"

He nodded and raised his eyebrows.

"Hmm. Maybe she left some behind?"

Active was already punching in Lucy's extension. "Hi, Lucy—what? Yes, I think Jeremy will be fine while you're gone. What? No, of course I won't ask him to stay on permanently. I promise, your job will be waiting when you get back from maternity leave, OK, now? Listen, would you get the Anchorage crime lab on the line for me? Thanks."

He punched off. "So where does that leave us for this week's hearing?"

"Nowhere we weren't before, but I've still got four days to find a hat with a rabbit in it," Procopio said. "Maybe on eBay."

Active shook his head. "Anybody you can call about how we get into the files in Wise v. Mercer? Old law school prof who specializes in this sort of thing? Another prosecutor in the law department?"

"I don't know, there's gotta be somebody."

His phone rang and Lucy's extension lit up. He punched her on. "Hi, you got the crime lab on the line? Thanks, put 'em through."

"No, there's somebody here to see you. A Bill Ashe from the Alaska Police Standards Council? Did you make another appointment without telling me?"

"What? Who?"

She said it again.

"OK, send the guy up." He looked at Procopio, whose mystified expression mirrored his own.

"Police Standards Council?" she said. "What do they

want?"

Active tried to mask his unease. "God knows. Maybe one of our criminal masterminds actually figured out how to file a complaint against a cop."

Procopio grimaced. "But why would they send somebody all the way up here as soon as they get it? Don't they normally do some kind of review before they spend their travel budget?"

Active shrugged. "Normally. Maybe it's a special case."

"Should I go?"

"Stay. I may need a witness."

They waited in silence. Within a couple of minutes, Bill Ashe was in the doorway introducing himself. He was gray-haired and wore bifocals and a gray goatee. And civilian clothes, Active noted. No uniform. Probably another ex-cop or Trooper racking up a few final years in the state system to beef up his retirement check. "Chief Active, pleasure." His voice was gray, too.

He offered a card, which Active took, and kept his hand out. Active gave it a shake as he glanced at the card.

"Mr. Ashe," Active said with a nod. "Theresa Procopio, our local prosecutor."

They shook, exchanged banalities, and Ashe took a chair next to Theresa.

Coffee was offered and declined. Ashe set a brown leather satchel on the floor beside him, unbuckled it and pulled out a folder. "It might be better if we talked in private."

Active shrugged. "We don't have many secrets in Chukchi. I don't mind, if you don't."

"I do, actually. No offense, Ms. Procopio."

"None taken," Procopio said.

"And if you'd close the door," Ashe said.

"No offense taken whatever," she added in a tone that made clear a great deal was. She shut the door behind her with considerable emphasis.

"Quite the little support group among the Chukchi law-enforcement community, I see," Ashe said.

Active grinned. "Pretty much. But how can I help you today? One of our guys make a wrong move, allegedly? None of the citizenry has complained to me."

"Actually, it's you. Allegedly. This complaint is from the governor."

"The governor?"

"She claims you made advances in a tent on the— how do you say it?—the Isignaq?

Active nodded. "Close enough."

"Mm-hmm. On the Isignaq River after your plane was forced down."

"Horse shit."

"Conduct unbecoming a sworn police officer was how she put it in the complaint."

Ashe pushed a copy across the desk. Active scanned it and tried not to let his face heat up.

"The gist of it is, she says you tried to seduce her during the night and assaulted her when she resisted, causing scratches on her neck."

"I can see that."

"Do you have anything to say? We need to get this cleared up and as an ex-cop myself I just want to help you help yourself here." He extended his hands, palms up. "Let's get it straightened out, OK?"

Active felt a momentary spasm of pity for Ashe, reduced to trying such an old trick on an actual living, breathing, cop who had so often used it himself. But only momentary.

"Sure, I have a statement. This is bullshit. She did it herself on the zipper of a sleeping bag, just like she said in that video she put on the Internet. Claimed it proved what a tough Alaska gal she is."

Ashe looked at his own copy of the complaint. "I believe she covered that in paragraph twelve. Maybe you should read it a little closer."

Active found the spot on the second page, reread it, and looked up at Ashe. "Helen Mercer suffers from battered woman syndrome?"

"So she says."

"You mean from Brad? Her husband beats her?"

"No specifics. But she claims it's why she couldn't tell the truth about what happened in the tent at first. Now she feels she has to take positive action for her own mental health."

"But a complaint to you guys? Why not a sexual assault complaint to the Troopers if she really wants to regain her mental health?"

"I haven't spoken to her personally—I'm given to understand she hand-delivered her complaint to our chairman—"

"Who would be the state commissioner of public safety, if I remember right?"

Ashe nodded. "She delivered it to him in person—"

"And he was appointed by her and serves at her pleasure, is that also correct?"

Ashe nodded again. "None of which will affect our investigation in the slightest, of course."

"Of course not. But please continue."

"Where was I?"

"You were explaining why she didn't file a criminal complaint if I assaulted her."

"I have the impression she thinks it would create too much publicity. She doesn't think it looks quite right for a governor to be a battered woman—she'd seem weak and helpless—and this will be quieter. We do our investigation, we pull your Alaska police officer certificate if we find cause, you get yourself a job as a legal investigator or something, everyone's happy, right?"

"I'm happy being a certified peace officer and head of the Chukchi Public Safety Department, thank you very much."

"Seriously, Nathan. I'm your friend here. If you could just—"

"All right, Bill. I can see you're a nice guy in a tight spot. I do have a further statement to make."

"Great, very wise. I'll just record it, if I may." He dug into his satchel.

"Oh, it's quite short," Active said. "I'm sure you'll be able to remember it: Talk to my lawyer."

Ashe pursed his lips. "You sure? My report will have to reflect your lack of cooperation. It will not work in your favor."

"Talk to my lawyer."

Ashe sighed. "If that's the way you want to go. What's his name?"

"When I hire him, he'll let you know." He stared at the door until Ashe took the hint, packed up his satchel, and walked out.

Active got coffee from the pot in the corner, set the cup on his blotter and stared at it for ninety seconds before drinking half of it down in a single scalding gulp. He punched Procopio's line and told her about Ashe's visit and the Jason Palmer case being reopened.

"No shit," she said. "That's some pressure."

"Yeah. I was just wondering—you getting anything like this from your chain of command?"

Procopio snorted. "No chance. The head of the criminal division's been around too long for even Mercer and her hack of an AG to fuck with."

"Must be nice," he said as he rang off.

The phone buzzed and Lucy's line lit up.

"What?"

"*Arii*, you don't have to yell at me. I'm hormonal right now. I cry when I see a diaper commercial."

"OK, I'm sorry. Hello, Lucy. How can I help you."

"I have the crime lab on the line. Just like you wanted."

He thanked her and punched the button when his outside line lit up. Then he asked for the technician who'd worked over Brad Mercer's snowgo, and asked the technician if they'd checked for blood on the top edge of the windshield. They had checked, and they had found traces. Enough to tell if it matched Pete Wise's blood? Active held his breath as the technician pulled the analysis up on his computer. Inconclusive, the technician said. Might be from Pete Wise, might not. Active punched off.

He finished the coffee, closed his eyes for several seconds, then punched the line for the fire hall.

"Gabe," he said. "Got a minute? I'd like to come over and catch up on the Jimmy Shaw case."

"Well, for us it's a search, not a case, but, yeah," Gabe said. "Come on over. Or I could come over there. Or we could just jaw on the phone. Ain't much to report, I'm afraid."

"Nah," Active said. "If I have to sit in this office one more minute, I'm gonna punch out a wall."

"I know the feeling," Gabe said. "I'll make new coffee. What I got left from this morning is down to street scrapings."

CHAPTER TWENTY-SEVEN

Monday, April 21

BEFORE HE COULD get out the door, his cell rang in its Bluetooth headpiece. He looked at the caller ID and sagged back into his chair.

"Morning, Suka."

"Morning, Nathan. Just calling to say hi. Hope your weather's nicer than here. We got the rain, the wind—I'm gettin' a terminal case of capital fever!"

"Well, we've got wind and snow today, but at least it's not raining."

"God, how I miss Chukchi! Why did I ever think I wanted to go to Juneau?"

"To what do I owe the pleasure?"

"Oh, I was just wondering—how's that Pete Wise thing coming? You know how much I want to help Grace and you on that ABI investigation but I just can't, not with that stupid Pete Wise business still hanging over us."

"You know I can't talk about Pete Wise," he said. "We'll say what we can at the hearing on Friday. But I can tell you we don't have any leads yet on whoever stole Brad's snowgo and dumped in the bay. You guys had any brainstorms on that?"

"Posilutely nothing," Mercer said. "It's a mystery!"

"That it is," Active said. "One of a great many going on in Chukchi these days."

"Oh, you mean like poor little Jimmy Shaw? Can you give me a report?"

"Gabe Reeder and his people from search and rescue are still at it, with public safety pitching in as I can spare my officers. Plus a lot of volunteers from the community, of course. But so far there's nothing."

"Is it a criminal matter?"

"Not yet. Not enough to go on. For now, all we can do is search."

"You need an Air Guard helicopter?"

"I don't think so. I think this is a ground search. Little kid like that can hardly have gotten out of town."

"You think it could be dogs?" Mercer asked. "Like last year?"

"God, I hope not." A year earlier, a pack of loose huskies had attacked a four-year-old on the street and mauled him to death before any of the adults nearby could drive them off.

"That was awful," Mercer said. "You beefed up animal control with the money I got, right?"

"Definitely. We have an animal control officer or a cop with animal-control certification on every patrol shift now. But I don't think it was dogs that got Jimmy Shaw. Even if nobody was around, dogs would have left something—clothes, bones, something."

"Let's change the subject," Mercer said.

"Certainly. As a matter of fact, Suka, there is something I was wondering about."

"Uh-huh?"

"I had a visit this morning from a guy—Bill Ashe, by name—from the Alaska Police Standards Council. He tells me you want them to yank my certification because I attacked you in Cowboy's tent up on the Isignaq."

Mercer said nothing. So did he. When it came to waiting it out, nobody ever beat him.

"Well," she said finally.

"We both know that's bullshit, if you'll pardon my French."

"That's no way to talk to a governor."

"And what you said is no way to talk to the people in charge of my peace officer certification. Only two people know what happened in that tent. We're both of them and we both know I didn't attack you. You said it yourself on YouTube and everywhere else on the Internet: You put those scratches there yourself with the zipper of Cowboy's sleeping bag."

"What can I say, Nathan. That's not how I remember it now that I've had time to think about it."

"Yeah? What changed your mind?"

"I don't know, I've been under a lot of stress lately. It all just got me thinking. What do I really know, and how do I know it? Who's my friend and who's not? The legislature blocking me at every turn, the lamestream media constantly calling me a twit and an airhead, even something as small as Brad's snowgo being stolen, and now this Pete Wise thing."

"Ah. So if the Pete Wise thing went away, that might reduce your stress level?"

"Oh, I'm sure. All I know is, it looks like you and Grace could use a friend in Juneau, and I could sure use one in Chukchi."

"I see."

"And I guess we'll see each other at the next hearing, huh? Maybe we can have a good chat then?"

"Maybe so, Suka."

Active shook his head to clear away the call, and backtracked to where he was before. Ah, Gabe Reeder.

He galloped downstairs as he debated transportation. The Chevy or the Yamaha? The debate lasted maybe a quarter-second. What he needed today was some wind and snow on his face and enough noise in his ears to drown out the din of unknowns about what had happened to Pete Wise and Jimmy Shaw, and about what Stuart Stewart and Bill Ashe were cooking up.

He cranked up the Yamaha and headed north up Third Street for the firehouse on Musk Ox Avenue. It was only a long block from Public Safety, but the ride was just what he needed. The wind, the noise, the snow freezing to his eyebrows—they made him feel like...like what? Like life might be worth living, like problems might be solvable. By the time he arrived, his mood had lifted to the point he spun a couple of donuts in the parking lot before he shut down and headed inside.

"Nathan," Gabe said as he came into the fire chief's office.

Active nodded, turned a chair around, and straddled it before the desk with its sign identifying Gabe as the chief. "Nothing new, I'm guessing?"

Gabe hooked one thumb in a suspender and scratched the tobacco-streaked beard as Active looked around the office. Familiar and mundane as the room was, it nonetheless reassured Active every time he entered. An all-business office—Gabe's helmet and grimy turnouts hanging from hooks on a wall and giving off the stench of smoke, three battered steel bookshelves stuffed with ring binders and crested with a row of manila folders in vertical racks, a corkboard with printouts pinned to it, a television that Active had never once seen on.

"Of course there's nothing new," Gabe said at length. He squirted tobacco juice into the water bottle he kept at hand for the purpose. "I would have called you."

"Of course," Active said. "But where are we? I know it's a search for you guys, but it's starting to look like a case to us."

Gabe sketched the effort again for Active—contacts with the boy's friends as identified by the family, searches of vacant buildings near the Shaw home on Beach Street.

"And your guys didn't get a funny feeling from any of the folks you talked to?"

He shook his head. "Nothing. I'm no cop, of course, but I do know most of them."

"We can re-interview them, if it comes to that," Active said.

"We're starting to widen out the area, now, so the search is gonna get slower and slower."

"I guess we should bring in a cadaver dog."

Gabe grunted. "Yeah, it's been close to forty-eight hours. If he's been outside in the weather all this time..."

"I think the closest one's in Anchorage. I'll see what I can do."

He was on the steps in front of the fire hall, blissed out again by the weather on his face, when his cell rang. He checked the caller ID.

"Hi, baby," he said. For now, he wouldn't think—or talk—about Bill Ashe's visit or Mercer's new version of their night in the tent. Grace, he knew, would believe and disbelieve it at the same time and they might never untangle it. He'd maintain.

"I have to see you," Grace said. "Can you come to the overlook on Beach Street?"

"What? Why not in my office or yours? Or home? Or how about the Arctic Dragon? It's almost lunchtime."

"Not on the phone or indoors. Just come."

She looked the loneliest he'd ever seen her as he parked his Yamaha behind her snowgo in front of the Dragon and crossed Beach Street to the overlook built as part of the seawall project. Her shoulders were hunched against the wind moving up the shore and her head was deep inside the hood of her parka.

"Baby," he said. "What gives?"

She mimed talking on a cell and pointed at the pocket where he kept his. He squinted in puzzlement, then pulled it out. "You need to borrow this?"

She shook her head and thumbed a slashing motion across her throat.

"Turn it off?"

She nodded, and he did. Her shoulders relaxed a little.

"What's this about?"

"I had a visit from the Chukchi social worker just now. They're doing an assessment."

"An assessment? My god, of what?"

"What do you think? Of whether I'm a fit mother. I know the gal pretty well—Minnie Wilkins—and she was really sympathetic, but apparently they got a referral from that Stewart guy that I'm an uncooperative witness and probable suspect in his investigation of Jason's murder and now they have to do an assessment of whether I can keep Nita."

"What did you tell her?"

"That she had to talk to my lawyer. But Nita told her something."

"Oh, no."

She grinned wryly. "She was home for lunch and Minnie asked her how she was. Before I could tell her not to answer, she said pretty good, except her mom wouldn't let her get a tattoo. Minnie said she agreed with me, so maybe I got a couple points there, ah?" She grinned again, but it stayed even farther from her eyes.

"You call Fortune?"

She nodded. "He said refer Minnie to him, which I

already did." She said it with a shaky little catch in her voice, almost a sob. "Which I suppose makes me even more uncooperative and suspicious. Oh, Nathan."

She rolled into his arms and he bear-hugged her for a long minute until her breathing steadied. She murmured something too muffled by his parka to be heard.

"What, baby?"

She pulled away a little. "Nothing, really. That bitch isn't getting Nita, is all."

"Minnie? I doubt she—"

"Helen Mercer. You know she's behind this." She watched his face and caught something. "And that's not all you know, is it?"

He looked away.

"Come on, dammit."

"The famous scratches?" He touched his neck. "Mercer filed a complaint with the Alaska Police Standards Council. There was an investigator in my office this morning, a guy named Bill Ashe. She says I gave them to her."

"She's accusing you of sexual assault now?"

He shook his head and briefed her on the complaint and the talk with Ashe.

"And what can this police council do if they find you...guilty, is that what it's called?"

"If they find the complaint justified, is the terminology. They can yank my certification. I'm out of work. Out of a career, basically."

"That bitch," she said through clenched teeth. "She's not getting you either."

"Oh, she made me an offer. Right after Bill Ashe dropped in."

"What?"

Active told her about the weird, elliptical conversation with Mercer.

"That bitch," Grace said.

"Yeah, you said that. Think I should cut a deal and call off the Pete Wise investigation?"

"You'd do that? You?"

He looked away. "For you."

"Hell, no," Grace said. "A, if she forces you to sell out, she'll still be getting you, in a way. And, B, how do we know she wouldn't want something else someday and hold all of the same crap over our heads." She grinned. "I said it before, I'll say it again, that bitch is not getting Nita and she's not getting you."

"Excellent," he said. "So I guess I need a lawyer now."

Her lips curved into a wolfish grin. "How about Alex Fortune? I've heard he's pretty good. And I guess we're both dirty rotten scoundrels now where Helen Mercer's concerned."

He grinned back. "I'll give him a call." He pulled out his phone and remembered it was turned off. He showed her the blank screen. "What's this about?"

She shrugged. "I don't trust that bitch. I have to assume she's tapped everything we own or use."

"I don't think even Helen Mercer can..."

"Can what?"

"Can..." He thought about it for a long time. "I don't know what she's capable of any more," he said. "You're right. We shouldn't say anything on the phone we don't want her to hear."

"Or at work or at home, either," she said.

"You do realize she's driving us both crazy?"

She grinned and kissed him goodbye and they promised to keep each other posted. She started across Beach Street as he turned on his phone and leaned on the rail of the overlook to call Alex Fortune, trying to decide how much to say now that somebody might be listening to everything he said.

The phone vibrated to let him know it had powered up, and he looked down to find the lawyer's name and number in his contacts, or, if it wasn't there, to search for it with the phone's tiny web browser.

Over the top of the screen, his eye caught something fluttering deep in the smashed ice along the seawall. He turned his attention back to the phone, then swore a silent oath and peered into the ice, his head suddenly hot.

It was dark down in the ice, and whatever was fluttering was dark, too. He needed a flashlight. Why hadn't he brought the Chevy? Getting down there was hopeless—the space was too narrow.

He galloped across Beach Street, cadged a flashlight out of the owner of the Arctic Dragon, and returned to play it into the chasm. Nope, just a bag of someone's trash. Even here, the ravens had been at it, with papers and disposable diapers spilling out, even a sheefish head.

He dialed Gabe Anders' number from memory and the fire chief came on.

"Gabe, Nathan," he said. "Have your guys searched the ice jammed up against the seawall from that storm last fall?"

There was a long silence. Then, "Shit. I'll get 'em started."

"I'll put everybody we've got available on it, too. And bring lights. It's dark down there."

Active ended the call to Gabe, then poked in 911 for Dispatch.

CHAPTER TWENTY-EIGHT

Monday, April 21

THE CALL CAME two hours later.

"We found him," Gabe said. "Looks like an accident to me, but I thought you'd want to see before we move him. We're up Beach Street near the docks."

Minutes later, Active pulled up and got out beside a cluster of police and firefighters gathered along the seawall. An ambulance was pulled up nearby, lights flashing.

Alan Long, he saw, was already as far down in the crevice as possible, at work with a department camera. He eased down beside Long, which still left his feet nearly a yard above the boy's head.

"Anything?"

"Nothing," Long said, his eye still on the viewfinder. "Take a look."

Active flicked through the camera's LCD. Long's flash had picked up a few details not visible to the naked eye in the gloom of the crevice. The boy looked like a frosted statue, his face surprisingly relaxed under the gray pallor, his mouth slightly open and even showing the hint of a six-year-old's gap-toothed smile.

"He looks kind of at peace, ah?" Long said.

"Maybe he just let go when the hypothermia set in and he started to feel warm."

"You see his right hand?"

Active studied one of the pictures. The boy had his arms raised, as if signaling for a basketball pass. His left hand was still mittened, but the other was bare, with bloodied fingertips. "He put up a good fight anyway."

He climbed out and Gabe walked over.

"Any hope of pulling him out?"

The fire chief shook his head. "Not a good idea, probably. Even if we could get a rope on him, I wouldn't wanna pull too hard. We'll get after it with chainsaws and cut the ice away till we get him loose."

Active nodded. "Take him to the hospital till we can ship him to the M.E. in Anchorage."

"You gonna talk to his folks?"

"Yeah, I guess it's on me. They here?"

"Nope," Anders said. "But I'm guessing they know already." He waved at the crowd gathered across the street. "Probably can't bear to watch and hope."

ACTIVE CLIMBED THE steps to the deck and passed through the *kunnichuk* of Urban and Sally Shaw's house on Second Street, a block back from Beach Street. Like most Chukchi houses, it was small—not more than seven hundred square feet, he guessed.

He knocked on the inner door and checked out the *kunnichuk* as he waited. A washer and dryer, a shotgun and two rifles in a corner, away from the moisture inside the house, an outboard motor in another corner, an empty dog cage with boots and shoes stored on top and inside, and a collection of the flattened cardboard boxes that women spread on the floor to use for skinning and cutting game.

Inside, someone turned off a TV, then the door opened to reveal a mid-forties Inupiat woman with wet, red eyes behind her glasses. Active took off his hat and dipped his head. "You heard?"

She raised her eyebrows. "My sister call us from where they find him. You come visit?"

She led him down a hall into the house's main room—two rooms, really—with a kitchen on one side and a living room on the other, separated by head-height cabinets in the kitchen. There was no dining table, he saw, a fact no doubt explained by the tininess of the kitchen and the presence of—he took a moment to count—five kids on the couch and floor, and a very old *aana* in a recliner who appeared oblivious to all around her. The three kids old enough to know what was happening stared at him and their mother. A man about her age emerged from a bedroom and came down the hall.

"Mr. Shaw? I'm Chief Active." He put out his hand. "I'm sorry for your trouble."

The man put out his hand for a single pump. "Urban Shaw."

"Can we go talk in the *kunnichuk*? He gestured at the kids.

"Maybe down there." Shaw pointed down the hall.

"Me, too?" said his wife.

Active nodded and they moved down the hall. He heard the TV come on behind them—a Pokemon cartoon from the sound of it—and they moved into a bedroom and closed the door.

"I know you've talked to one of our officers already, and somebody from the fire department, but could you tell me what happened?"

Urban Shaw started to speak, then stopped and pinched the bridge of his nose. "Two days ago," he said, "Jimmy's being bossy around the house, same like always, so we tell him, 'Go play out.' When he's not back around midnight, we call you guys but nobody never find him till now. He was down in the ice by Beach Street?"

Active nodded. "Between the ice and the seawall. It looks like he fell in and couldn't get out."

"Or maybe he crawl in to see what's down there," Urban said. "That's Jimmy, all right, he always *pukuk*." He chuckled a little bit. It ended with a catch in his throat. His wife started to sniffle, and wiped her nose with a tissue from a pocket in a pilled and baggy pair of flannel pants.

"Did he go out by himself a lot?"

Sally Shaw raised her eyebrows. "He's not like our other kids. He won't sit on that couch and watch TV for nothing. If none of them other kids won't go play out, he'll drive us crazy till we let him go by himself."

"He always pester me to caribou hunting already," Urban said. "I was gonna take him, all right, but I tease him he's not big enough yet and he sure get mad."

"Did he ever get lost before or come home late?"

Both Shaws squinted in negation. "Not never ever," Sally said.

HE CALLED PROCOPIO from his office and told her about the discovery on Beach Street.

"Was he injured before he went into the crevice?"

"No idea yet. We couldn't get closer than a couple of feet. They're having to cut the ice away with chainsaws before they can even get him out."

"Poor kid," Procopio said. "These Chukchi parents. You see little kids playing out by themselves all hours, it's a wonder this doesn't happen more."

"You know the the official Chukchi motto, right?"

"Let 'em."

"About pretty much everything," he said. "Anyway, I called the hospital on the way back to the office and asked the doc there to look him over before they get him ready to ship down to the medical examiner and let me know what he finds. I'm guessing it'll be nothing except whatever he got while he was down there."

"My guess, too," Procopio said. "I won't even open a file on it unless something turns up."

THE NEXT MORNING, Active's outside line lit up while he was still unloading his briefcase. "Chief Active," he said.

"You check your email yet?" asked the voice of Theresa Procopio.

"Sorry, I'm running a little late today. Wrote a major equipment violation on a broken tail light on the way in, just so the borough assembly will know we do something around here. Then I went by the hospital to ask about Jimmy Shaw."

"Oh, yeah. They find anything?"

"Nothing to indicate he was hurt in any way before he

went in. I doubt the M.E. Will find anything different. No need to start a file on it, I guess.'"

"I'm guessing that's the only good news we're gonna get today. The Mercers just got a two-week postponement on the Pete Wise hearing."

"What? How?"

"Stein granted the motion without talking to me is how. I think he's hoping it'll all go away and we'll come in with some kind of agreement on getting into Pete's files."

Active dropped into his chair and turned on his computer. "What grounds?"

He could hear the shrug in Procopio's voice. "They need more time to prepare."

"Two weeks? That's—"

"I know, total bullshit."

"Can we undo this?"

"I'll go over the motion again and look for any chinks. But Stein is seeing things their way so far."

They rang off and Active put away his briefcase as his computer booted up.

He was just launching his email program when his cell phone went off. He froze for a moment when he saw the caller ID. He took a deep breath and tapped the call online.

"Morning, Suka. How are things in Juneau?"

"I thought you were my friend."

"I am. You know that."

"I know you violated a court order and I will have your ass for it. You're hanging out there now."

"What are you talking about?"

"You're saying you didn't do this?"

"Do what?"

"Check your email and call me. And don't talk to Theresa Procopio about it. Or Grace."

"OK."

"And if I don't answer, leave a voicemail. I'll be on a plane."

"A plane?" Now he recognized the noise behind her call. She was in an airport.

"I'm on the way up there. I'm in Anchorage and I'm booked on the next flight. In fact, don't call me. Meet me at the house at, what time does it get in, hang on, eleven-thirty, supposedly, but it is Alaska Airlines. Meet me at the house at noon."

"The house? Whose—"

"My house, Nathan. Be alone and don't be late."

"Will Brad be there or is—"

"He's at the mine. It's just me."

She hung up, and he stared at his phone in disbelief for several seconds.

He turned to his email screen. At the top, the usual clutter of official stuff, fun stuff, and spam—the Division of Retirement and Benefits, the Alaska Peace Officers Association, Groupon, a "Private email" from one Y. Fang about a major opportunity, the usual "Good morning, Sweetie" from Martha and "Kasmooch" from Grace, the message from the Mercers' lawyer about the hearing postponement.

And one from Pete Wise, with the subject line, "The files you wanted."

CHAPTER TWENTY-NINE

Tuesday, April 22

ACTIVE AND THERESA Procopio bent their heads over his printout of the DNA results attached to Pete Wise's email.

"You sure you don't know how this happened?" Procopio asked. "You got a friend in the court system you never told me about?"

"Scout's honor," Active said. "I'm as dumbfounded as you."

"Any guesses?"

"Can I plead the Fifth?"

"Why not? I'm in contempt of court just looking at this. At least I can plead ignorance about where it came from when I get busted."

They resumed their scrutiny of the report. "One more time, OK? I need to make sure I got it."

"All that matters is what it says at the top and bottom."

"'DNA Paternity Inclusion,' " he read at the top. "'The alleged father is not excluded as the biological father of the child.' "

"And there you have it."

"You sure? It says Pete can't be excluded. Isn't that theoretically true of every male on earth? And there's no results from Brad here. It could still be him, right?"

"Read the fine print at the bottom again."

Active bent over it. "'Based on the genetic testing results obtained by PCR analysis of STR loci, the probability of paternity is greater than nine-nine-point-nine-nine percent.' Yeah, I'd take those odds in Vegas any time."

"Mm-hmm."

"So that's why Mercer was so worried? If Pete had gotten into court with this, it would have been game over?"

Procopio shook her head. "Not hardly. Pete ordered this thing off Amazon and took the samples himself and—"

"How would he get a swab from Pudu?"

"Fuck if I know. But he did, according to this. The point is, a DNA test is only admissible if the court orders it and the samples are taken by an independent third party and tested by an approved lab."

"And so that means...Where does it leave us, actually?"

"Oh, Mercer would have fought it like hell in court, but there's not much doubt about it for practical purposes. Pete Wise was Helen Mercer's baby daddy, at least for Pudu."

"Last thing she needed was having this dragged out into public view, I guess. You want a copy?"

She stood and headed for the door. "Absolutely not. I haven't even seen it yet." She paused on her way out. "I'm just glad I didn't get that damned email, too."

Minutes later, Active stopped his Chevy before the women's center. There was no sign of Grace outside, so he called on his cell.

"Can you come out for a minute?" he asked when she answered. "And leave your phone inside."

He dropped his own phone into the cupholder, got out and crossed Beach Street, and leaned on the seawall rail.

"What?" she said from behind him.

He turned. "Is Sonny safe?"

"Ah. You figured it out." She wore a quizzical grin.

He winked in acknowledgment. But he said, "Not officially, no."

"Interesting reading, huh?"

"Very. But, again, Sonny. He does work on the computers at Chukchi Telephone and Pete did have his email with them. That's a little close for comfort, isn't it?"

"Terms like the Tor client were mentioned," Grace said. "And anonymous relay servers."

"Ah. The traffic passes through so many servers and and so much encryption, nobody can track it? Or something like that?"

"Maybe the NSA could untangle it, but Helen Mercer can't," Grace said.

"We may both have to lie about this."

The grin came back. "Of course. But you'll put it to good use, yes?"

"Absolutely."

At noon, he went through the *kunnichuk* and knocked on the inner door of the Mercer house. It was dead silent inside and he started to wonder if Alaska Airlines was behind schedule today. Or if Mercer had pulled a Mercer and changed her mind. No, the *kunnichuk* door would be locked if the place was empty.

He knocked again, waited a half-minute, and was pulling out his cell phone to call her when the knob rattled and the door opened to reveal her with a thick white towel wrapped turban-style around her head and some of the rest of her clad in a satiny bathrobe in her signature scarlet. A bathrobe short enough to display the thigh gap that had contributed to her fame in the rancid swamps of the Internet, and with nothing under, judging from how it draped off her nipples. Her feet were bare.

"Hi, Nathan. Sorry to keep you waiting." She waved at the robe and towel. "I just got out of the shower. I didn't have time for one before I left Juneau this morning. Your email was quite the attention-getter."

"Again, it wasn't mine. I was as surprised as you."

"Mm-hmm. Well, be that as it may, come on in." She nodded toward a sofa and a jade-topped coffee table, no doubt from the big mine on the upper Isignaq. "Did you bring a printout?"

"I think I can remember the gist of it."

"I'll get mine." She vanished into the kitchen and returned with a black crocodile-skin tote, the robe swinging out a little as she set the bag on the coffee table and opened it. She met his eyes for a moment, then re-belted the robe. "Sorry. I'm a bit distracted."

"No problem. Just tell me why we're here."

She sat beside him on the sofa and opened a file folder labeled "Wise." The DNA report was on top. "Assuming you weren't behind this leak, which I'm not conceding, how on earth did somebody do it? Get into Pete's email and re-send all this stuff?"

"So this matches what you guys got as respondents in the suit?"

"Identical. And however it happened, why would Pete think he could get away with this?"

"With what?" he asked. "I mean, a DNA test—"

"Oh, that's bullshit. There's no way he could get a

sample from Pudu. He forged this."

"How would he do that?"

"I don't know. The Internet."

"There's an easy way to prove it."

"You mean a real test?"

"I had the medical examiner take a sample from Pete's body. We can get a swab from Pudu, run the test, and it's over. If you're telling the truth."

"If? Fuck you, Nathan. I oughta know if I ever slept with Pete Wise and I didn't!"

"Then why not end this?"

"Because it's the kind of bullshit I get all the time. If I start going along with every crazy demand some wacko bird comes up with, it'll never end."

"Wacko bird? Pete was a pretty straight shooter, from all I've heard. If he's not the father, why would he do this?

"He had a crush on me in high school when I was coaching basketball and he never got over it. Calling the house all the time, my office in Juneau, practically a stalker. Brad got into it with him a couple times, including the night before this all happened, but it didn't make any difference. I think he actually believed he was Pudu's father." She leaned back on the couch, unwrapped the towel, and raked her fingers through her hair, eyes closed. "God, this is exhausting."

The robe slipped off of one thigh, and the top gapped open to show a pretty nice breast, suspiciously nice, considering her age and the fact she had four kids.

This time she didn't notice, or didn't mind. He watched the show, wondering if she was watching back from the corner of her eye.

After a couple of minutes, she shook her head as if to clear it and sat up. The robe gapped open a little more. She closed it and tightened the belt and caught his gaze with a knowing smile.

He rose from the sofa. "That's it? This is why you got me over here?"

"That's it. I thought you were my friend. I thought if I looked you in the eye, you'd believe me and we could get this out of our lives." She shrugged and bit her lip.

"One more question before I go?"

"Sure," she said in an exhausted tone. "Anything."

"Everything you say makes sense. But none of it explains why you killed Pete Wise."

"You still don't believe me."

"Of course not. Why did you do it? You wouldn't be the the first politician with an active sex life. You won't be the last. You could have talked your way past a love child."

She buried her face in her hands. "Nathan."

"Yes?"

"It was Brad. I'm sure it was Brad."

CHAPTER THIRTY

Tuesday, April 22

"BRAD KILLED PETE Wise? You expect me to believe that?"

"I don't know what to expect from you anymore. I thought you were my friend. God knows, I need one." She stood and the robe slipped off her shoulders a little. She turned her eyes full on him, the eyelashes jeweled with tears. "And now I think my husband's a murderer."

"You pull that up and I'll listen."

She sighed, adjusted the robe, and tightened the belt. "Coffee or something?" She pointed at the sofa.

"No thanks, just the story." He slipped his notebook out of a pocket.

"That morning, what was it a week...?"

He nodded. "A week ago today, yes."

"It seems like a year."

"It does. I can imagine what it's been like for you."

"You can't, but thanks."

"So. That morning."

"It was about five-thirty, six, maybe. The phone goes off on Brad's nightstand so I figure he'll get it and I try to ignore it and go back to sleep. Then it rings again and I poke Brad to wake up and get it, he always sleeps like a hibernating bear, because it might be my folks with some kind of problem with the kids. But Brad's not there, so I figure he's in the john or already out getting packed or something and I grab it and it's him."

Active wrote "phone—5:30/6?" in his notebook. "And then what happened?"

"I answer it and he tells me he's out for a ride and he's lost his snowgo through the ice up by the mouth of the Katonak and he wants me to come get him on mine."

"Mm-hmm. So off you go."

"I knew roughly where the spot was so I go up there and call him on my cell when I get close and he talks me in. I pick him up and we come back here and go back to bed for a couple hours before we have to get organized for our Juneau trip."

"Why did you lie about the snowgo being stolen when we called about it?"

"Brad swore he wasn't the one who hit Pete and didn't want me to get dragged into it. I give him credit for that."

"And you believed him?"

She only nodded. He cocked his head and waited her out for a thirty-count. He kept his eyes on her face to avoid distraction, and noticed for the first time that she seemed to have had time to put on makeup after her shower. She didn't speak.

"Did you and Brad fight after Pete showed up the night before? Is that how you got the cut on your forehead I saw when I took you to the airport that morning?"

She raised her eyebrows in assent and touched the spot, which still showed a faint bruise. "Brad had been drinking some and he got a little out of hand, yeah. The bastard, he always suspected Pete was telling the truth about Pudu."

"But you didn't file a domestic violence complaint?"

"Of course not. I couldn't stand the publicity."

"There was a 911 call from your place a few years back. Same thing?"

"Uh-huh. Pete came over that time, too, Brad went after him, and they got into it. Pete left and then Brad came after me so I made the call. He calmed down, and I canceled it."

"Uh-huh." He put it all into his notes.

"That's why, as soon as I heard Pete was dead, I started to wonder. Brad denied it, but I guess if your lab says it was his snowgo that hit Pete, then it's over?"

"Not exactly. The lab can't tell us who was driving yet, but there was blood on the windscreen. Can we get a sample from you for comparison purposes? That would take you out of the picture and point the finger at Brad even more."

She gazed off to the right for a moment. "I suppose I should ask my lawyer first."

She returned her eyes to his. Summer was in them, and a smile on her lips. "Or maybe there's another way to handle this." The feline rumble he had heard on the Isignaq was back in her voice.

"Such as?"

"I see what I can do about Grace's murder investigation and the children's services inquiry into Nita's situation and I withdraw my complaint to the police standards council against you."

"And me?"

"You see what you can do about the Pete Wise investigation."

"No, thanks," he said. "Not my kind of deal."

"And we spend the afternoon together. Trust me, you'll never forget it." She slipped the robe off her shoulders and let it drop away and untied the belt. She put a hand between his thighs and winked. "That a Glock in your pocket or are you just happy to see me?"

He pulled her hand away and stood up. "Not really."

She eyed him, one hand on a confident, cocked hip. "Seriously. You don't see anything you like?"

"Actually, I see a couple."

She gave her implants a quick glance and chuckled. The triumphant grin returned and she spread her arms. "They're all yours." Her eyes widened in invitation and perhaps even real anticipation.

"I see you're still playing me. And I see you're desperate."

"What?" Her face went rigid and her lips flattened to a thin slash.

"Besides, you're too old for me. And I'm allergic to silicone." He pointed.

She raked her nails across his cheek, eyes lethal with fury, focused like a wolf circling a caribou.

"Jesus," he said.

She drew back for another slash but he grabbed her biceps, shook her hard once, and immobilized her. He realized with shock that her nipples were erect and he scented musk in the air. Could this be what she liked?

The tension drained out of her.

"OK now?"

"Sorry, Nathan," she said with something like a sob. "No woman likes to hear something like that."

He gentled his face and handed her his handkerchief. "I'm sorry, too. That was unkind of me."

She blew her nose and passed back the handkerchief, then pushed his arms apart and tried to fold into them.

"Probably better if we don't touch. And if you put this back on." He scooped the robe off the sofa. She slapped it away.

Her nipples, he noticed, were normal-sized again, but the eyes were still like a wolf's.

"Thanks for trying to rape me, asshole." She gestured at the finger marks forming angry and red on her arms. "These plus those wounds on your cheek plus your little number in the tent—you're done."

He touched his cheek and came away with blood.

"Powerful evidence, all right," he said. "How about we get some pictures?"

He pulled out his phone and and took a selfie of his damaged cheek. Then he pointed it at her nude upper body. "You?"

"Get out, asshole! Get the fuck out! And get yourself a fucking lawyer."

ACTIVE CLICKED OFF the voice recorder on his phone and looked around the little audience gathered before his desk. Patrick Carnaby, Theresa Procopio, and Alan Long were still processing what they'd just heard with various expressions of disbelief.

Active cleared his throat. "Well?"

Finally Carnaby spoke. "She was naked?"

"Like the day she was born."

The Trooper chief shook his head. "How'd she look?"

"She wore it well, actually. Seemed to take to it naturally."

"But you told her she was too old and her boobs were fake?"

"I did."

"That was cold, Nathan."

"You didn't even squeeze them to make sure?" Long asked. "*Arii!*" he said as Procopio elbowed him in the shoulder.

"You kidding?" Active said. "I'm gonna touch that woman after what she's already accused me of? I mean, except for restraining her when she was trying to rip my face off." He gestured at his lacerated cheek.

"I'd'a ripped off more than your face," Procopio said. "And gouged out your fucking eyes with my other hand."

There was a silence as the three men involuntarily checked her chest for signs of enhancement.

Procopio noticed. "Shut up," she said.

Nobody continued to speak, until Active screwed up his courage. "You told me to push her when we talked about this before I went over."

Procopio grimaced. "But that? What is wrong with you, saying that to a woman? And she's standing there naked, offering you everything she's got, and you're not tempted? Not even slightly? Not even for a quickie?"

More silence. This time, Active sensed, the other two men were picturing the scene. Especially the governor's part in it. And imagining in the consequence-free fantasy world of the male libido what they would have done with the opportunity.

"Leave my DNA in that woman?" Active said. "Sure, for her rape kit." He tapped his phone and looked at the prosecutor. "That voice recorder app has a time-stamp feature. Any forensics test will show that it ran continuously from the time I turned it on here in this office in your presence, as verbally instructed, until I turned it off, also in your presence under verbal instruction, when I got back."

Procopio said "Still" and left her seat to pace in front of Active's window. Six feet right, six left, repeat.

"If she does file rape charges against you with the state, we'll need a copy of that," Carnaby said. "We play it for her, tell her it'll come into evidence at the trial, that'll surely be the end of it."

"How you doing, counselor?" Active said.

"Fucking patriarchy," she muttered. "Woman gets into a position of power, first thing happens is, the patriarchy uses her sexuality to bring her down."

"So you're on her side now?" Carnaby said.

"Actually, it seemed like she was using her sexuality to bring me down," Active said.

"Fuck all of you and your fucking XY chromosomes and your fucking testosterone and your fucking measuring contests!"

"Maybe this is the first time it ever didn't work for her," Carnaby said. "Like the queen in, what was it? Cinderella? With the mirror, mirror, on the wall?"

"It was Snow White, moron, and fuck you anyway," Procopio growled.

"Maybe some coffee," Active said. He called and asked Lucy to bring some up.

"Tea for me," Procopio growled.

"And tea for Theresa," he said into the phone.

Time passed. They gossiped about the sheefish derby and the sex lives of various Chukchi luminaries excluding themselves. The coffee and tea arrived. Procopio scooped up her cup and resumed pacing by the window. They gossiped about when the sea ice might go out, who was the dumbest state legislator, and whether the U.S. Supreme Court was more of a threat or a menace when it came to undermining law enforcement.

Finally, Procopio left the window and set down her cup and cleared her throat. "Sorry, gentlemen. Sometimes my inner feminist gets the better of me. So what do we have here?" She settled into her chair.

"Well," Active ventured. "She did seem to finger Brad, which, if I understand cor—"

"You do understand correctly. Spousal privilege always makes this kind of thing iffy. If she refuses to testify about it, we can't make her."

Carnaby and Long nodded.

"But if she did file a rape charge and I did use the recording in my defense, then it would be on the record, yes?"

"Hmm," Carnaby said with a look at Procopio.

Procopio thought it over. "It might open the door a crack, but probably not one wide enough to be useful and only after a huge fight. The murder case against Brad would be a separate and unrelated proceeding from the rape charge. Better if Brad told the same story in his own words for some reason. Confessed, essentially."

The other three nodded.

"So what do we have?"

Procopio ticked the points off on her fingers.

"One, for whatever good it will do us, Helen Mercer does implicate Brad big-time and her story does fits the known facts."

Her audience nodded, and Active made notes.

"Two, she herself is an accomplice after the fact, by trying to scare Nathan off the case except, if we do manage to get her to testify against Brad into court, we don't want to be charging our own witness with a crime in the same case. So that's off-limits.

"Three, she tried to bribe Nathan with sex to drop his investigation."

"Yeah, except does that count?" Carnaby asked. "I mean, he told her it was valueless. What kind of bribe is that?"

"Fuck you very much for that helpful analysis, captain. If I may proceed?"

Carnaby grinned and fell silent.

Procopio was up to the little finger of her left hand as she ticked off the next one. "Four, she offered to use her influence to terminate the children's services and murder investigations of Grace, and the police standards investigation of Nathan. That's definitely official misconduct, times three."

Procopio switched hands. "And, five, the rape charge, if she files it, might be considered false swearing, if the recording makes her look ridiculous enough."

"What a woman," Long said.

"And, six, now what?" Active said. "I'd like to see the phone records from the morning in question. Can we get a warrant or will Stein think it's a fishing expedition like McConnell said in court the other day?"

"Fishing expedition's ass," Procopio said. "Give me a copy of the DNA tests, I'll take that into court along with an affidavit saying we had nothing to do with the leak and don't know how it happened. Then, after Judge Stein's head explodes and he finishes gluing it back together, I'll play the recording for him, he'll ask if you got a picture of her naked, damn his eyes, and, then, yeah, we'll get a warrant for the phone records. The landline records will be pretty quick, and the cells, too, if they're from Chukchi Telephone Co-Op. Longer if they have some other provider."

"Hers is from Chukchi Telephone, all right," Active said. "His, I've never called or had a call from."

"If Chukchi Telephone's got it, they'll give it to us. If not, we can figure out his number from her records and go after his calls, too."

Active scratched his chin. "I'm assuming I don't have enough yet to arrest Brad?"

"Not quite. If we're going after these people, we can't afford any loose ends.

"Then I think he oughta hear this recording. Agreed?"

All parties nodded.

"But what if she gets to him first?" Carnaby asked.

"And tells him what?" Procopio asked. "'I just hung Pete Wise's murder on you and the cops are on their way'?"

CHAPTER THIRTY-ONE

Tuesday, April 22

CLIMBING INTO COWBOY Decker's Cessna was like a visit to a planet where things were simple and concrete. The smells of avgas, oil, and upholstery, the groan that built to a steady rumble as Cowboy cranked the engine, the squawk of the radio in the headset as he talked to the FAA across the field.

"How ya been, Nathan?" Cowboy asked over the headset as the plane moved out of the Lienhofer tiedowns. "Haven't hardly talked to you since our little adventure on the Isignaq."

"Don't remind me," Active said.

"Grace believe you about those scratches on the governor's neck?"

"I think so."

"Long as she does, I do. Smart woman."

"Very," Active said.

"So what's this trip about?"

"Police business. Very hush-hush."

"Want me to wait?"

Active pondered. The first half hour of ground time for the Lienhofer Cessna was free, but after that it was half the air-time rate. And his department budget was always in a bind. On the other hand, if Cowboy left, it would cost another round trip to call him back. Plus, it was possible Active would have the governor's husband in shackles while he awaited Cowboy's return, no doubt in some highly visible location.

"Give me the free half hour," he said. "Then take off

if I don't show up or send somebody out to talk to you."

"We taking a prisoner with us? That's extra."

"Don't know yet."

Cowboy turned east to taxi down the runway for takeoff. The stiff west wind left over from yesterday rocked the wings and battered the Cessna's control surfaces.

"Breezy day," Active said.

The pilot shrugged. "Twenty-knot winds, gusting thirty. No problemo."

"How about at the mine?"

"Little worse than here. Two-thousand-foot ceiling, ten-mile visibility, wind about thirty, gusting forty, which could be a problem if it wasn't blowing straight down the runway, which it is. Some turbulence close to the mountains. Another beautiful day in paradise."

Halfway down the runway, Decker pivoted the plane to point west and pushed in the throttle. The engine roared, the Cessna rolled, then a gust caught them and they were airborne. "Feel her kind of relax there?" Cowboy asked. "She's more at home up here."

They crawled across the white landscape just below the cloud layer. Active watched the wind-driven snow stream off the pressure ridges in the ice on Chukchi Bay, then ghost over the tundra and scrub spruce as they crossed into the Katonak Flats. There was nothing to do and not much to say, so he leaned against the Cessna's door for a nap.

He awoke when his head jolted against the door frame. Turbulence never seemed to bother Cowboy, presumably because he knew when it was dangerous to the Cessna and when it wasn't. But Active didn't, and something in the back of his mind always told him the next jolt would rip off the wings. He tightened his harness.

STAN JONES

"Here we go." Cowboy pointed through the snow haze blowing off the ridges.

Active picked up the web of roads surrounding the mine, then the diagonal slash of the runway, then the central complex a mile past that.

From the air, the scene looked so sterile that, except for the snow on the ground, it might have been a moon colony. The treeless mountain bowl, the huge, blocky industrial buildings with pickups, SUVs, earth movers, ore haulers, and snowmobiles scattered around, a dirt-walled tailings lake iced over in the cold. And the scar of the mine itself, surrounding everything in tiers that marched up the sides of the bowl like terraced farmland in China or India, except that the crop here was dollars.

"Can you get security on the radio?" Active asked through the headset. "I called ahead and a guy named Danny Kavik is supposed to meet me at the airport."

"Hang on." Cowboy switched frequencies, identified himself, and got Gray Wolf security to come up. "Yeah, I've got Nathan Active from Chukchi Public Safety here. He's supposed to meet Danny Kavik?"

"Roger that," security said. "He's on his way."

Cowboy throttled back and lowered his wing flaps a little to set up for landing. Cowboy, Active knew, could grease a plane on smoother than anybody. Sometimes, a Cowboy Decker landing was so soft Active wouldn't awaken from a mid-air nap until the pilot reached the tiedowns and cut his engine. Not today. Today, the approach was like driving a pickup down a staircase. Active tried to tighten his harness again, but there was no more give.

The plane finally banged into the runway and bounced, bounced again, then touched down a third time and stuck. Cowboy taxied to the Gray Wolf tiedowns and they waited for Danny Kavik as the

Cessna rocked in the gusts.

Finally Active spotted a Suburban painted in the official Gray Wolf colors of blue, white, and green barreling down the side of the runway. The driver stopped in front of the plane. Active zipped up, pulled on his gloves, and pushed his door open against the wind, then fought to hold it open with his shoulder as he climbed to the ground. He raced to the Suburban, grabbed the handle and wrenched the door open, then squeezed into the cab.

The driver put out a hand. "Danny Kavik."

Kavik was a lean, young Inupiaq in a uniform and buzz-cut and the look of a man either born or determined to be a cop.

Active gave the hand a single pump. "Danny."

"We got it set up like you wanted," Kavik said as he started for the central complex. "We told him you were coming in to update him on a new development in the Pete Wise case. His shift's over in a few minutes, so we didn't even have to pull him off duty."

"Any idea if he's talked to his wife since lunch?"

Kavik thought it over, then shook his head. "His crew's been on shift all day, wiring up some new housing modules. Personal calls are against the rules, unless it's an emergency."

"Thanks, man."

"Still got my application?"

"I do," Active said. "Still no openings, but you're on the short list for the next one that comes up."

"Thanks. I need to get back to Chukchi if I can. My mom's pretty sick and she needs help riding herd on the other kids."

"You bet. And I need more local people on my force. Nothing against the Anchorage and Mat-Su guys that sign up for the two-on and two-off, but some actual community policing would be nice."

Kavik pulled in at an office with a "Gray Wolf Security" sign outside and turned off the Suburban. "We got a conference room in here you can use. Somebody's gonna bring Brad over in a few minutes."

Kavik showed Active in, waved at a uniformed woman at a radio console, and led him to the conference room.

"You want coffee or something?"

"Sure," Active said. "And bring some for Brad, too."

Kavik left. Active shrugged out of his parka, checked the recording on his phone and put it on the table. Then he pulled his digital recorder out of his briefcase, started it, and put it into the front pocket of his uniform shirt. Finally he put two pens and a legal pad on the table in front of him.

Kay-Chuck played from somewhere nearby, but not loud enough to interfere with the recording. Two women passed in the hall outside, discussing a boss who was either cute or creepy, Active couldn't quite make it out. Kavik returned with a thermos of coffee, two cups, and Brad Mercer.

"Mr. Mercer." Active stood and put out his hand.

Mercer looked wary, but took it. "Chief."

Active sat. Mercer didn't look ready to sit, but couldn't seem to think of an alternative. He took a chair across the table. Kavik eased out and let the door shut behind him without a sound.

"Coffee?"

Mercer waved it off. "They said there's news on the Pete Wise case?"

"Well, as a matter of fact, your wife—"

Mercer looked even warier now.

Active tapped his phone. "Look, why don't I play something for you before we talk? It'll make more sense. Your wife flew into Chukchi today, did you know that?"

"She what?"

"Uh-huh. And she asked me to meet her at your house, which I did. And she came to the door in a scarlet robe with a towel on her head."

"The satin one?"

Active raised his eyebrows.

"I got her that in Vegas!"

Active put his phone on speaker and started the playback from where he'd cued it, when Helen Mercer had said, "I just got out of the shower."

Active let it run to the the point where he left the house, climbed into his Chevy and called in to Dispatch. He looked at Mercer, who sat in silence for perhaps thirty seconds.

"She said I killed Pete Wise?"

"You heard it."

"The lying bitch!" Mercer slammed a hand down on the table. "Goddamit, if somebody killed him it was her. Everything she said about that morning is true, except the names are reversed. She was the one called me from out on the ice, then I was the one went and got her. That bitch, I should have figured something was screwy when I saw she took my snowgo. I had to take hers. It's purple. Purple!"

"What would she be doing out there that time of morning?"

"She spent the night with Pete so he'd drop his lawsuit. But when they woke up, he told her 'thanks for the *quiyuk*' and said he wasn't gonna drop it. So she got pissed and took a ride to cool off. That's what she said."

"Wait. You knew they were together that night? And you went along with it?"

"Sure, Pete and me was *nuliagatagiik*."

"*Nuliaga*...I don't know that word."

"It's what the old-timers used to call it when a woman

would have two husbands and they were friends. She was pregnant when I married her, and neither Pete nor me knew for sure which one of us—"

Active struggled to keep his mask on. "You shared her? And you both knew? And neither one minded?"

Mercer nodded. "Right up till Pete got killed. That's what I'm saying, we were *nuliagatagiik*. A few people still do it around here even if they don't talk about it any more. Pete and I were close to the same age, good buddies in high school, played basketball together, which is when it started, hunted and fished together, I taught him to mush. But when she got started in politics, she told Pete and me to stop buddying around so it wouldn't attract so much attention, so we did.

"What about her?"

"No way was she gonna stop. Even though Helen's not Eskimo, she took to it like she was. Just a woman who needs more than one man and a lot of *quiyuk*. And Pete could light her on fire even better than me. Whenever she was in town, she'd try to slip over to his place and spend some time. That's why he lived alone and never had a girlfriend, even on the side, as far as I know. He couldn't see past her. I still don't know how the hell they got away with it all this time. I mean, this is Chukchi. Everybody knows your business."

"I still—but you guys were both OK with this?"

"Not at first. At first we beat each other up. Lots of times. Finally we all three figured out one of us would kill the other one if we didn't become *nuliagatagiik*, so we did."

"That's what the old 911 call was about?"

Mercer raised his eyebrows. "Me and Pete got into it again and she made the call. Then she told us to stop our bullshit or she'd cut us both off. So we promised we would and she canceled the call. After that, we was *nuliagatagiik*."

"What about the cut over her eye the morning Pete was killed?"

Mercer shrugged. "I dunno. She said she got it when the snowgo went through the ice. Doesn't make much sense, now that I think about it. Maybe she banged herself up when she hit Pete?"

Active made notes on his pad to stall for time. "All right, how about we back up and go through that whole day and evening before Pete was killed? Pete comes to your place to make his offer about the suit, or he does it by phone, or what?"

"No, it was at the conference."

"Conference?"

"Yeah, it was that Monday afternoon before the mushers' banquet. Pete and us, plus our lawyer, that McConnell guy. We were all on the phone so nobody would see Pete with Helen."

"And what happens at the conference?"

"Pete wants to keep on with this village arrangement we've had all these years, just make it official so she won't take Pudu away from Chukchi permanently—"

"Village arrangement?"

"We always let Pudu spend time with Pete."

"I thought you didn't know Pete was the father."

Mercer shook his head. "Didn't know, but figured. So did Pete. Pudu looks a lot more like him than me. Or any other guy around here."

Active made notes and kept silent. Why interrupt the flow?

"But Pudu never knew Pete might be his father," Mercer went on. "He thought he was just a family friend, some kind of distant cousin, maybe, who'd take him hunting and fishing, coach him in basketball, that kinda stuff."

"If it worked all this time, why did Pete want to stir up trouble with his lawsuit?"

"Helen never did really like them hanging out. She doesn't want Pudu to go village, is how she puts it, and she was jealous of how much he liked Pete. So Pete was afraid if she got a job in Washington, she'd take Pudu away and he'd never come back. That's when Pete filed his suit."

"Pete thought she could get elected to national office?" Active asked. "Seriously? After what happened the last time she tried it? Not to mention what happened when our last female governor tried the same thing?"

"No, that's not her plan. I don't understand how this political stuff works, I'm just an electrician and a dog musher and a caribou hunter, all right. But I think she said she was trying to get enough influence going into the convention to horse trade for a big job if the ticket won. Ambassador to Russia, maybe?"

Nathan marveled for a few moments. Helen Mercer in Moscow? Wining and dining oligarchs and the Russian president? "So you have your conference and Pete won't agree to anything but a formal custody arrangement because she might take Pudu to Washington?"

Mercer raised his eyebrows. "I didn't like the idea either. Pudu's a Chukchi kid, like Pete and me. He'd go crazy back there, especially if she went to Russia, probably get into all kinds of trouble and stuff. So when Pete wanted to do the DNA test, I said I'd get the sample from Pudu—"

"You took it?"

Mercer raised his eyebrows again. "Oh, yeah. And one from myself. Like I was saying before, we both wanted to know if he was Pete's kid or mine or even somebody else's, since we didn't know for sure who all she was sleeping with back then. We figured if the test confirmed it was one of us, Helen would have to back off and let the boy stay here with me and Pete, even if she got her big job."

"You weren't gonna go with her, either?

"No way. I'd go as crazy as Pudu back there. Not Eskimo country for sure, even worse than Juneau. But I was gonna visit her from time to time between my shifts up here at the mine, at least when there's no hunting and fishing going on. You know, catch up on the *quiyuk*. I'm like Pete was. I can't stay away from her very long, either."

Active laid down his pen. "I never heard of anything like this."

Mercer's grimness eased a little and he chuckled. "It's Chukchi, Nathan. Makes sense if you don't think about it. Anyway, we have the conference. Pete and Helen both won't back down. She tells him to go fuck yourself, you're not getting my kid, no matter what, and she says she's done with him, they're not gonna be getting together any more. Pete thinks about that awhile. Then he says, if she'll keep it up with him, he'll drop the suit and take his chances on seeing Pudu whenever he's back here from Washington or wherever."

"And Helen went for that."

"Not exactly. She says, OK, but you and me are done after tonight, I never want to see you again or hear your name. He still agrees, so she walks over there after the mushers' banquet, after we drop the kids off at her folks' place, and I go to bed. The next thing I know she's on the phone. Her story was, they spend the night together, then Pete tells her 'thanks for the *quiyuk*,' but he still isn't going to drop the suit and she can go fuck herself. He takes off to run his dogs, she takes off to cool down and puts the snowgo through the ice and calls me. That's what she said."

Active made more notes on his pad to give himself thinking space. "So this *nuliagatagiik* relationship you two had with your wife. How did that get started?"

"She was the boys' basketball coach at the time, so there was a lot of travel to the villages, regional tournaments in Nome and Barrow, the state tournament in Anchorage."

"Wait. She coached the boys? Not the girls?"

Mercer raised his eyebrows. "Best coach we ever had. She was a helluva player in high school herself, better than a lot of the boys. One time, she even tried to go out for the boys' team, but the coach said no and she called him a bed-wetting needle-dick."

Active couldn't help grinning. "To his face?"

Mercer grinned back. "Oh, yeah. If her parents hadn't both been teachers, she probably would have been expelled. Anyway, Helen always said she didn't have any interest in coaching girls because they weren't good enough. Just boys. And there was always a lotta tepee-creeping on those trips. That's when we'd get together with her."

"At the same time?

"Never! What kind of people do you think we are? Anyway, she and I got married right after I graduated and then Pudu was born a few months later. That's why I always wondered if Pete was the father, or even somebody else. That's kinda when we started fighting over her."

"And Pete was still in school when you graduated?"

"Yeah, he had another year to go at that point."

Active paused once more and looked at his notes as he spooled back through the interview in his mind.

"Let me line it up here," Active said. "They spend the night together, she takes off in a rage, Pete goes out to run his dogs and winds up dead, your snowgo ends up in Chukchi Bay banged up like it would be if it hit somebody, which we're pretty sure it did."

Mercer thought it over. "Yeah, that's about it. If my snowgo hit Pete, she was driving it."

"So she killed him and set it up so you'd take the blame."

"Unless it was an accident, I guess. Maybe she followed him and his dogs out there to talk to him one last time?"

"Except she took your snowgo, not hers."

"God damn her, yeah," Mercer said. "She told me at the time she never saw him again after he told her to screw herself and she took off."

"So when I called you both knew the snowgo wasn't stolen and that story you told was—"

"Yeah, it was her idea and it was total bullshit. She acted like she came up with it on the spot, but I bet she planned it out all along. She told me what to say, and I said it. You know how it is when your woman looks at you that certain way."

CHAPTER THIRTY-TWO

Tuesday, April 22

"THESE PEOPLE," PROCOPIO said as Active clicked off the digital recorder with Brad Mercer's interview.

"Indeed."

The prosecutor rattled her nails on her desk and knit her brows as she studied her notes on the recording.

He took a hit of the coffee she'd served him on arrival. It was awful, scorched from too long in the pot. "So what do we have here, counselor?"

"The makings of a pretty good erotic romance, maybe. Let's see, we got a love triangle and a love child, a gorgeous governor baring her all for a hunky young cop. Yep, you write it, I'll be your agent, it'll be the next *50 Shades of Grey*."

"That's all? But they incriminated each other and one of them—"

"Yeah, one of them surely killed Pete Wise, by accident if not intentionally," Procopio said. "You got a feel for who and how?"

"On the how, I'm guessing accident. Too stupid a way to commit murder, even for these people, starting with the problem of dumping the snowgo. As for who, I go back and forth. Helen hates being crossed, but she's probably too calculating to expose herself like this. Which leaves Brad. He did admit fighting with Pete in the past, and he might be enough of a knuckle-head to screw up like this and panic."

"But even if we could get around the spousal immunity problem, it could still go nowhere. If one testified, they both would, and they'd just cancel each other out."

Active nodded. "It's a hall of mirrors."

"Any luck with the search warrant for the phone records?"

"Oh, majorly. I think Stein's getting as sick of these people as we are. In fact, Chukchi Telephone is supposed to email them over any time now." She looked at the clock on the wall behind Active. "Let me check." She turned in her chair and clicked her email open. "Here we go, come look."

Active moved around the desk and peered over her shoulder.

"Hmm," they said together two minutes later.

"Lot of calls that morning," Procopio said. "First one was to the Mercer landline at 5:43, a series of calls between the cells after that till, what, almost half past six."

"Hmm." Active pointed. "That call to the land line at 5:43? That's her cell. I recognize the number."

"So that had to be her calling from the ice."

"Yup. Print that for me?"

"Think we can get a search warrant on Pete's house now, see if she spent the night in his bed?"

"With the phone records and the recording from Brad, plus the other stuff I already filed? Puh-leeze. Maybe even by quitting time today, and your guys can tear through the place like wolverines in rut. I'll get on it now." She opened the word processor on her computer and began typing.

"So, then—a warrant also for hair samples from her?"

Procopio paused at the keyboard. "Of course. One follows the other."

"Head and pubic?"

"Of course pubic. Unless she's got a Brazilian."

"She, ah, does not. At least not as of this morning."

"We'll also go for a DNA sample," Procopio said.

"DNA?"

"Yeah, it's in saliva."

"Right, sure. Her saliva might be—"

Procopio nodded. "Almost anywhere on Pete's body, depending on how lucky he got. Plus, her DNA might be on the sheets if she's a squirter."

"What?"

"It's in female ejaculate."

"Seriously? That's a real thing?"

"You don't know about that?" Procopio said. "Poor Grace."

"Shut up. But it's real and it contains DNA?"

"Yep. CSI 101."

"So now I know."

"She can probably drag the search of her person out in court for a while, by the way. She'll have to be served with a warrant, go to a lab or maybe the hospital here or in Juneau, or you'll have to get a crime technician in to see her. So, brace yourself for another fight."

"First step is to get the warrant, right?"

Procopio nodded.

"What about interviewing Pudu?"

"They'll fight that like hell, too," Procopio said. "Probably drag it out even more. I'll set the wheels in motion if you like, but maybe the search warrants first?"

"Yeah, let's at least see what the search at Pete's house turns up. Ditto for questioning Helen's parents, I suppose. The kids spent the night in question with them, so they aren't likely to know where Helen slept. And even if they did, why would they tell us? They can go to the bottom of the list, too."

Procopio resumed typing as Active pocketed the phone-record printout, pulled on his parka and tapped a contact on his cell. "And you?"

"I'm off to atone for my sins."

"You pissed Grace off again, huh?"

SHE ANSWERED AS he reached the stairs.

"Suka? Look, I'm sorry for the way I behaved today. I, er, I haven't stopped thinking about you since I saw... since you...and, ah, well, I was wondering if your offer is still open. I'd like to come over and apologize properly."

There was a long silence at the other end. He crossed mental fingers, hoping her husband hadn't called about the interview at the mine. Maybe he was still on shift. Maybe he was too furious. Maybe he was getting his own lawyer.

"After what you did? I'm not sure I ever want to see you again."

He relaxed a little. The feline throatiness was back in her voice. "I don't blame you, but—"

"Oh, all right. But it's going to take a lot of apologizing. Do I need to cancel my flight? Will you be staying the night?"

"Only part of it. I don't want Grace to know."

A few minutes later, he parked in front of the Mercer house on Beach Street, just south of the start of the seawall. Like everything about the governor, it made a statement and a loud one. Not only was it two stories, it was also cedar-fronted with a glass wall by the door and had an unequal-pitch roof, the only one he had seen on a Chukchi house.

He parked the Chevy in front and walked through the *kunnichuk*. The inner door was unlatched and swung open a crack at his knock. He took a deep breath and stepped in. "Suka?"

She came to the door and took his hand. "Nathan, good to see you again. I hope."

This time, she was at least dressed—painted-on jeans, a scarlet satin top, a necklace with a tiny jade seal pendant. Except not fully dressed. She was braless once more, it appeared, and her feet were bare again. "Likewise," he said. "And, I do apologize for before."

She stepped back a little, studied the red stripes on his face, then touched his cheek. "Wow, I did that? I should apologize to you. "

"No, I had it coming. Really. I cleaned up at the office. It's good now."

"Well, let me get something for it. And I'm having some chardonnay—join me?" She waved at the jade coffee table, set with a bottle of white wine and two glasses, one empty, one half full.

"You do recall we're a dry village, right?"

"Wanna bust me?" She grinned, filled the other glass, and disappeared down a hall. In a moment she was back with band-aids and ointment. She squirted some on her fingertips and massaged it into his cheek.

"You have nice hands," he said. "And a soft touch."

"Just wait."

She finished and eyed her work, then the band-aids. "Well, these are pointless. You'd look like a chainsaw accident if I put on enough to cover the damage."

He shrugged. "No complaints. But don't you need a uniform to practice nursing?"

She giggled. "Don't have one or I'd model it for you. Just let me put this away and then we can discuss why you're here." She padded off to the bathroom and returned to perch on the sofa. She tucked her feet under her, threw an arm along the backrest behind him, and gazed into his eyes. Hers were wolfish again, but this time like she was circling a caribou carcass and trying to sniff out the trap. "So," she said. "That apology."

He touched her knee, put on his flustered face, and pulled back his hand. "Well, um, I, ah..."

"Oh, Nathan, you're adorable. No wonder Grace likes you so much. Look, you haven't touched your wine." She handed him the glass. "Relax, I won't bite. Unless you want me to."

"Maybe some music to set the mood?" He pulled his phone out of his pocket. "I think you'll like the playlist I put together. It starts with 'At Last.'" He winked.

"How romantic! I love that in a man."

"Will this plug into your sound system?"

She nodded at an expensive-looking setup on smoked glass shelves under a huge wide-screen TV. "Oh, posilutely. It plays everything. Music, radio, TV, DVDs, flash drives, those little memory cards, I don't know what-all. Brad set it up. A guy thing, you know?"

He walked to the system and set his phone in a dock under a corner of the TV. He squatted in front and found a remote with a vast array of buttons. But one did say "On" and another said "Aux. He pressed them in order and the system lit up. Then he started the playback and turned to watch as Mercer heard not Etta James but "I just got out of the shower."

At first she looked puzzled, then she figured it out and her cheeks blazed. "Goddammit, you recorded me? Turn that thing off!"

He paused the playback.

"That's illegal, I'm calling the attorney general right—"

"It is legal, trust me. Cops do it all the time."

"Well, get the hell out. Fuck you and fuck your recording. I don't want to hear it."

"Really? I thought maybe you'd like to refresh your recollection before you hear Brad's version of events?"

"You recorded Brad, too?"

"I did."

"Are you recording me now?"

He shook his head. "Nope. This is just us. My phone's hooked up to the system and this"—he pulled out the digital recorder—"is turned off. He showed her and she reached for it. "Sorry, I can't let you touch it, it's got Brad's interview on it. But you can see the display is dark."

"How do I know you're not wearing a wire? Is that what they call it?"

"They do, and you don't know, but I'm not. Care to frisk me?" He grinned, like they were still in the opening round of this match.

"Fuck you."

"Then you'll have to take my word for it."

"I suppose cops can lie, too?"

"We can. But, again, I'm not. Let's play the recordings, then have a talk."

She folded into herself on the sofa, arms around her shoulders. She she looked half the size she had before. She drained her wine glass, then his, and waved at the entertainment center. "Go on."

He watched alarm and fury play across her face as she listened. "Pretty good sound quality, don't you think?" he said when it was done.

"I said all that?"

"You did. And it's all in evidence now. Would you like to hear what your husband had to say?"

She gave an exhausted nod and poured more wine. She missed the glass at first, and chardonnay spread across the jade table top. She sipped as he found a cable for his digital recorder, plugged in, and started Brad's interview.

Once again fury and alarm fought for control of her face. She was silent for a long time after the interview finished and he pocketed the recorder.

"You can't possibly believe all that," she said at last. "He's lying. I never had sex with Pete, I certainly wasn't sleeping with both of them, and now Brad is trying to frame me for what he did. The lying sonofabitch."

"Well, there is this." He pulled a sheaf of papers from his pocket and handed her the phone records. "You'll notice the first call the morning Pete died was from your cell to the landline here at the house. That would be you calling from out on the ice after you dumped the snowgo, I presume?"

She studied the printout in silence.

"Forget something when you came back from Pete's place and borrowed Brad's snowgo for your little morning drive?"

"This doesn't prove anything. Brad obviously took my phone with him so it would look like me calling."

"So you didn't spend the night in Pete's bed to get him to call off the custody suit?"

"Of course not! What kind of woman do you think I am?"

"More interesting all the time, actually. But never mind that. Let's talk about this." He handed her the custody petition.

"So? We've both seen this before."

"Right. But what I didn't notice was the birth dates, not till Brad told me you were having sex with Pete while he was still in high school. Pete was seventeen years old when Pudu was born and you were a teacher, and the coach of his team. Ever hear of our Satch Carlson Law?"

This time, he thought, she paled. But she did keep her game face on.

"I think so, yeah."

"From your lawyer, perhaps?"

She didn't speak, but clenched her teeth. A jaw muscle twitched.

"Maybe a refresher won't hurt. If a teacher sleeps with a student, the age of consent in Alaska rises from sixteen to eighteen. If you do the math here, Pete was only sixteen when he fathered Pudu. And that makes you a child rapist. Welcome to some jail time and the sex offender registry. And goodbye to your political career."

"This is just more of your bullshit. I told you Pete faked these results. He was not Pudu's father!"

"With these birth dates, there's absolutely no doubt the court will order a DNA test for Pudu, and we've already got Pete's at the crime lab."

"You still won't have a case. We did have sex, but Pete raped me."

"And you didn't report it because..."

"I felt so stupid for letting him into my room that night—he said he needed advice on his jump shot—and I didn't want to put him in jail and land him on the registry for the rest of his life."

"Well, your husband's testimony about your ongoing relationship with Pete might undermine that claim—"

"More bullshit! He can't testify against me because of spousal privilege."

"Sure he can, if he wants to. The privilege only protects him from being forced to testify. Your lawyer didn't tell you that?" He waited. "I can't wait till a jury hears this. Talk about a paragon of family values."

She still didn't speak.

"There's one more thing," he said. "We're in the

process of—actually, let me make a call." He tapped the contact on his phone and in a few moments Theresa Procopio was on the line. "Madam Prosecutor. Did we get those warrants—already? well, damned fine work!"

He clicked off and tapped another contact. "Alan? Nathan. We got a warrant on Pete Wise's place. Head over and secure it till I get there, OK? Dust for fingerprints on anything we can't ship to the crime lab, otherwise wait for me."

He clicked off and studied her.

She was, if possible, even smaller now. "A warrant on Pete's place?"

He nodded. "And another one for samples of your hair and DNA. If there's so much as a trace of you in that house or on Pete's body or on his clothing—"

"Women don't leave DNA," she said in a feeble voice. "That's men."

"Actually, some women do. It depends on how much they enjoy the experience. It's in female ejaculate, just like with men."

"Well, I didn't...I don't...I mean..." She stopped and gave a half-sob. "That sonofabitch!"

"Pete or Brad? Or both of them, seeing as how they were *nuliagatagiik*?"

"Fuck you, Nathan."

He waited, but said no more. "Mm-hmm. But if we do find something that puts you in that house, you know what that means, right?"

"I think it means I should call my lawyer before I say anything else."

"Sure, you have the right to do that. But it might be worth your while to hear what I have to propose first."

She closed her eyes and laid her head against the backrest. "Whatever."

"I'm offering you a deal. One where you get to keep

your clothes on, though I'm starting to think you do your best work without them."

"Drop that shit. It's not gonna work now."

"You plead guilty, or at least no contest, to manslaughter, leaving the scene of an accident, and destruction of evidence—that's for dumping the snowgo—and you call your dogs off me and my womenfolk."

She opened her eyes and raised her head from the backrest. "Did you say accident?"

He nodded. "I know it wasn't. I know you ran Pete down on. I knew it when I the rage in your eyes when you did this." He touched his damaged cheek. "But Theresa's not sure we can get a murder verdict, whereas the accident version is a slam dunk. So you're getting a break here."

"A break? It'll ruin me."

"You didn't notice I haven't mentioned the matter of you raping Pete when he was still a minor, or of him fathering Pudu?"

She tilted her head and studied him. "What's that about?"

"Insurance."

"Insurance. I figure you'll be able to talk your way past the manslaughter plea in public, at least to some extent. You're out for a ride on the tundra on a cold, clear morning, thinking how much you love your Chukchi and how much you'll miss it in Juneau, and there's a tragic accident. In a moment of panic, you don't know what to do, you make a stupid mistake, and now you've got a local cop and an overzealous prosecutor on a vendetta and you had no choice other than pleading no contest so it doesn't drag out forever." He read her eyes for a moment. "Something like that on your mind, maybe? Anyway, as long as

I've got the child rape charges and the paternity tests in my pocket, you'll have to leave Grace, Nita, and me alone. Otherwise, it'll all go before the grand jury, and on the Internet, too, if I need it to."

"Why should I believe you'll stick to your piece of this? I mean, sitting on my allegedly raping Pete Wise?"

"Again, insurance. If I use the child rape now and you wiggle off the hook, I'm out of ammo. With child rape, polyandry, and a love child in reserve, I can go several more rounds if I need to. Think of the birth dates on that custody petition as candles on a great big birthday cake I can light any time."

She sipped thoughtfully at her wine. "What kind of sentence?"

"Sixty days, which you can serve under house arrest in the governor's mansion."

"Can I start it after my trip for the primaries next week?"

He nodded.

"And Theresa's OK with all of this, including letting the rape issue slide?"

"That part she's not aware of. When I first got the files, she didn't even want to look at them because they were sealed. The only thing she has now is the DNA tests on Pete and Pudu, which she used to get the search warrants. And the birth dates aren't on them."

"So—"

"So it's our little secret. Yours and mine."

"Unless you change your mind."

He nodded. "Or you do."

"But she's in on the rest—the plea and the sentence?"

"I think I can sell it to her.

She thought it over. "It'll take a while to call off the dogs, as you put it. And if I've already pleaded, I may not be able—"

He nodded. "Have your lawyer get a draft plea agreement to us by this time tomorrow, with an offer to show up here and enter it in court on Friday."

"Friday? That's only three days."

"That's your deadline to make the investigations go away."

HE CAUGHT UP with Procopio as she was locking her office and pulled her back inside.

"Say what?" she said when he told her of the deal with Helen Mercer.

Active nodded.

"Sixty days is pretty fucking light. You record her this time too?"

He shook his head.

"That would be because...?"

"The circumstances were not such as to, ah, permit another surreptitious recording."

Procopio's eyes narrowed. "Wait a minute. Do we need to test you for her DNA now? Talk about a conflict of interest."

"No, nothing like that, I swear. I played the two recordings for her and of course she suspected I was recording her again, so I had to prove I wasn't."

The prosecutor whistled. "You played the recordings of her and Brad? What did she do?"

"She buckled and I moved in for the kill and I got the deal. And no damage to my face."

"Why would she cave? The evidence so far is just conflicting testimony we may not get in and telephone evidence for which she has at least a superficially plausible explanation."

"Maybe she's afraid the search will put her in Pete's house."

Procopio chewed her lip for a moment, then nodded in acknowledgment. "Make me love that sentence."

"I think she'll fight rather than take a longer sentence. Six months, a year, she'd have to leave office. This way, she might conceivably survive. The legislature might try to impeach her, but they're out of session now and they love her, anyway, and this will be old news when the next session starts."

"I admit, I'd hate to take her on in front of a jury. She struts out there in that push-up bra, bats her eyes, and tells them she just wanted to talk to Pete one last time and she hit him by accident, God knows what they'll do. Especially the men, fuck all of ya. Hung jury for sure, if not outright acquittal."

"What I'm thinking," Active said. "We shouldn't let the perfect be the enemy of the good."

"Who said that?" Procopio asked.

"Someone wise, I'm sure."

"He was right. Or she. God damn, I'm tired of this case."

ACTIVE CLICKED OFF the first recording and looked at Grace over his teacup. "You never heard that. It's part of an official police investigation."

She tilted her head and shot him a fierce don't-bullshit-me look. "Helen Mercer is standing there naked inviting you into her bed and you're not tempted? Not one little bit?"

"Not even. You know she's a psycho. And you heard what she was setting me up for. A rape charge."

"Of course she was. But how'd she look?"

"You heard. Old and fake."

"You expect me to believe that?"

"OK, she looked pretty good, actually." He saw from her expression he was off track, and realized this was actually a test. Conversations with females usually were. "For a woman her age, of course, and in comparison with you, well...what I mean is, there is no comparison. Whatever."

"Nice recovery, Chief Active. But those implants of hers—they really looked that fake? You didn't squeeze one to check? As part of your investigation?"

He rolled his eyes. "You sound like Carnaby and Long."

She pointed at his cheek. "And she did that when you told her she looked old and fake, and by the way, thanks telling her that, the bitch."

"She did, and, you're welcome. It was well worth it."

"Did you like it? I mean, if you did, I could, we

could...?" She formed her right hand into claws and swiped it before his nose.

"No, thank you. Now, do you want to hear Brad's interview or not?"

"Let me get dinner and I'll listen while we eat." She went to the stove and returned with salads and caribou stew.

Active started the second recording and they ate and listened. At least, he ate. Grace kept stopping open-mouthed, spoon in mid-air.

Her mouth was full stew when the interview ended. She chewed and swallowed and chased the cracker with tea. "My God. That's a pair to draw to."

"Altogether."

"Two men simultaneously—"

"That we know of."

She nodded. "A love child and..." She paused. "Anything more you want to tell me?"

"Much more." And he told her about the rest of his afternoon—the phone records, the search warrants on Mercer's house and person, the second meeting with the governor and the plea deal with the birthday cake as leverage.

"You told her you had a romantic playlist on your recorder and she bought it?"

"She did. And the fact that she did and was ready to jump into bed was just more confirmation of how desperate she was."

"Serves her right, the bitch. I would have loved to be there when she came out of those speakers instead of Etta James."

She was silent for a long time. "I'm glad you caught the birthdays," she said finally.

"Figured you'd spotted that," he said. "Miles ahead of me as usual."

She smiled and lifted her eyebrows. "But I don't know about giving away the child-rape charges. I mean, don't we want her in the coffin with a stake through her heart and the lid bolted on and every rock we can find piled on top?"

"Like I said, we need the insurance. A trial could take forever, and all that time she could be pushing her people on those investigations of you and Nita and me."

"Oh, baby, I love you so much. Thank you."

"And I love you." He looked around what was now Grace's house. She and Nita weren't completely moved in, but it was enough to give the place a woman's stamp. Grace's pictures, her furniture, her—what did women call them, tchotchkes?—filling just enough of the empty space on shelves and table and counters. Clutter, he would have called it, until he saw what it did for the look and feel of the place. "And thanks for making this house a home."

Grace's phone pinged. She glanced at it, then pulled up a text. "What? I swear, I will kill that child! And Nelda Qivits too!"

He threw up his hands in hopes of opting out of whatever mother-daughter stuff was about to boil over. It was not to be.

"Look at this! Nita got her tattoo! And Nelda gave it to her!" She pushed over the phone and made him look.

"Didn't she say—"

"Shut up, Nathan. You stay out of this."

"OK, well, I really should be go—"

"No! You sit right there! You're the male authority figure in her life. She'll be here in a minute and you're going to back me up about having the damned thing removed."

"Removed? Won't that be pain—"

"I hope so, the little smartass! Now sit there and shut up."

Soon the door flew open, Grace jumped up from the table, and Nita burst in, face alight. "Mom, you're really gonna like this."

Two sets of eyes raced over Nita's face.

"I don't see any tattoos," Grace said. "Is this another one of your jokes, because if it is—"

Nita held up her right arm, which had a bandage around the wrist. "Wanna see?"

Grace's face softened. She took her chair at the table again and pulled one up for Nita. "Come over here, *bunnik*."

Nita did. Grace pulled her arm onto the table and unwrapped the bandage.

"See, Mom? That's OK, right?"

Active stepped over for a look. The tattoo was a tiny *inuksuk*, no more than a half-inch tall, inside the girl's wrist.

"Nelda says it will always keep me on the right path."

"Oh, *bunnik*." Grace pulled her into a hug.

Active started to ease out, to give them this moment, when Nita looked at him over Grace's shoulder. "Can I name him Nathan?" She looked at her mother. "Mom?"

Active nodded.

"Of course, sweetheart," Grace said. She pushed the girl back and gazed into her eyes for a moment. "How about some caribou stew and pilot bread!"

"You bet, Mom. While you're making it, I'll take a picture and put it on Facebook."

Grace handed over her phone and Nita rushed into the living room and planted herself on the sofa, wrist in the air.

"That daughter of yours is quite something. Wonder where she gets that."

Grace smiled.

He looked at his watch. "I guess—"

"You need to get over to Pete Wise's for the search."

"That OK? You OK?"

"Don't worry, we'll be fine. I've got my princess back. Till next time."

"It may not take that long to search the place. Fast check for any of Helen Mercer's clothing or possessions, which I'm doubting will produce results, then bundle up everything we can test for DNA or hair matches and ship it off to the crime lab."

"Don't forget the shower drain. She's the type to leave it completely clogged. The bitch."

Not only was the shower drain clean at Pete Wise's house, so was everything else. Empty trashcans, empty drain traps in the bathroom and kitchen, a fresh bag in the vacuum cleaner, no hairbrushes in the bathroom or bedroom, even a new, still-in-the-wrapper toothbrush in a cup in the bathroom.

Active stood with hands on hips as Alan Long rolled up the bed sheets and pillowcases and stuffed them into a plastic bag. "You smell that bedding?"

Long raised his eyebrows, yes. "Fresh, like it was just washed. No hair or stains on it either."

"I'm thinking this stuff hasn't been slept on since it was put on the bed."

They were both dressed in official CSI gear—latex gloves and paper booties, even hairnets. The getup made Active feel a little ridiculous, but less so than he would if the crime lab found traces of Long or himself in the evidence they sent down.

Active dropped to his knees and crawled around the bed, his eyes on the carpet. "Not even a dog hair. What musher doesn't have dog hair on this carpet?"

"Think the place was scrubbed?"

"My guess." He shook his head. "Let's vacuum the carpet and the bed and the furniture anyway and send the cleaner bag down to the lab along with all this other stuff. Maybe we'll get lucky."

"We'll sure get a lot of bitching and moaning," Long said. "They hate a wild goose chase like this."

"Just get the vacuum from your rig and do it, OK?

AT MID-MORNING THE next day, Active studied Procopio over the rim of his coffee cup as she studied the plea offer from the Mercers' lawyer.

"It's all here, I guess."

"It is."

Procopio sighed. "Still feels like we coulda done better."

"Or struck out altogether. I have a very bad feeling about that search. Place looked like she cleaned it up and I'm guessing we'll end up with no trace she was ever there. In any case, it could drag on till breakup. Last I heard, the crime lab was backed up something like six weeks on this kind of DNA testing. Hair samples, I don't know how long they take, but—"

"'Bout the same," she said. "They have to send it to some expert Outside. We don't have one up here." The prosecutor shrugged and gazed absently around Active's office. "Probably best to get what we can and call it good. I'll let McConnell know."

"But it wasn't a total loss," he said as she stood

up and made for the door. "I did notice something interesting when I went over to Pete Wise's place last night."

She turned. "Yeah?"

"His lot is back-to-back with the Mercers' lot."

"Huh."

"Huh, indeed."

"Pretty handy for tepee-creeping."

"Yep."

The next forty-eight hours were like a storm breaking up, if not quite vanishing.

First Minnie Wilkins, the social worker, let Grace know the children's services investigation had been suspended with a finding that Nita was deemed safe in her care, subject to later review.

He came home that night to find Grace sobbing on the couch. He sat down beside her and she grabbed him and swung her legs across his lap. He cradled her like a baby. "Almost over," he said.

"'Suspended.' What does that mean?"

"I think it's Helen's insurance policy. Like the child rape is ours. Can we live with it?"

"I guess." She buried her face in his chest and tears wet his shirt. "The bitch."

"Besides," Active said. "She won't be governor much longer. Even If she doesn't leave for a big job in DC, she can't run again here because of term limits. So, who knows? Maybe our search of Pete's place will turn up something interesting and I'll sit on it till the coast is clear. Or maybe somebody will light the birthday cake someday and take her out."

The next day, Active's phone rang and Lucy told him Stuart Stewart was on the line.

"You know people in high places, huh?"

"Not that many," Active said.

"One that counts, apparently," Stewart said. "The AG's office just called to say we should let you know your woman's off the hook. Her father's case stays cold, subject to reopening as needed."

"Subject to reopening."

"All you're gonna get, at least while this crew's in office."

"I'll tell her."

"Might as well," Stewart said. "You know we never make it official. The subject just doesn't hear from us again."

"Thanks, and, ah, just thanks."

Stewart hung up without so much as a "no problem."

"Thanks, baby," she said when he called. Then she broke down in sobs.

"You OK? Should I come home? I'm coming home. I'm leaving now."

"No, no, not now. Let me pull myself together. I've been that bitch's basket case long enough. I never want you to see me like this again."

"It's OK. Let me come home."

"See you tonight."

That afternoon came the final call, from Bill Ashe, the investigator for the police standards council.

"Let me guess," Active said.

"Yep, you get a pass, at least till next time," Ashe said. "Bullshit end to a bullshit case. Remind me to be on vacation the next time the governor calls."

"Me, too," Active said. "Maybe we should go fishing. Ever catch a sheefish?"

"I want to piss away my time and money, I'll go to Vegas," Ashe said.

"You're off the hook, too?" Grace said after he told her of the call.

He raised his eyebrows. "She's a woman of her word, it appears. Gotta give her credit, I suppose."

Grace considered for a moment. "Not yet. Not till your hearing tomorrow."

CHAPTER THIRTY-FOUR

Friday, April 25

HELEN MERCER, AS Procopio had predicted, sported the push-up bra and abundant cleavage when she arrived in court. Also, the painted-on jeans and scarlet blouse Active had seen the night he shared his playlist. Brad Mercer wore Sorels, rust-colored Carhartt jeans, a wool shirt, and a Gray Wolf ball cap that he parked under his chair.

McConnell, the Mercers' lawyer, proved to be a small and fussy-looking man in gray pinstripe, and rimless glasses so shiny it was impossible to see his eyes. No doubt the prim, buttoned-down exterior he showed the world was one reason for his success in criminal defense. It would be easy to misread that.

Judge Stein rapped his gavel and the courtroom settled down. "Everybody here? Everybody set?"

Everybody nodded.

"For the record, this is a closed hearing on the matter of the death of one Peter Aqpattuq Wise on, ah, April 15 of this year. I understand we have a plea today?"

McConnell rose. "We do, Your Honor," he said in a high, thin voice. "If we could pass these around?" He waved a sheaf of copies at Doris, the court clerk.

"We have ours already." Procopio said. She tapped the folder in front of her. "Mr. McConnell was kind enough to send it up by email."

"Actually," McConnell said, "We have a revised version. I think the prosecutor and Chief Active will want to take a look."

Doris came out from behind her railing, took the copies from McConnell, and put two on the table where Active and Procopio sat. She took the rest back to the bench.

Active and Procopio gave the document a casual scan, looked at each other, picked it up in disbelief, and read it again. Active read it a third time before he could believe it.

"Brad Mercer?" Procopio erupted from her chair. "Brad Mercer is pleading? That is not what we agreed to and it is not what we got from Mr. McConnell two days ago. His offer was that Helen Mercer would plead. This is outrage—"

Stein held up a restraining hand. "We try not to raise our voices in this courtroom, Ms. Procopio. And it would appear that Mr. McConnell wants to offer an explanation. Shall we hear it?"

Procopio nodded and sank back into her chair.

"This is bullshit," Active hissed into her ear. "Total bull—"

"Yeah, I know. Let's just listen."

Active shot a fast glance at the governor. He thought she shot back a smirk, but it was too quick to be certain.

McConnell pushed back his chair and rose. "Your honor, Ms. Procopio is right. We did send a different plea offer on Wednesday. But as I subsequently observed the demeanor of my clients in discussing with them the events of April 15, including listening to both of the state's recordings, I came to entertain doubts, serious doubts, that Mrs. Mercer's plea was an accurate account of those events."

He gazed down on his clients. The governor kept her chin up but Active was pretty sure it trembled.

"I became concerned, Your Honor, that Mrs. Mercer, might be pleading in an effort to protect her husband because she was so moved his the devotion to his family, the devotion that led him to make that fateful trip out onto the tundra on the morning in question in one last effort to resolve the Mercer family's differences with Mr. Wise, with the tragic but accidental result that brings us here today. It's that devotion that is reflected in his affidavit and our new plea offer."

McConnell paused and seemed to look into himself. "It was foolish of the governor, I know. But who among us has not been a fool for love at least once? And who, having done so, does not pity those who never have?"

The lawyer paused again and gazed around the courtroom.

"Cut the crap, Mr. McConnell," Stein said with an expression of disgust, or amusement, or both. "Save it for when this gets in front of a jury, if it ever does."

Active shot another glance at the Mercers. This time, it was Brad Mercer who looked sheepish. His wife cast down her eyes. The lashes looked to be jeweled with tears, just like the first time she'd tried to blame Pete Wise's death on her husband.

"Of course, Your Honor," McConnell went on. "I counseled with my clients. I told them of my concerns. I implored them to consult their hearts and their consciences in this matter. I even indicated I might be unable to continue representing them unless I could achieve a satisfactory level of confidence regarding the veracity of the materials we were filing with this court. And they did, after praying for divine guidance, as I understand it, come to me with the account we submit today. As you can see, it is identical to the previous version in every material respect. Only the names have changed."

McConnell gazed around the courtroom again. "So, if we're ready for Mr. Mercer?"

"This should be good," Active said.

Procopio shrugged. "I'll kill him on cross."

Stein waved Brad Mercer up and administered the oath.

McConnell led the First Mate through the new version of Pete Wise's death. He had, it seemed, been distraught over Wise's refusal to back off the custody suit during the previous day's conference, and had gone to his house early that morning for another talk. Seeing Pete's sled and dogs gone from behind his house, Brad had surmised Wise was out for a morning run with his team and had followed him by snowgo along the usual route of Chukchi mushers, past the airport, the cemetery on the ridge, and onto the Isignaq trail.

Surface visibility was poor that morning because of the layer of blowing snow, Mercer said, and as he came over a rise, he was suddenly upon Wise and his team and hit the musher from behind before he could react and swerve aside.

After that, he said, he must have panicked, fearing not only for himself but also for the damage to his wife's career that would result from public knowledge of the accident. The next thing he remembered clearly was shoving the snowgo through the ice on Chukchi Bay and calling his wife for rescue.

And how, McConnell asked, had he come to make the call on her phone?

That he didn't know, Mercer said, unless it was because he picked it up by mistake as he fumbled around in the darkness of the bedroom before his ride to Pete Wise's house for another talk about the custody suit.

And what about his wild stories of sharing his wife with Pete Wise, of Helen Mercer spending the night with Wise before he was killed, and of helping Pete

Wise get a DNA sample from Pudu?

All concocted, Brad said, and he was sorry for doing it. But when he heard the recording of his wife trying to seduce Chief Active, he had he lashed out in blind fury and struck back in every way he could, never stopping to think she only did it to protect the family.

"But it was lies, all lies," Brad said. "It was my wife who told the truth about what happened and when she tried to take the blame after all, I saw how much she loves me and I realize how much I love her. So now I'm confessing to what really happened."

"FML," Procopio muttered.

"What?" Active whispered.

"Eff My Life. McConnell stole our cross-examination."

"Cross, Ms. Procopio?" Stein said.

"Your Honor, this comes as a complete surprise to us, not to mention an outrage. We need some time to go over this material before we can respond."

"Very well." Stein looked at the clock at the back of the courtroom. "How long will you need?"

"Not long," Procopio said.

"Let Doris know when you're ready and we'll resume."

Active and Procopio found a conference room a few doors down the hall from the courtroom and slumped in chairs at a little table under framed copies of the state and federal constitutions.

"Shit," Procopio said as she flipped through Brad Mercer's plea and affidavit. "That's what we've got here. Shit."

"Same as we had yesterday, but with a different name on it," Active said. "Should we take it?"

"I could rake Brad over the coals a little. But there aren't many coals to rake here with the search of Pete's place looking to come up dry."

"It is remotely possible he's telling the truth, I suppose."

"Is that what your gut tells you?"

"I still don't know. But here's the thing. If Brad's telling the truth, he deserves to go to jail. If he's lying under oath, he still deserves to go to jail. In which case, if he has a little time in his cell to think it over, maybe he'll come to his senses and rat her out."

Procopio tilted her head and narrowed her eyes. "You fight dirty."

Active raised his eyebrows. "I try."

"I guess I'm in," she said. "Let's go break the good news."

"Not yet, I'm thinking."

Procopio sagged back into her chair. "What now?"

"What's to stop Mercer from giving him a pardon or clemency or something the minute we walk out of here?"

"Again, FML. Nothing except bad publicity maybe."

"At which point she'll blow it all off as a vendetta by a small-town cop and an overzealous prosecutor."

"So what, then?"

"They have to stipulate that Brad serves at least a year before she takes executive action."

Procopio shrugged. "Why not? Probably get laughed out of court on constitutional grounds if she ever contests it, but this case is already a clown car."

"And no possibility of parole till he's done the year."

The prosecutor shrugged again. "Sure, that, too."

They left the conference room, and Procopio popped her head into Doris's office to let the clerk know they were ready.

"That was not our agreement!" McConnell protested when Procopio laid the counteroffer before the court. "A year is not—"

"Your agreement was never our agreement," Procopio said. "Ours was with Helen Mercer. This is the new one."

"And this business of the governor stipulating, I'm not sure it's even...I've never run into..." McConnell sputtered to a halt and and whispered for a moment with the Mercers. "Now I'm afraid we need some time, Your honor."

"Thought you might," Stein said. "Be my guest." He stood and slipped out the back to his chambers.

"Third door on the right," Active said as McConnell and the Mercers filed out.

No one thanked him.

Active and Procopio waited in the courtroom, for lack of a better idea. Active checked email on his phone. Procopio pulled a laptop from her briefcase and started a draft of the new plea agreement.

Less than ten minutes later, Stein and his clerk entered the rear of the courtroom as McConnell and the Mercers filed in from the hall. McConnell's expression was unreadable. The Mercers were stone-faced. Active caught Brad Mercer's eye for a moment and shot him a little smirk. The First Mate's expression got stonier.

Stein gaveled them to order. "Mr. McConnell, what say you? Do your clients accept the state's offer?"

"This is highly unusual and I'm not sure it's legal, your honor, but we do."

"All right, guys, put it in writing, get signatures from the Mercers and Ms. Procopio, file it with Doris and we'll call it good," Stein said. "Anything further? No? Then we're done here." He looked at Procopio and Active, then McConnell and the Mercers. "And I wish I may never hear of this matter again."

They all stood as he slipped out the rear door. Doris gathered her papers and followed soon after.

"Nathan?" the governor said as they moved toward the exit. "A moment?"

Everybody started back toward the tables.

The governor shook her head. "Just Nathan, Brad, and me."

"Governor," McConnell said. "I seriously advise against this. We have the matter wrapped up. Further conversation cannot possibly be in your interest."

Mercer gave him a frosty stare.

"I advise against it is all I can say." He started for the door.

"Me, too," Procopio told Active. "This is not a boat to be rocked."

Active touched her arm. "I won't do anything stupid."

She left, too. Active and the Mercers took seats on a front bench in the public section of the courtroom.

Mercer gave him a searching look. "So this is really over?"

"You know the deal. You stick to your part, I stick to mine. The cases stay closed, the birthday cake stays unlit."

She looked at her husband. "Brad?"

"I said I'll do it and I will."

"I do have a question," Active said.

Mercer widened her eyes in inquiry.

"That ridiculous business about drafting me for your bodyguard, the Trooper job, the scratches in the tent. What was that about? Pete Wise wasn't even dead yet. Were you already planning to kill him?"

"What happened to Pete Wise was an accident! There was no plan—"

"Don't bother. We're off the record here and the deal's done anyway."

She got back a little of the smirk he had seen earlier. "The truth is, I was worried about Pete's suit right from the get-go because of the birthday cake issue. With your reputation, I figured if word got out, you'd be asking me about birthdays before I knew it. I needed leverage. Then Cowboy put us down in Shelukshuk Canyon and I never let a good crisis go to waste. I got you into the Arctic Oven, scratched my throat, and there was my stick to back up the carrot of the Trooper job."

He chewed his lip for a moment. Was she telling the truth for once, or just working a new angle not yet obvious?

"I surrounded you, Nathan." She flashed him the campaign smile.

He looked at her husband, who had taken it all in, chin on hand.

"How about you, Brad? You know what really happened, but you'll be the one sitting in a cell while she's out doing what she does, maybe with a new man. Why you doing this?"

Now the First Mate wore the smirk. "You should have spent that afternoon with her."

"What? Why?"

"You'd know why I'm doing this if you were ever inside her."

"Told you," the governor said.

Her husband chuckled. "She's gonna have'em put me in Lemon Creek at Juneau so we can have conjugal visits."

The governor winked and left with her husband.

EPILOGUE

Saturday, April 26

ACTIVE PUSHED HIMSELF up on his hands and looked down the length of Grace Palmer's body, the hills and hollows, to where they were still joined in the middle, her ankles locked behind his knees. "Baby? You there?"

She opened heavy-lidded eyes, now limpid and silver. "No, I'm in heaven." She closed them again. "I guess it's true what they say. There's nothing like the real thing."

"No argument here." He rolled off and stretched alongside her on the narrow little cot in Leroy's sheefish camp. "That boffo splibo still going?"

She groped around on the cooler beside the cot and came up with the boffo. "Nope, it's out. Why?"

"I was thinking I might give it a try. Walk on the wild side a little in honor of...this. Today. The first time I was ever inside you in the biblical sense."

She propped herself on an elbow. "You? Smoke a boffo?"

"I'm thinking it might speed up my recovery."

She handed him a lighter off the cooler.

He lit the boffo and inhaled cautiously, not having smoked marijuana since college.

She took a hit and laid it on the cooler. "Again? Already?"

"Soon. But I have a question first."

"Ask me anything."

"Wanna get married?"

"Seriously?"

"Of course seriously. A, we love each other to pieces. B, this, here today, makes me think you've, how do I put this, finally exorcised your demons enough to give informed consent. C, if we're gonna propagate the species, we don't wanna wait too long to start. And, D, if Helen Mercer does come after us again, we can invoke spousal privilege."

She chuckled. "Not the most romantic proposal a girl ever had, I suppose, but, then, it wouldn't be you if it was. So, A, hell, yes, and B, fuck Helen Mercer."